37

This has been a strange few years for the book industry. There have been many changes and realignments, and these changes have led countless commentators to predict that (a) reading is dead; (b) books are dead; (c) publishing is dead; (d) all printed matter is dead. Or that all of the above, if not already dead, will be dead very soon. ¶These are upsetting predictions, given they're based on assumptions and attitudes, and not data. Instead, they point to the one reliable aspect of the literary world: that every decade, no matter the climate or the realities of the business, excitable people, many of them inside the industry themselves, will claim that reading is dead, that books are obsolete. It's a common but ill-informed line of thinking, and it leads to some bad decisions and bad outcomes. ¶Back in May of 2010, amidst some of the most dour prognostications about the state of the industry, we asked fifteen or so young researchers to look into the health of the book. Their findings provide proof that not only are books very much alive, but that reading is in exceptionally good shape—and that the book-publishing industry, while undergoing some significant changes, is, on the whole, in very good health. ¶Let's start with some bedrock data that disproves any statements that the industry is in freefall. According to Nielsen's BookScan—a sales-monitoring service widely regarded as representing 70 of 75 percent of trade sales—Americans bought 751,729,000 books in 2010. Excepting 2008 and 2009, when sales reached 757 million and 777 million, respectively, that's many millions more books sold than in any other year BookScan has recorded. (Five years earlier, in 2005, the total was just 650 million.) The decline from the all-time high of 2009 can't be overlooked, but it's worth remembering—in 2010, in the middle of a crippling recession, with unemployment in the double digits, people still bought more than 750 million books. (In all likelihood, quite a few more, considering BookScan's tendency to underestimate.) And that figure doesn't include e-book sales, which are now thought to make up as much as 9 percent of the overall book market—and which are growing by the year, representing at least a partial antidote to declining hard-copy sales. So: despite the prognostications, and the poor economic circumstances, total U.S. book sales in 2010 remained well above a billion books. ¶Other statistics—literacy, library circulation, overall book production—paint a similarly reassuring picture. Here are some examples, with each statistic using the latest available figures:

- In 2008, there were more original book titles published in print than ever before: 289,729 different titles in the U.S. alone.

- In 2007, there were more U.S. publishers than ever before: 74,240 (that's compared with 397 in 1925). This figure has been rising every year since the data began being collected.

- In 2005, there were more published authors living in the U.S. than ever before: 185,275 (compared, for example, with eighty-two in 1850).

- Adult literacy in the U.S. is also at an all-time high: 240,220,540 adults (98 percent of the adult population) were considered literate in 2010.

- Library membership in the U.S. is at an all-time high: 208,904,000 Americans held library cards in 2009. (That's 68 percent of the population, the greatest number since the American Library Association began keeping track in 1990.)

- Library circulation is at an all-time high: 2.28 billion library materials were circulated in 2008 (that's 7.7 circulations per capita) compared to 1.69 billion in 1999 (6.5 circulations per capita).

¶That's all good news. So much good news that we hope you'll feel armed with the numbers to combat the next lazy assumption that books, reading, novels, or literacy in general is dead. It isn't, by any available measure. ¶Still, though, there persists the idea that Reading Is Dead, and this assumption requires a corollary assumption, which is that there was some other, Golden Age of Reading and Writing Somewhere in the Past. For those who lament the death of reading, there is never a clear sense of just when this Golden Age was, but the idea is always there—that we are a fallen society, and that some earlier era was when books were read in greater volume and with greater depth and enthusiasm. ¶So let's consider this Golden Age of Reading and Writing that every successive generation and age is measured against. When would such an era be? ¶Let's start with Dante. Surely 1321, when *The Divine Comedy* was published, was a time wherein the majority of citizens were walking around piazzas, reciting Ovid and Sophocles and talking about Dante's latest works? Not exactly. At that time, barely 10 percent of the Italian population could read. And given that Dante toiled at a time before the arrival of Gutenberg's press, books were incredibly scarce, and prohibitively expensive. The average Italian citizen—even if literate—had virtually no access to books. In the Italy of the fourteenth century, and indeed across Europe, reading for pleasure was an activity enjoyed by precious few. ¶So maybe it wasn't Dante's era that was the presumed Golden Age. How about Shakespeare's? People were coming to the Globe Theater to see his plays performed mere weeks after he'd written them! Surely this was the era that marked the pinnacle of literate society, from whence our decline began. ¶But no. The statistics from his lifetime, 1564 to 1616, aren't much better than those from Italy during the time of Dante. In Shakespeare's era, the vast majority of the books and pamphlets that were printed, bought, and read were practical hexes and quasi-religious tracts. Shakespeare himself was not read widely, in part because by 1600, only 40 percent of the English population was literate (about 1,680,000 people). Books read and bought for pleasure were rare, and still expensive. As it had been for hundreds of years, the reading life was one for the very well-educated (and wealthy) few. For example, the first printing of John Milton's *Paradise Lost*, in 1667, was a mere 1,300 copies, and it took two years for them all to sell. So while those years were a time of some monumental writing, it was not our Golden Age of Reading. ¶Let's jump forward a century or so. Certainly the time of Jonathan Swift and William Blake was one of great and widespread literary awareness? Not exactly. In 1792, the most widely circulated newspaper in England, the *Times*, made it into the hands of a mere three thousand customers a day, about .04 percent of the population. By 1800, literacy in England had reached just 62 percent for a population of roughly 8 million (having risen only about 20 percent in the previous two hundred years). The most popular books were still religious texts, and most households were lucky to own a handful of books—and those were not likely literary in nature. ¶Back in the nascent United States, things were worse. At the time of the signing of the Constitution, in 1787, only about 60 percent of about 3 million American adults could read. And though Jefferson might have had a vast personal library, most citizens did not. Owning large numbers of books was still prohibitively expensive for most. ¶So let's set aside the lifetimes of Dante, Shakespeare, Milton, Swift, and Jefferson. Their eras, remember, were without systems of public education, and thus literacy was not equally accessible to all. Given the tiny percentages of people who could not only read, but had the time and money to read literature, their times cannot provide our Golden Age. ¶Would the nineteenth and twentieth centuries qualify? These were the years when literacy rates in America exploded. In 1870, about 80 percent of 38.5 million Americans were literate; by 1940, almost 95 percent of 131 million citizens could read. ¶But today, as we noted, more than *240 million* American adults (aged fourteen years and older), of about 245 million altogether, are literate. ¶In 1950, 5,285,000 Americans aged twenty-five and over had attained a bachelor's degree—about 6 percent of the twenty-five-and-older population. ¶In 2009, about 60 million Americans in that age group had one, making for a 29 percent share of the same population. So those more recent decades don't eclipse our own time, either. ¶To state the obvious: there are more people in this country and on the planet than ever before, and that means that there are more potential readers. More widespread and democratic access to education here and around the world means that there are more literate people—over 3 billion, by the last calculation. And with book production at an all-time high, it follows that more people are reading that at any time in human history. So that's good news.

INTERNS & VOLUNTEERS: Annie Atura, Alex Colburn, Merany Eldridge, Alexandra Finnegan, Jill Haberkern, John Knight, Melina Mance, Jeffrey Mull, Anna Noyes, Zohar Perla, Eric Podolsky, Rebecca Power, Lauren Ross, Zack Ruskin, Ben Shattuck, Angelene Smith, Noah Sneider, Jenn Snyder, Molly Stack, Matthew Tedford, Michael Valente, Valerie Woolard. ALSO HELPING: Eli Horowitz, Andrew Leland, Michelle Quint, Greg Larson, Jesse Nathan, Meagan Day, Laura Foxgrover, Katrina Ortiz, Andi Mudd, Walter Green. COPY EDITOR: Oriana Leckert. WEBSITE: Chris Monks. SUPPORT: Sunra Thompson. OUTREACH: Juliet Litman. CIRCULATION: Adam Krefman. ART DIRECTOR: Brian McMullen. PUBLISHERS: Laura Howard and Chris Ying. MANAGING EDITOR: Jordan Bass. EDITOR: Dave Eggers.

COVER AND INTERIOR PAINTINGS: Jonathan Runcio, courtesy of the artist and Ratio 3, San Francisco. BORDER ART: Sophia Cara Frydman and Henry James. Images in "The Life of Richard Onyango" appear courtesy of the Pigozzi Collection, Geneva, and *Richard Onyango: The African Way of Painting*, and are © Richard Onyango. Thanks to Elisabeth Whitelaw and Ed Cross.

AND FIVE NEW STORIES FROM KENYA,
SELECTED BY BINYAVANGA WAINAINA AND KEGURO MACHARIA

DEAR MCSWEENEY'S,

Well, I've arrived here in Paris! *McSweeney's* first foreign correspondent! Haven't had a chance to leave the apartment yet, but I'm telling you, I simply cannot wait to tackle this amazing city! A dream come true! Very, very, VERY excited! Europe, here I come!

MIKE SACKS
PARIS, FRANCE

DEAR MCSWEENEY'S,

I recently invited my students to ask me any questions they had about a story I was teaching, Poe's "The Tell-Tale Heart." One student asked, "Hey, have you ever met anyone famous?" His classmates, many of whom have never met anyone more famous than me, were quickly enraptured by my answer, and seemed highly impressed by the ease and grace with which I interact with the rich and famous. Hence my reason for sharing several celebrity encounters here. My hope is that you and yours will be, at the very least, equally impressed.

Bill Cosby (1986)

When I was seven, my grandparents took me to see Bill Cosby's standup act. My grandfather knew the guy who owned the venue, and he took me backstage to meet Dr. Cosby. However, upon laying eyes on him, I backed off and said "That's not Dr. Huxtable." As we shuffled out, Dr. Cosby looked at me with an expression I can only describe as equal parts bemusement, surprise, and hurt.

John F. Kennedy, Jr. and either Madonna or Daryl Hannah (1987)

My parents and I once stood next to John F. Kennedy, Jr. in a deli in Hyannisport. We said hello to him and he shook our hands. He had a blonde woman with him who I was pretty sure was Madonna. However, I've since been told that it was actually Daryl Hannah he was with. John told me his favorite sandwich on the menu was corned beef. I told him that mine was turkey and mayo, which he said sounded quite good, "quite good indeed."

Jay Leno (1988)

My father and I once stopped by his friend's auto-repair shop while Jay Leno was visiting. Jay posed for a picture with me and a bag of Doritos. After the picture was snapped, he giggled and offered me the bag. I said "I don't really like those chips" and he said, "Hey, hey, who's the comedian here?" Everyone laughed.

Arnold Schwarzenegger (1989)

I was with my grandparents at a seafood place on Cape Cod when Arnie and three big guys walked past us, smoking cigars and making crude jokes about women. I said, "Hey, it's Arnie!" Arnie winked at me and said "Hello, little man." I was surprised to see that he's actually about five-foot-nine. "I don't care for his stupid robot movies," my grandfather said quite loudly.

Malcolm Jamal Warner (1999)

I passed Malcolm Jamal Warner outside of Tower Records in Boston. I said, "Yo, Theo!" and he said, "What's up, my man?" I said, "Not much, I guess," and he said "All right! Good seeing you!" and kept walking.

Dennis Franz (2000)

Dennis Franz—the fat guy on *NYPD Blue*—and I once stood next to each other outside a Gap dressing room. I told him I'd just seen a rerun of *Hill Street Blue*s he was on. He seemed very concerned about where the show was being aired and at what time and how often. I told him what I knew. He jotted notes down in a small notepad, looked around the store, and said "Okay, thanks for this" and patted me on the shoulder.

Darryl Hall and John Oates (2009)

While boarding a plane in Washington, DC, I passed Hall and Oates sitting together in first class. I pointed and said, "Hey, say it isn't so, Hall and Oates!" "It isn't so," Hall said, rather flatly. I was impressed that they flew together and were still such close friends. My mother once told me that they were probably lovers, "or at least in love," but I don't know.

Also, I think the "Don't taze me, bro!" guy was briefly a student in a composition class I taught at the University of Florida. If you have any questions about these celebrities, or my encounters with them, please get in touch.

Best,

JAMES FLEMING
ORLANDO, FL

DEAR MCSWEENEY'S,

Out of here. Just didn't like it, truthfully. Will be back in Brooklyn day after tomorrow, if you need me for anything. Thanks for the chance.

MIKE SACKS
PARIS, FRANCE

DEAR MCSWEENEY'S,

Have you ever noticed that Band-Aid boxes are lettered in Braille? My husband, a business professor, suggested that perhaps Johnson & Johnson labels all their personal healthcare products in Braille as a way to (a) indicate their sensitivity to the disabled, and (b) increase market share. But I checked Walgreens—besides Band-Aids, there are no other products with Braille lettering, Johnson & Johnson or otherwise. Neosporin and generic antibiotic ointment come in boxes of identical shape and size; Bengay and Preparation H are perilously similar. Just for kicks, I closed my eyes and felt around in the pain-reliever section, and let me tell you, there is no way to tell Motrin from Tylenol. (With a little box-shaking, I could distinguish between liquigels and caplets.) But the Band-Aids! They're labeled in Braille according to type: assorted sheer strips, clear strips, clear spots, extra-large flexible fabric, waterblock plus, antibiotic waterproof. Disney's *Princess and the Frog*. If you're blind and have a cut, Johnson & Johnson has got you covered. If you're blind and have a headache, cold/flu, fungal infection, poison ivy, jock itch, hemorrhoids, or anything requiring Benadryl, though, you're just totally screwed.

All the best,

JAMIE QUATRO
CHATTANOOGA, TN

DEAR MCSWEENEY'S,

I just got into an argument with my wife over a song on the radio. The song was "Crazy Love" by Van Morrison. My wife thought it was a cover version, but it wasn't;

it was the original. I am sure of this. So now I'm up here in my man attic, fuming.

We actually don't fight much, so we should consider ourselves lucky. Or not. Experts on *Oprah* say fighting with your spouse from time to time is healthy. It gives you a chance to vent and to share feelings and stuff. When my wife and I do argue, though, it's usually over something trivial. We never fight about money, or our feelings. Instead we bicker about where else we've seen that actor in the movie we're watching, or whether sharks are mammals or fish, or if Dr. John and Dr. Hook are the same musical entity.

I won't mention who's won the majority of these quarrels or just how lopsided the outcomes have been. But when it comes to this particular argument, the one about "Crazy Love," I'd like to point out a few things:

1. Van Morrison is my favorite recording artist ever. I first heard his album *Astral Weeks* as a junior in high school, and a week doesn't go by when I don't listen to part or all of it. The album's liner notes reference Cambridgeport, Massachusetts, the neighborhood I grew up in[1] and where Van Morrison lived when he wrote much of the record. This has nothing really to do with my argument, I just like mentioning it.[2]

2. There have been quite a few cover versions of "Crazy Love." Rod Stewart sang one. As did Brian McKnight, Helen Reddy, and a guy who came in eighth place on *American Idol* a few years ago. None come close to matching the original, and for this reason they weren't hits and are rarely, if ever, played on the radio, especially the radio station we were listening to, which is an independent, crunchy, AOR-type station that never plays songs by Brian McKnight, Helen Reddy, or former *American Idol* contestants. Yes, they do play Rod Stewart,[3] but for the most part just "Maggie May."

3. My playing "Crazy Love" on my computer right after the song ended on the radio should have been the final word. I mean, it was the song we had just heard on the radio, and there it was moments later coming out of my computer. I admit that me angrily singing along probably didn't help my wife discern the integrity of my argument, but just the same, *it was the exact same song that had just played on the radio.*

4. My wife likes Van Morrison—not nearly as much as I do, but she (a musician herself [4]) respects his talents and has

---

[1] My wife grew up in Kansas.

[2] Also, to be clear, "Crazy Love" wasn't a track on *Astral Weeks*, it was on *Moondance*, his more commercially successful follow-up to *Astral Weeks*. At any rate, I love Van Morrison.

---

[3] Not for nothing, but Rod Stewart is an artist whose merits my wife and I disagree on, as she fails to see how great his early albums were and instead rigidly focuses on his later disco/vapid-pop years.

[4] She plays the flute and was a member of her high school's marching band. The flute, incidentally, is a featured instrument on *Astral Weeks,* which, in

accompanied me happily to several of his concerts. She even agreed to have "Tupelo Honey" be our wedding song. So, yes, great, wonderful—I love her. However, a couple years ago we were in the car, listening to the radio, when the first few bars of "Tupelo Honey" came on. Without blinking, she mumbled "I hate this song" and changed the station. She admitted later, after I had pulled the car to the side of the road and banged my head quietly against the steering wheel, that she hadn't realized that it was "Tupelo Honey" and had confused it—the first song we danced to together as husband and wife—with another song.[5]

5. So after playing "Crazy Love" on my computer failed to make her see the light, I went to the radio station's website and found the listing of its most recently played songs. Right there at the very top of the list, surprise surprise, was "Crazy Love" by Van Morrison. Now, it's not out of line to believe that most fair-minded people would see this as putting me over the top as the be-all end-all winner of the dispute. I know I did. So much so, in fact, that I proceeded to climb atop our dining room table, pump my fists, and scream, "HA! I WAS RIGHT! I WAS RIGHT! YOU WERE WRONG!" In

retrospect, I regret doing that. I should have shown more restraint and acted like I'd "been there" before. If I'd done that, in all likelihood my wife wouldn't have challenged the veracity of the radio station's website and dismissed the listing as an eager-yet-uninformed intern's mistake. In all likelihood, she wouldn't have called the radio station.

I didn't wait for their response. I climbed down from the dining room table and stormed up here to my man attic. By now, my wife has surely spoken with the smoky-voiced Stevie Nicks–ish DJ, and realized that, yes, that was Van Morrison's version of "Crazy Love."

In a few minutes, I'll probably make the journey downstairs. We'll share a weary hug and apologize to each other. But I can't bring myself to do it just yet. I'm still angry.

Anyway, thanks for letting me vent and share my feelings and stuff,

CHRISTOPHER MONKS
ARLINGTON, MA

DEAR MCSWEENEY'S,
My friend Keith and I were wandering through the Virginia woods when we came across a large, dead turtle half submerged in a bog. It was of the snapping variety, and even dead, its powerful beak-like jaws were imposing. We were curious thirteen-year-old kids, so we stood staring. After a while a sleepy-looking man wearing a flannel shirt came and stood next to us at the glorified puddle. He looked down at the turtle for a while, and then he asked a question. I knew it was a question

---

my opinion, represents the pinnacle of all rock-flute recordings. Sorry, Ian Anderson.

[5] I don't think I really need to add anything else here to support this section of my argument.

because of the upswing in tone at the end, but every other aspect of it was so unrecognizable as any kind of language I was familiar with that I remember looking up slack-jawed, my attention drawn away from the dead turtle by sheer incomprehension.

Without looking up Keith said, "Yeah, it's a turtle."

The man's attention went back to the turtle momentarily. Then he turned back to us, his lips moving, and I heard a long string of sound. It was like a harp tumbling down a mountain.

Keith said, "Yeah, it's dead."

The man looked back at the turtle. Then he nodded slowly, his mouth turned downward, before continuing on through the woods. Which is what Keith and I did eventually.

Sincerely,

TED TRAVELSTEAD
BROOKLYN, NY

DEAR MCSWEENEY'S,

As the child of a father with a mother whose parents were Irish immigrants, I've battled a sense of "otherness" all my life. You probably didn't know that, because I've been so brave and private with my struggle. But growing up in the city of Denver, all I wanted to do was pass—to hide my Irish features beneath an innocuous Western costume. I went shoeless, rubbed dirt on my face, wore a turquoise bolo tie, traded beads for steer…

I was totally kidding. Do you really think people from Denver are like that? You harbor some pretty small-minded stereotypes, don't you? See, this is exactly why I didn't want to tell you about being one-quarter Irish. Let me guess—now that you know, you think I'm a raging alcoholic. Please. I said *one-quarter* Irish, not "two-thirds." I bet you think I wake up at night and ravage a seven-pound bag of potatoes in a single sitting. Or maybe you think I make grown men weep when I get my hands on a Celtic harp. Well, the truth is, potatoes are an excellent source of soluble fiber. And most people say I have the hands of an angel.

Here's my point: You're Irish, aren't you? I could tell you were battling your own demons. That's why you're so hard on everyone around you. But listen, Irish people aren't so bad! I know, because I just traveled to Ireland with my family. And I have tons of tips and tidbits from my journey that will make facing your own pasty countenance a little more palatable.

Here's one: when preparing for your trip, make sure you learn all the words to Don McLean's "American Pie." Every Irish person knows them, and you're going to look like a total jerk if you don't.

Also, why not make it a family trip? What better way to learn to love the Irish part of you than by doing it with kin? And don't feel self-conscious about using the word *kin*—you're Irish! That's how you talk! Besides, as long as you're not old (this wasn't printed in *TV Guide*, was it?), going with your family means going with your parents, and that means not having to pay for anything. Even beer! Or risky horse bets!

Be warned, though—if you travel to Ireland with your family by car, avoid sitting in the front passenger's seat. Your father is not used to driving on the left side of the road.

This means you'll be in a particularly vulnerable position when he hits a lot of curbs, trees, and side-view mirrors. You'll think you're justified in screaming when he sideswipes a car full of passengers, but he'll still pull into the parking lot of a Tesco and try to make you walk back to the hotel. Your dad's getting pretty crotchety in his old age, isn't he?

You're going to face another hard truth pretty early on in your trip. You know how when people find out you're Irish, they always say, "Oh, you *look* Irish!" You probably thought they were complimenting your rosy cheeks and alabaster skin. Actually, they were saying "You look like a dead body the cops just pulled out of the river. You're bloated, and nothing with blood in its veins has skin that color." Bummer, I know. But you've still got a great personality when you're drunk.

Here's another upside, though: Irish people are waterproof! As you'll notice, God weeps miserable sheets on the Irish all day, and all that moisture just rolls right off their Shetland woolies. This is because in Ireland, humans and seals have been crossbreeding for centuries.

But above all, take time to appreciate the deep, genuine kindness of the Irish. Like when you have that thought about Irish people looking like cadavers, and you write it down because you think it's funny, and then you're checking into your hotel and you accidentally leave the notebook where you wrote it wide open because you had your confirmation number written on the same page, and the awkward young lady who's checking you in reads it. Sure, her face will crumple into sorrow and bewilderment, but she'll still give

you really good service. And maybe, being stock of the Emerald Isle yourself, you're capable of that kind of generosity too.

HALLIE HAGLUND
NEW YORK, NY

DEAR McSWEENEY'S,

While dining recently at a Mexican cantina in Atlanta, I had a nice chat with L. (male) and A. (female). They are one of my favorite couples in the world, only in part because they are so much younger than me. I am but a greedy old weed next to their flourishing promise and gumption, which smells, at least on the lovely A., like something that blooms pinkish-purplish. As a weed, I like sucking up what they have to say.

Our discussion turned to various things having to do with love. As of this writing, L. and A. have been dating a long while. They are not yet engaged, but you know the deal: if they don't make that happen soon, their families and friends will step in.

On this night, they talked about another couple they knew, who were planning a wedding. There was to be a bachelor party in Rio during Carnival and a bachelorette party in Sonoma. I've been married before, and mahogany, the money that's thrown at weddings, you know? L. and A., however, felt no obligation to compare their future nuptials to others'. It heartened me, to see them unperturbed.

The conversation then veered toward A.'s recent trip home to Chicago, where she met up at a bar with her "first love" and "first sexual partner" (the same man). He brought along a female friend, a scientist from Greece. They all got on really well, A. said.

McSweeney's, there is no observer on the planet that could look at A. and not think, "Criminy, that is one pretty girl." The curly hair, the fresh face—it's undeniable. Slathered over the top of all this is a daring, intellectual personality. And as A. relayed this story, I felt myself thinking, my mind crimped in a defensive posture for L., "Yeah, well, it's no mystery what that guy was hoping for."

A. continued. She and her former lover had told their relationship story to the scientist: how they had fallen for each other, how they had had fun sex, how they had stayed together for years too long. And the scientist asked, "Why aren't you still together?"

Here I looked at L. and thought, "You are better than me, sitting there so calmly."

But A. finished by saying how healthy it was to sit with an old beau and explain to someone (a scientist, no less) why they'd broken up. So, I thought, this is what people do now with their exes. I felt inspired by it.

Next it was L.'s turn. As it happens, the girl he had dated in high school had fatefully stepped into the same Mexican cantina where we presently dined. She was across the room. He hadn't seen her in years. She was on crutches. He would say hello to her later. I don't know if there is symbolism in this. But her presence opened the doors to a story.

Their relationship had fallen apart, of course—college, craziness. But L. remembered fondly how he used to sneak over to this girl's house and stand outside her window, waiting for a hook-up session. (A. seemed to really enjoy this part; I don't know how these kids are so healthy.) You are familiar with this romantic setting.

This is when I, the out-of-touch weed, jumped in. "Let me guess—you'd throw a rock against her window? And she'd sneak you in?"

L. looked perplexed. The needle scratched on the record. A. turned to me and said, "Wait, you've actually thrown *rocks* against someone's *window?*"

Then L., attempting to help, hoisted his cell phone. "Well, no, actually," he said. "I had one of these." L. and A. chuckled knowingly.

And my very first thought was, "You threw your *cell phone* at her window?"

But no, thankfully, I did not say that, and anyway L. made a gesture that indicated he had used the cell phone to contact his temporary sweetheart from outside her window and arrange the make-outs.

Call me old-fashioned, but this information floored me. I didn't have a cell phone in high school. I'm almost completely sure they weren't invented yet. We had only pebbles and rocks and sticks to conjure love. Which is why I'm writing.

We live in fast times, we all agree. Emotional maturity may well be at an all-time high. But let us stop a moment to record this: Sometime in the last ten to fifteen years, the act of using a pebble and a window to woo a high-school hook-up passed from literal practice into the figurative, irresponsible-seeming sort. Try a rock on a window now, and the object of your affection will probably just respond with an angry text.

For an old weed like me, it's difficult to keep up.

Yours,

JAMIE ALLEN
ATLANTA, GA

HEY MCSWEENEY'S,

While making my latest crossword, I had to stop for a good couple of minutes to contemplate two answers I'd managed to fit in the southwest corner: VIMEO (clued as "YouTube competitor") and AMANPOUR ("News anchor Christiane").

Both fit; that's always a plus.

Both were new, never-before-used entries, and us puzzlemakers love being the first to debut new words in crosswords.

But the fact that VIMEO crossed AMANPOUR at the M really bothered me. Was that unfair? Just how well-known are those entries? Would most people have heard of both words?

I think about things like this all day. Crossword constructors are supposed to go out of their way to avoid obscure crossings. When we have to rely upon an ungainly entry, like the Belgian river MEUSE, to hold our answer grids together, we'd better be damned sure that the words going the other way are all common entries. If we crossed the first E in MEUSE with something like SOTER (you recall the years of his papacy, 166–175 AD, no doubt), we'd be stuck with a blind crossing. *Blind* because that crossing square is essentially unsolvable without either an encyclopedic knowledge of arcana or mad Googling skills.

Among certain circles, these blind crossings are called Naticks. I should know, because one of my puzzles led to the coining of that term. In my Sunday *New York Times* crossword of July 6, 2008, two obscure entries crossed at 1-Across, of all places. "*Treasure Island* illustrator, 1911" clued N C WYETH, while "Town at the eighth mile of the Boston Marathon" clued (you guessed it) NATICK.

The N was completely blind.

I remember thinking at the time that it was a tough but essentially fair crossing. Then again, I live in Boston and have at least thought about running the Boston Marathon. So NATICK to me would have been a no-brainer. Not so to pretty much everybody else. Since WYETH's name began with two initials, that first letter could have been anything. Which meant the Boston town could have been BATICK or HATICK or MATICK. You get the idea.

This move was deemed extremely dickish, and the Natick Principle was formed: "If you include a proper noun that you cannot reasonably expect more than one-quarter of the solving public to have heard of, you must cross that noun with a reasonably common word or phrase."

So what do you think? Is VIMEO crossing AMANPOUR a Natick? Let me know.

BRENDAN EMMETT QUIGLEY
CAMBRIDGE, MASSACHUSETTS

DEAR MCSWEENEY'S,

At some point it's probably happened that someone has come into a room where a lot of people are watching that movie *The Red Balloon* right at the moment when all those bullies throw rocks and pop the namesake balloon. Coming into that room, seeing that scene, and then finding everyone in the room crying all of a sudden, that has to be confusing. If I were that guy, I'd probably think "Why's everyone crying?! It's just a balloon!"

Sincerely,

STEVE DELAHOYDE
CHICAGO, IL

DEAR MCSWEENEY'S,

I think most people have a screwy impression of what it's like for the journeyman actor to live here in Hollywood on a daily basis. Well, first of all, nobody lives in Hollywood because it's a toilet. But all over the suburbs of Los Angeles, you'll find that most of the "celebrities" do the same things everyone else does—we go to the market, we walk the dog, we go to the dry cleaners, we carpool. And to quote Norman Bates, "We all go a little mad sometimes." This is my story.

I spent many years happily skipping through the routines of motherhood and work. I had regular gigs on several animated series that only required a few hours of my time each week. I was surrounded by incredibly funny people who made me laugh my guts out, and I got paid for it. The rest of my time was spent with my daughters—and with my husband, when we still had the strength for date night.

My life took on that feeling I'd get as a kid at the beginning of summer, when school's out and you have no homework and nothing's ahead of you but some ass-kickin' fun. And then I discovered Mommy and Me.

Mommy and Me was a structured playtime in a clean and controlled environment. It allowed me to play with the girls and not worry about the countless deathtraps I envisioned at the park: swing-chain strangulation, monkey-bar limb dislocation, sandy snacks, sandy vaginas.

I adored Mommy and Me. I belonged to any and all Kid Gyms that offered it, to Temple programs, even to a Methodist church. I was a Mommy and Me whore.

But as it should, my daughters' need for me waned. I became less of a playmate and more of a functionary, and eventually I found myself entombed by my kid's carpool schedules. I drove two carpools for their two different schools, which were on opposite sides of town. There was also religious school and tutoring, both of which took place during rush hour. Around this time one of the animated shows I worked on was canceled. Shlepping became my career.

I didn't for a moment resent the kids. My first-born did stand-up comedy in West Hollywood; the "baby" did all-star competitive cheer in Pasadena because nobody has any cotton-pickin' spirit on the west side. I was thrilled they had their passions. It was just the suffocating monotony of being in the car all day, every day. I began to feel like the actress who takes a part-time job as a waitress. After several years, she realizes "Hey, I'm a fucking waitress!"

My boredom turned into a malignancy. My free time began to feel like a work-release program. And I was getting old doing it! If you'd done a time-lapse series of photos of me in that car, you would see my face morph from thin to fat, then thin again, then fat, my teeth gritted, jowls sliding down my face. My once-glorious hair would give in to its inevitable thinning and take on an "I give up! I don't care, but I really do and I'm cursing the darkness!" look. My hands, gripping the steering wheel, would become freckled and gnarled.

On the road my self-pity turned into a sense of malevolent entitlement on the road. "Thou shalt not stop my driving flow" was my commandment. My coping mechanisms were road rage and sexual fantasies. Certain driving routes I'd depended on to keep the rage at bay began to betray me. I no longer sailed past those sorry bastards stuck in traffic, chuckling to myself, knowing my ace in the hole was Ohio Street; the vermin had found my secret route and backed it up for blocks! Slamming the steering wheel, cursing, I would conjure images of a punishing Rapture vacuuming up those individuals I deemed unfit to be on the road. It was like in Anne Lamott's book *Bird by Bird*, when she quotes a friend telling her "You can safely assume you've created God in your own image when it turns out that God hates all the same people you do."

When stuck in traffic, in my mind's eye, I could vividly see the asshole that was causing the backup. It was a feckless hotshot lawyer/agent on his cell phone, head thrown back laughing, or a narcissistic teenage girl, neither one of them noticing that the light had changed and then accelerating just slowly enough to make me miss the last chopper out of Saigon. Either way, McSweeney's, I was dead certain it was someone stupid, and that sickened me.

And then I began to turn my ire toward the kids in my carpool. It started with one boy's family—devoid of any sense of humor, this kid's parents were the kind of conservative Republicans who voted for their candidate because of a single issue: Israel. I love Israel, but I felt like grabbing her by the ears and screaming in her face, "The Evangelicals want to hasten Armageddon, you harpy!" I blamed this family personally for the crimes of the Bush administration. Also, once, when I finally, reluctantly, accepted an invitation to come inside their home, the husband came down the stairs and started gushing at me: "Laraine Newman is in *our* house! We have a big star in our house!" I was thoroughly mortified, and more so when the mother turned to me with an expression resembling someone smelling cauliflower cooking and said "I've never heard of you."

I also grew to loathe a boy I'll call Henry. Nobody liked the kid, unfortunately, and though this stirred some compassion in me at first he beat it out of me by routinely launching the most noxious farts imaginable. If I ended up consigned to the personal hell of being alone with him as my third and final drop-off, I'd resort to putting on Lil Wayne or an old Sam Kinison CD to block him out. I knew this was insane. What if he complained to his parents? If I lost this carpool, I'd be driving even more!

Eventually, in trying to make the rides fun for myself and the kids, I came up with a little diversion I called "Mr. Toad's Wild Ride." I would drive in a rubber-burning zigzag, and the kids would shriek with laugher. But when I found myself alone with Henry, he would invariably begin to chant "Uncle Toad's, Uncle Toad's" in a nasal monotone. "It's *Mr.* Toad's, you rodent!" I would scream, silently, inside my head. Then I would go to my happy place.

Don't think I wasn't aware of how shameful it was that I was behaving this way. What had happened to the good, tolerant, and forgiving person I'd thought I was? It had been easy to be that person when I wasn't in a perpetual state of abject fear and anger. But when stripped of everything I thought defined me—my career, my youth, my creative participation in the world—I became someone I couldn't recognize. Even though I wasn't actually wearing "mom jeans," and I didn't drive a mini-van (which is code for "Okay, I'm ready to be invisible to all men"), for me that carpool represented the death of hope. How can you reinvent yourself when you're in the fucking car?

But I survived, McSweeney's. Kids graduated, went to different schools, or got their driver's licenses. I'm acutely aware now that I'll soon be staring into the gaping maw of an empty nest. Then the focus will be back on me. My friends will come to me and say, "Hey, you've got the time now; maybe you should do a one-woman show." And I'll nod my head, thinking, "Yeah, because that's exactly what the world needs, another one-woman show." I'm so fucked.

Your pal,

LARAINE NEWMAN
WESTWOOD, CA

DEAR MCSWEENEY'S,

While researching my forthcoming book about the renegade psychoanalyst Wilhelm Reich, I went to see Alexander Lowen. Lowen, who died in 2008, was in analysis with Reich from 1942 to 1945, and spent twelve years studying Reich's eccentric variety of hands-on analysis. He claimed to have spent more time with him than anyone, apart from Reich's third wife.

Lowen was ninety-five when I met him, but several people still made the pilgrimage from New York to New Canaan, Connecticut, to have therapeutic sessions with him. As a result, all the cab drivers waiting at the train station knew where he lived. A ten-minute drive away, a large stone gateway announcing THE CENTER FOR BIOENERGETIC ANALYSIS led to well-kept grounds and a large clapboard house. Two sun loungers sat neatly next to each other on an immaculate lawn; an old Buick station wagon was parked in the drive.

Lowen's secretary, Monica Souza, met me at the door and led me into a large living room, where the doctor was on the phone. The room had a '70s bohemian grandeur, with gold-colored sofas and a large pool table that had been turned into a display case for Lowen's many books, whose titles include *The Language of the Body*, *Joy*, and *Love and Orgasm*.

His phone call finished, Dr. Lowen stood up to shake my hand. "Shall we start work?" he asked. I followed him into his study, expecting to conduct my interview over his cluttered desk, but he continued on through his office into his cork-walled therapy room. Monica was already there, putting a freshly laundered sheet onto the single bed that served as his analytic couch. There was a framed notice above it that simply said BREATHE.

Lowen asked me if I did any exercise, and I answered in the negative. "You have to do exercises every day!" he shouted in disbelief. "Get undressed and I'm gonna make you do it. You know how to do a somersault?" I quickly explained that I'd come to ask him some questions about Reich, rather than for therapy. "I was in his classes," Lowen replied.

"Let me tell you about Reich—you put this down in your book: breathing is the essence of life. If you stop breathing, you know what they say about you? The moment you don't breathe, you die." He sat down and told me to strip to my boxer shorts. "I've always been something of an athlete," he said. "I do three somersaults every morning, and I'm one hundred," Lowen added, adding five years to his age.

Within minutes of our meeting, I was doing somersaults in my underpants on a bed in Alexander Lowen's office. "You've got to look at the distances," he instructed me, watching me fling myself off the side. "You throw yourself like that and you're going to get killed. Go a little slower. Come on, do thirty-five or fifty of those. That's good. Can you hear your breathing? Well, that's what therapy's about. Reich thought breathing gives your body life and if you do enough breathing your emotions become alive and suddenly you're crying and talking. BREATHE!"

By the time I'd finished my prescribed number of somersaults, the mattress had almost come off the bed. I felt a little nauseous. I'd found time for a coffee at the station, and all the movement and hyperventilating had made me giddy. But without letting me pause for rest, Lowen had me bend backward over what looks like a padded sawhorse—he called it a "breathing stool," and considered it his major therapeutic innovation—and instructed me to reach back and lift an iron bell. This "sexual exercise," as he described it, was designed to stretch and relax my pelvic muscles, allowing for "vibrations" in that region.

Arching back, I noticed a large bottle of massage oil and two cushions on a shelf above the bed. One of the cushions was embroidered with the words, *Mirror mirror on the wall, I've become my mother after all*. A patch of the ceiling above me was scuffed and dented. Later, pointing to a tennis racket that hung on the wall, Lowen explained that "Sometimes people are angry and they beat the bed with it to get their anger out, or to try to get it out."

Therapy with Lowen was more like having a personal trainer than an analyst. I was told to lie on the bed and kick my feet up and down, and then to assume a position that Jean-Martin Charcot described as the "hysterical arc-de-cercle" when it was displayed by his patients at the Salpêtrière in the nineteenth century. "This is a basic exercise that Reich used," Lowen explained. "Now get your knees up, hold your feet, pull your ankles back, and lift your ass off the bed. Now arch more, move back on your feet, that's it, that's what Reich did. Arch, arch, that's it, now you've got the idea, now put your knees together, breathe, breathe!"

After almost an hour of such contortions, my body started to give out. "There you go, you've got vibrations!" Lowen exclaimed as my legs began to shake and shudder. "There's a strong charge in your body now. Can you feel the breathing going through the whole length of your body? It's alive. That's it! You're doing very well—Vibration is LIFE!"

Best,
CHRISTOPHER TURNER
LONDON, ENGLAND

AMBITION

by JONATHAN FRANZEN

ANTONIA'S VERY GOOD-LOOKING younger sister, Betsy, knew better than to expect even minimal tact or sensitivity from her husband, Jim—he had, after all, proposed to her with the words "If you want me to marry you, I'll do it," and she had, after all, accepted this proposal—and so she couldn't fairly be offended when Jim began to hint that she should have some work done. Jim's idea of a hint was to remark, while Betsy was seated at her bedroom mirror and doing her makeup, "Isn't it funny how people's noses and ears keep growing after the rest of the body stops?" Or to mention, apropos nothing, while the two of them were celebrating their twentieth wedding anniversary at a midtown steakhouse where every busboy knew Jim's name, that he used to have a moral problem with plastic surgery but was "totally coming around to it now." Or, when they were out eating lobsters with Jim's arbitrage partner Phil Hagstrom and Phil's young second wife, Jessica, to reach across the table and put his butter-smelling thumbs on Betsy's eyebrows and stretch the skin between them and say, with a wide, instructive grin, "You're frowning again, baby."

Betsy was proud of her natural assets, proud of the fact that they *were* natural— she could still, at forty-three, pass for thirty-six or thirty-seven—but she was also excited, in a dirty sort of way, to imagine reaping the benefits of augmentation, of compounding her native advantages, of strengthening her already impressive portfolio of looks, while being able to blame the procedures entirely on Jim and Jim's tactless demands, rather than on her own vanity. Almost every year on Election Day, she managed to "forget" to go out and cast her vote, or it was only after she'd fed the kids their dinner and filled her extra-deep custom-built travertine bathtub with hot and fragrant foamy water that she "remembered" that the polls were still open and wouldn't close for another hour. Instead of putting her clothes back on and shlepping through rain or sleet and participating in American democracy, she lowered herself into the tub and savored the unclean pleasure of not having voted against her conscience (which had been Democratic since her childhood in Cleveland) while Jim had gone and flipped every Republican switch the voting machine could offer and yanked the machine's big lever brutally, as if to emphasize his ever-deepening hatred of liberal Democrats, so that the household's only tallied vote would safely go to candidates who wanted to lower the taxes of high-income families and leave them more money for luxuries such as Betsy's bathtub, which Jim had bribed the co-op to the tune of thirty thousand dollars for permission to install, and which, as Betsy freely admitted to herself, it made her very happy to soak in on a raw November night.

People had always overestimated Betsy and Jim's ambition. In the beginning, her parents had imagined that she was secretly heartbroken to have been married in a hasty, colorless courthouse ceremony so unlike the California beach wedding of her sister, Antonia. Jim's parents had similarly assumed that their son was furious when Betsy, as soon as she had his ring on her finger, dropped all pretense of wanting to become a Catholic for him. Though Jim was frank about his lack of interest in anything but making money, and Betsy scarcely less frank about her motives in marrying him, nobody had wanted to believe them. Jim did dutifully spend a tasteless sum on a honeymoon in Paris, and there, for two days, Betsy did gamely try to do the romantic touristic things expected of newlyweds, but she was five months pregnant, and it was plainly a torment for Jim not to have hourly access to the markets, and their richly illustrated moneyed-yuppie travel guide to the authentic moneyed-yuppie pleasures of Paris was like an insider's guide to Hell. She'd never felt uglier and had seldom experienced more intense dislike of another person. On their third morning in France, out in the middle of the Pont Neuf under a white-haze sky, Jim began to abuse her viciously, shouting into her eyes, "What the fuck do you want to *do*? You haven't told me one single fucking thing you want to *do*!" and Betsy screamed back at him, "I don't fucking want to do *anything*! I hate this city, and my feet are killing me, and I want to go home!" Whereupon Jim, more quietly, and with a frown, as if some strange coincidence were confounding him, said, "But that's what *I* want to do." All of a sudden the two of them were laughing, and touching each other's arms and shoulders, and it was just about the most romantic moment of Betsy's life, there, sunburned and sweating in the middle of the Pont Neuf, surrounded by the Seine's atrocious glare, the two of them agreeing to throw in the towel and stop pretending. They went straight to the nearest McDonald's and then back to their deluxe moneyed-yuppie hotel room for a series of hair-raising romps punctuated by languid hours of English-language TV (Betsy) and highly technical phone calls to the New York office (Jim). How dirty and hot being terrible tourists together turned out to be! Their joint surrender to boringness, their rejection of ambition, became their exciting little secret. Some people, Betsy decided, just weren't as good at life as others: as good at culture and adventure, as good at being authentic and interesting. "I'm *this* kind of person," she thought with relief, "and not the other kind." Sitting on the Champs-Élysées, eating a farewell Big Mac before flying home three days early, she experienced a rush of gratitude to Jim so strong it felt like love. And maybe, she thought, it *was* love. Maybe this was what lasting love was all about. Not caring if your husband shouted English at French waiters, demanding food that tasted "more American." Not caring if your wife didn't have the patience to wait in line at the Eiffel Tower. Feeling sorry for your husband because his Catholic conscience had obliged him to propose to the first girl he happened to knock up. Feeling sorry for your wife for being too female about math and money to share your interest in tracking, to the fourth decimal, the franc/dollar exchange rates offered by various Parisian banks and kiosks, contrasting the best of these rates with the far better rate that a New York banker pal had given you before you left, and calculating how many hundreds more francs you'd received for your dollars than all the cheese-loving, French-speaking American yuppies who acted so knowledgeable and superior. Each spouse the keeper of the secret of the other's insufficiency and unambition. Like two lousy golfers encouraging each other to shave strokes, improve their lies, take lots of mulligans. Each obliged to the other for overlooking so much: could this be love?

Apparently it could. One by one, couples who'd initially seemed much happier than Betsy and Jim, more conversational and huggly-snuggly, began to separate and divorce, and the wives whose marriages had remained intact confided to Betsy that their sex lives, alas, had not, and meanwhile *Betsy*, of all people, lazy old *Betsy*, continued to enjoy intermittently dynamic relations with her mate. While other New York City parents networked and groveled to place their children in special incubators of genius, Betsy and Jim were content to send their own kids, Lisa and Jake, to the second tier of high-end schools, and to let them watch TV and help themselves to soft drinks, and it wasn't Betsy and Jim who were employing the child psychologists and family therapists now, was it?

The contrast with Betsy's sister was especially satisfying. Antonia had married a rabbit-faced Silicon Valley executive whose tales of soirées with Bill Clinton and George Soros delighted Betsy's parents, and with whom Antonia had raised three terribly interesting children. One son had a shaved head with a foot-long braided rattail and had shown his digital shorts at Sundance and Toronto; the other had dropped out of high school to read classics at Oxford by special invitation. The daughter once glued together eight thousand soda cans to form a prison cell in which she'd staged a three-day hunger strike, on the front lawn of Palo Alto High School, to protest the drowning of sea turtles by plastic six-pack rings. When Betsy's mother called to report on these achievements, Betsy took her cordless phone out onto her upper terrace, the one with open views of Central Park's emerald cumuli, and considered how pleasantly *normal* her own children were, and what a skinned rabbit Antonia's husband looked like compared to Jim. Jim was her towering, large-headed protector, her pit bull in pinstripes, her cuff-linked Great Dane. On the rare nuptial or funereal occasions when the entire family had to be together, her Cleveland relatives scattered at his approach. ("We need this headache?") Only Antonia was reckless enough to take him on. If she and Jim were left alone for more than a few minutes, they erupted in crude, joyless political shouting matches—

Lies nonstop on Fox—
Blame America first!
the NONSTOP LIES—
Jane Fonda and her—
Vile! Corrupt! Incompetent!
stab you in the back—

—and it was in the wake of one such fight that Antonia had taken Betsy aside and asked her, with a twisted face: "How could you *marry* that asshole? What were you *thinking*?" Betsy had said nothing in reply, just quietly buried the word *asshole* in her heart and let it fester there until her mother began to call her with stories of Antonia's domestic misery in Palo Alto and, later, Antonia's hermitlike existence in Manhattan, where she'd moved to be closer to her children. "She lives two miles away from you," their mother said. "I can't believe you won't even talk to her." Betsy, sitting on her upper terrace, looking out across the park, answered cheerfully: "It's actually quite a bit closer than two miles. I can see her building from where I'm sitting." Then she went out and spent thousands of dollars on tight-fitting skirts and dresses of the kind Jim liked her in.

One winter day, not long before Jim first mentioned cosmetic surgery, she got a call from Antonia's daughter, who was living in Brooklyn. The daughter and her girlfriend were having a party on the last night of Hanukkah, and they hoped that Betsy and Jim would come. It was a peculiar invitation, given Jim's famous dislike of Jewish holidays and Antonia's famous dislike of Jim—Betsy suspected that the daughter was trying to irritate Antonia by inviting them—but there wasn't much danger of Jim's saying yes. Or so she thought. That evening, when he came home from work, he laughed and said, "A lesbian Hanukkah party? Hey, hey! I better not tell Hagstrom, or he's going to want to tag along with us and check it out."

The party was in a brownstone in Park Slope. Jim may have gone to it intending to leer and give offense, but what he and Betsy found in the brownstone were thirty or so fresh-faced, dignified, intelligent-looking girls and boys drinking wine, eating Middle Eastern food, and discussing subjects that Betsy could feel, instantly, in her bones, she knew nothing about. Even Jim, who was ordinarily uncowable, hesitated in the entryway until Betsy's niece, a short-haired girl who was flushed with the exertions of hosting, came to their rescue and ferried them to a backwater suitable for invisible older relatives. Here they found bowls of hummus and baba ghanoush. Also Antonia, alone on a sofa.

Antonia had put on weight in the two years since Betsy had last seen her. Her hair was a half-gray witchlike haystack, and she seemed torpid and drifty, possibly drugged, as she greeted them. "Hello, fascist," she said. "Hello, wife of fascist." To Betsy she added: "I seem to recall that you and I used to be sisters."

"That was before I got married," Betsy said.

"Right." Antonia turned to Jim. "She's still mad at me because I think you're an asshole."

"Well, you're an asshole, too," Jim said affably.

"Exactly. There you go. Exactly my point." Antonia was slurring her words a little. "It doesn't make any sense, does it?"

Betsy went and found a bathroom and checked her makeup. She came out and had a conversation with a girl who was possibly as old as thirty and seemed astonished by Betsy's answers to polite questions about how she spent her days. "Aren't you *bored?*" the girl said. Betsy drifted into a corner and stood looking at other happy young girls who were talking about trade unions in *Ben*ezuela, and the rise of Soft Skull Press, and the demise of the bhangra scene in South London, and she thought she might cry. At more conventional parties, there were always men who stared at her, and it was disappointing to feel so invisible. She drained a glass of wine and poured herself another large one. Her daughter, Lisa, had started college in September. Her son, Jake, had lately turned fifteen and monosyllabic and private. She missed them both, and she was suffering from the loss of two of her favorite pastimes: staying up late with Jake and watching reruns on Nickelodeon, and religiously attending every field-hockey game and swim meet and tennis match of Lisa's, where she would nestle herself among the other mothers and feel like she was part of something. Several times, in October and November, Jim had told her to go and get some Prozac, for Christ's sake, he was sick of her moping.

She finished the second glass of wine and returned to the sofa where her husband and sister were now sitting side by side and having the same fight they always had, but in a different mood. Since when, Betsy wondered, was the word *fascist* an *endearment?* It was as if, over the years, by way of their shouting matches, Antonia and Jim had achieved an intimacy and ease with each other that Betsy didn't quite have with either of them.

"How much did you end up taking that loser for, anyway?" Jim said. "Five million? Eight million?"

"Does your crassness know no bounds?"

"I hope you didn't touch his pathetic little stock options."

"You should come over sometime and measure the settlement yourself," Antonia said. "I'll leave you alone with a yardstick and a calculator and a brokerage statement. Doesn't that sound fun? You can think about nothing but money all afternoon. Money and rage."

"I want to go home," Betsy said.

Jim looked up at her as if surprised that she was still at the party. "We're staying for the candle game," he said. "Sit down. Relax."

It was this candle game that drove Betsy, a few days later, to a Park Avenue psychiatrist named Frank Clasper. Numerous friends and neighbors of hers had portrayed Dr. Clasper as the easiest of touches, a human vending machine loaded with the most popular psychoactive drugs, and when she finally gained admission to his inner sanctum, after listening to his white-noise machine and reading more about Britney Spears's maternity than she cared to know, she was annoyed to discover that Clasper expected her to talk about herself—that it wasn't enough simply to say she was a little depressed. The doctor was wearing boarding-school horn-rims and had the manner of someone who'd stepped directly from precocious boyhood into late middle age; he could have been a very old forty or a very young sixty-five. He asked what she meant by "a little depressed."

Betsy mentioned sadness, low energy, insomnia, loss of appetite. Then she stopped and gave Clasper a tentative look, hoping she'd said enough. But Clasper wanted to know what *specifically* had prompted her to call him, and soon she was telling him all about Antonia and the party and the candle game. Was he familiar with the candle game?

"Describe it for me."

It was a tradition from her childhood. She'd forgotten all about it, but Antonia must have kept playing it with her kids while they were growing up. On the last night of Hanukkah, as the menorah candles were dying down, each person in the family made a guess about which candle would be the last to go out, and then everyone gathered around the menorah and rooted for their choice.

"I always hated the game," Betsy said. "It goes on *forever*. Because the flame can get incredibly tiny—tiny, tiny, tiny—and burn for the longest time. And then, if your own candle goes out, you still have to sit there while the other people root for theirs. And it's so stupid. It's just candles. And so anyway, on Friday, I don't know why it upset me so much, but I randomly picked a candle, and my sister picked a candle, and then it was Jim's turn to pick. *And he picked the same candle as my sister.*"

Clasper was writing on a notepad with a pen whose action was completely silent.

"I didn't understand it," she said. "There were other candles to pick. Like mine, for example. He could have picked *mine*. Or a third candle. And then to have to sit there for half an hour, with all these interesting young people who are so much smarter than me, while my sister and my husband rooted for their candle, even though they hate each other, supposedly, they can't stand each other. Supposedly. I had to sit for the longest time, watching all the other candles go out, and it was so *depressing*. One by one. One after another."

"What did it remind you of?"

"I don't know. People dying?"

"Yes. What else?"

She shook her head and lowered her eyes. She suddenly felt that she'd been talking too much.

"Did it remind you of marriages ending?" Clasper said.

"So anyway," she said.

"You felt your husband was being disloyal."

"You told me I had to talk."

"And this was what you chose to talk about. Your sister and the candles. Why?"

"Because I had to talk before you'd give me a prescription."

"You want a prescription? I'll write you a prescription." Dr. Clasper picked up an Rx pad and gave her a long, hard look.

"My sister always won," she said, turning her head away. "When we were little. I don't know how she did it, but, every single time, she picked the right candle. And that was *everything* to them. I swear to God, they loved to see her beat me. Even though she was the smart one, and I was the embarrassment, and they supposedly cared about justice."

"Yes," Clasper said. "But we should stop now." He put his pen down. "Will you come see me again?"

"Where was the justice?"

"I could see you at ten o'clock on Friday."

"Just tell me that one thing. Where was the justice? Then I'll go."

"We really have to stop," Clasper said. "We can talk about this again on Friday, if you want."

"Just that one thing," Betsy repeated stubbornly. It had occurred to her that if Clasper was an old forty he probably wouldn't be interested in a forty-three-year-old woman, but if he was a young sixty-five he might very well be swayed now. She bowed her head and waited to see what her looks were worth to him.

"There's a prejudice," he said finally, "that good looks are a matter of luck. Just something you're born with. Whereas brains are something you develop and earn with hard work."

Betsy sat very still, hardly breathing, thrilled.

"So, for some people, the beautiful girl is a symbol of social injustice. Of unmerited privilege. Sometimes, the girl feels this way herself. But we really have to stop now."

"It's so interesting to talk to you," she murmured.

"Mrs. Hanlon. You have to stand up and leave now. Will you come again on Friday?"

She told him she would.

Once she was outside again, however, and surrounded by phenomenally expensive real estate, by the mahogany and elevators of Park Avenue living, she had second thoughts. She imagined discussing Jim with Clasper, and figuring out things about Jim behind his back, and leaving Jim alone in his lack of ambition, and her heart filled with pity for him. He may have been clumsy and hurtful to her at the Hanukkah party, but he hadn't known any better, and this was what she loved about him, this was their agreement: not knowing any better. If the current situation were reversed—if Jim suddenly got ambitious on her and started having deep talks with a psychiatrist and realizing important things about himself—she would feel so abandoned and betrayed she didn't see how she could survive it.

The hinting began six weeks later, on Valentine's Day. That morning, before Jim left for work, he looked up from his newspaper and said, "You want to hear something ballsy? The Italian prime minister just had another facelift. He's running a major industrialized country, and he's having a facelift. Can you believe it?"

"Interesting," Betsy said.

Late in the evening, before sleep, after sex, he asked her if she thought that Jessica Hagstrom's breasts were real.

"Well, partly real," Betsy answered with a little laugh. "And partly not."

The following Sunday, before she was even out of bed, he brought her a bra and suggested that she put it on as soon as she got up, rather than waiting until after breakfast and letting gravity do its work for an hour or more.

"Okay," Betsy said.

She carried the bra into her dressing room and shut the door. A different, less interesting psychiatrist than Clasper had given her some pills that she now took one of every morning. The pills had a strong sulfurous odor, as of Hell, and they revved her up a little bit. She decided to take two of them, so as to be twice as revved. She'd unilaterally declined to enter therapy with Clasper, she'd lovingly foresworn that chance to *know better*, and now she was supposed to listen to Jim's hints for self-improvement? Swallowing the second pill, she set her jaw against ambition.

That night, when they were discussing a possible trip to the Bahamas, Jim suggested that perhaps, instead, they could take a surgical vacation. "Have some work done," he said. "You know, his and hers, you and me. I'm joking."

"I'll think about it," Betsy said.

She did think about it. More than thought about it: assumed that she *would* start having work done, soon, because it was the path of least resistance to do what everybody else was doing, and then blame it on Jim, and feel no guilt, and enjoy the results. But first Jim had to stop breaking their agreement. He had to cut out the daily hints. It was stubborn and perverse of her to deny herself a thing they both wanted, but she knew what she felt: he had to stop putting his fingers on her and pulling her skin around and trying to make her into something better.

Through April and into May the hints continued, and Betsy began to take, besides her Hell-smelling pills, little medleys of calming pills and sleeping pills that she got from her slut of a psychiatrist. She enjoyed the effects, and she enjoyed even more the thoughtlessness of her surrender, the laziness: just pop that pill! It was her own private drug rebellion. The sunny May days seemed overcast to her, they were over in a few hours. She was catching whiffs of pot smoke from Jake's end of the apartment, sometimes even in the morning, but whatever. Often, when she found herself in front of a mirror, she couldn't remember how long she'd been standing there. For the anxiety occasioned by the sight of her changing skin, the sudden waxy sagging of her face, there was nothing better than another calming pill.

And then Jim's hinting stopped. Just like that. As abruptly as it had started. At the very moment when Betsy was becoming certifiably bedraggled, he lost interest in the subject of improving her. An entire week passed without a hint. She reduced her pill intake, and the days brightened, and finally, one morning, after examining herself in the mirror, she felt emboldened to go and press herself against Jim and put her mouth on his ear and say: "About that surgical vacation…"

"I was joking," he said.

"Not for *you*. But I was thinking…"

He turned away from her and, with a trailing hand, gave her a pat on the bottom. "Don't worry about it. You're fine."

She took the kids out to Easthampton for two months. Between Jim's weekend visits to her bed, she ate a lot of salads, coated herself with sunscreen, got strenuous daily exercise with Lisa, bribed Jake with beer so that he watched TV with her, and observed with quickened interest the spectacle of augmentation that every cocktail party, beach, and restaurant afforded. The carved and rigid faces. The bronzed and beautiful ones. In the dry cool of her steel-and-glass rental, with a full-time cook and gardener, she felt like one of those infinitely pampered child pharaohs, like King Tut's sister or something, awaiting interment in the Valley of the Kings. To ascend to glamorous immortality, to be lacquered and golden and smiling on the outside and surgically cleansed on the inside, to complete her saturation in wealth by turning into cypress wood and precious metal and staying beautiful forever: this would be the little girl pharaoh's deliciously lazy final step.

On Jim's dresser, among the other contents of his pockets—his bill clip and Beemer keys and lucky golf tee—Betsy one Sunday morning noticed a stamped metal button bearing the logo of the Metropolitan Museum.

"Were you at the Met?" she asked when Jim emerged from his shower.

"Yeah," he said, toweling.

"Why?"

"I've been interested in learning about art."

Betsy frowned. "You mean, to invest in?"

"Yeah, maybe. But also just generally."

"What do you want to learn about it?"

"You know, the various schools and styles. Impressionism. Cubism. That kind of thing."

"Is this something I should be learning about, too?"

Jim shrugged. "I wouldn't worry about it."

He went back to the city, and a new dread settled over her, a premonition that deepened when she returned and found white dog hairs, quite a quantity of them, on the Persian runner outside the master bedroom.

"Who has a white dog?" she asked.

"I don't know," Jim said. "A lot of people do."

"Yes, but who has a white dog who was in the apartment in the last few days?"

"I've been at the office every night until ten or eleven."

He continued to work long hours all through September, except on weekends, when, uncharacteristically, he stayed home and wandered from room to room, hanging out with Jake, watching TV, and repeatedly asking Betsy what her plans were. If she said she had no plans, he nodded and disappeared. If she did have plans, he asked where she was going and what time she was coming back.

One Saturday, she went to lunch in Carnegie Hill with Jessica Hagstrom, who, for some reason, had wanted to see her alone. Betsy often encountered Jessica socially, but they'd never had an actual personal conversation, and she wondered if there might be some trouble in Phil and Jessica's marriage. What Jessica had to say, however, without preamble, as soon as they were holding glasses of Prosecco, was that Betsy should take better care of herself.

The dread that was lately always latent in Betsy came rushing to the surface. "I beg your pardon?"

Jessica rolled the stem of her glass between the palms of her wonderfully young hands. "I just thought somebody should tell you," she said, not looking at Betsy, "that you might want to watch out for yourself a little better."

Betsy withstood this apparent comment on her looks; she took it like a man. "Okay," she said. "Although I would say in my defense that I've been giving the matter a lot of thought. In fact, since you and I are being frank with each other, maybe you can answer some questions I have about the whole experience."

"Experience?"

"I'm thinking of having some work done."

"Oh my God. Is this Jim's idea?"

"Well, he brought it up first. But now it's my idea more than—"

"But this is exactly what I'm saying!"

"I kind of lost control last spring," Betsy said. "But now I'm working out again, and being more careful about the chemicals I—"

"What I'm saying," Jessica said, "is that you should be careful about how much you love Jim."

Betsy stared at her.

Jessica shook her head emphatically, as if to disavow her own words. "I don't know how else to say it. I guess I'm just worried that you're not as careful as the rest of us are."

"The rest of us?"

"As everybody else. As other women. But, you know, I'm realizing this might not be… that I probably shouldn't…"

"You mean," Betsy said, her voice rising, "*all the people who took other people's husbands? That's who I'm not as careful as?*"

Jessica was shaking her head, opening her purse. She slid to the edge of her seat and dropped two twenties on the table. "I'm really sorry," she said, "I just remembered I actually have to be somewhere else in ten minutes."

"Jessica—"

"This was a huge, huge mistake."

"Wait!"

"I'm sorry," Jessica said, standing up. "I thought I should warn you, because I always thought there was something nice about you. All the other women who were friends with Christine were so nasty to me. But you didn't seem to care. You hardly seemed to notice I was new, and I thought it was because you were nicer than the others. And that's why I wanted to do something nice for *you*, and try to warn you."

"Warn me about what?"

But Jessica was gone. Betsy drank her own Prosecco and finished Jessica's. Under their influence, as she headed down Madison Avenue, she found herself disoriented by the length of the midday shadows, by the sudden reality of fall. In the low, vision-doubling light, she saw how she might come across as self-satisfied and insufferable to her friends, because of Jim, and how her friends all seemed closer to each other than she felt to any of them, and how this had never bothered her, because she hadn't needed them, because of Jim. Her eyes were on the sidewalk, still battling the changed light, when she passed a Jack Russell terrier outside the Corner Bookshop. Its leash was looped around a parking meter, and it was gazing intently at a person inside the store. The person looked a lot like Betsy had looked at twenty-five. The person was holding the arm of Betsy's husband, who was holding an open book. His back was angled toward the window, but there was no mistaking the breadth of his shoulders, the size of his head. He wasn't a fiction reader, but he was standing in the fiction section. The person clutching him had her fingers in his armpit.

Betsy spat on the dog.

The dog flinched and Betsy spat again. The dog turned its head, trying to see the spittle on its back and neck, becoming agitated. Betsy, horrified by herself, ran away down the sidewalk, jostling people, stumbling, nearly falling.

When Jim came home, an hour later, she was sitting in their big formal living room, the one they used for entertaining. She sat like a throned pharaoh, her back straight, her arms resting comfortably at her sides. She didn't move at all as Jim approached her. She said, "I just saw you at the bookstore."

Right away, he began to nod and smile impatiently, as if she were giving him an earful, rather than sitting perfectly still. It was interesting to watch.

"Okay," he said. "You caught me." And then, angrily: *Did you spit on the dog?* Some disgusting creep sociopath spit all over the dog. Was that you?"

To sit perfectly composed, to be a lovely statue. Her voice fluttered up from inside her like a bird emerging from a burial cave. "Does this mean we're breaking up?"

"I don't know." Jim stamped around the room, as if to counteract her stillness. "But now that we've got things out in the open, I'm going to be spending some nights and weekends elsewhere."

Another bird fluttered up from the cave: "Don't bother coming back."

"What? Don't be stupid," Jim said. "Or was there something you were getting from me a year ago that you're not getting now? Huh? I can't offhand think of anything you're not still getting. So just calm down."

It was a strange thing for him to say, given that Betsy couldn't remember ever feeling calmer. "If you go away tonight," she said, "I never want to see you again."

Jim laughed at this the way he laughed at Democrats. He strode from the room and slammed the front door behind him, and when, a day later, he still hadn't come home, Betsy sent Jake to a friend's and took a cab to the other side of the park, where Antonia gathered her in her arms and gave her Kleenexes and Chinese food and got her thinking about lawyers.

"Move *out*?" Jim said three nights later, when he finally resurfaced. "You're blowing this way, way out of proportion."

Betsy had been lying awake in the dark when he came into the bedroom. Without raising her head or reaching for a light switch, she began shouting out Jim's crimes. He went and shut the hallway door, in case Jake was still up.

"Okay, okay, guilty as charged," he said. "But this means you can cheat on *me* now, and then we're even."

At this, Betsy sat up and turned on a light, to make sure he saw her look of disbelief.

"At least consider it," he said. "Before things get out of hand here."

"Out of hand? Out of hand? You're screwing some—child—and going to museums, and bookstores—"

"You could go to museums. No one's stopping you."

"But you hate museums!"

"They're a little boring, yeah," Jim conceded. "But once you start learning about the history, the Medicis and whatnot, it gets less boring."

"If you'd come to me and said, 'Let's take a class at a museum together, let's go learn about art together—'"

Jim made an exasperated gesture.

"But no, instead, it's 'Go get your tits fixed!' 'Go get your face fixed!'"

"Since when do *you* like museums?"

"I don't need fixing! I'm still in great shape!"

"Right. For your age. I realize. It's just that I'm in a phase of being interested in young people. In spending time with young people, and finding out how they look at things."

"Your children are young people. Your son down the hall is a young person."

"I'm trying to say this doesn't have to be such a big deal. We get through this, you do what you need to do, I do what I need to do, and we can still get old together."

"Except apparently I'm already old."

"Bets. There are millions of guys who'd want to have an affair with you. Believe me. Or you can go take a class at a museum. You can do whatever. I thought that was basically our *agreement*. That we cut each other some slack."

Betsy stared at him.

He gave her a big smile. "Right?"

"Yes," she said deliberately. "That was our agreement. I was willing to put up with your being an unbelievable asshole. But you wouldn't put up with me not being twenty-five anymore. You broke the agreement, and now you have to leave."

"Whoa. Jesus. You're sounding like your sister."

"I am *not* the ambitious one here," Betsy said.

"Oh yeah?"

"Do you think I would have married you if—"

"There is *no reason* you have to be such a Nazi about this. You could just chill, like we always have."

"I demand that you move out!"

"Where am I going to go?"

"Go live with your young person."

"That's really not such a good idea."

"Then go to a hotel."

"Look, I'll stay in the guest rooms. You won't even see me."

"You can stay one night and get your stuff together. But then you're gone."

"Baby, I was *joking* about having work done. Didn't I keep telling you that? It was jokes."

"I loathe you," she said.

He reeled back. "You better cool down," he said. "You better take some time and cool down."

The next day, he rented a furnished high-floor bachelor pad at the Mondrian, but it took him nearly a month, plus a stern phone call from Betsy's lawyer, to forsake the guest room he was camped out in and pack some suitcases and actually move out. Soon after this, he and the dog owner stopped seeing each other, according to Jake, who also reported that there was no food of any kind in the kitchen of the bachelor pad, not even peanuts or martini olives, and that Jim had taken to using an online dating service. Betsy had to be careful not to imagine him dating. Nothing made her unhappier now than feeling obliged to pity him for his clumsiness and crassness. When her cleaning woman reported that somebody was spending nights in the guest room again, Betsy was quick to tell her lawyer to tell Jim's lawyer to tell Jim to stay the hell away. Jim called her on her cell phone the same afternoon. He said he missed his home and didn't see what was wrong with discreetly crashing there, if he arrived very late and left very early. Betsy hung up on him. He called back and said that even if they got divorced he didn't see why they couldn't still share a house, and grow old together, and take care of each other. She turned her phone off. Late that night, unable to sleep, she wandered around the apartment and noticed a light on in the largest guest room, behind a closed door. She stood in her pajamas, looking at the door, picturing the shrunken man on the other side of it. Of all his betrayals, his weakness in crawling back to her was the one that hurt worst. She'd always lied to herself about settling for a small kind of life; the truth was that she had *idolized* him. Only now, after she'd lost it, did she see the immensity of the pleasure she'd had in making herself stupid, and how once-in-a-lifetime lucky Jim had been to have a wife as innocently forgiving as she was, and how grievous, therefore, his own loss was, too. If he stayed away he was an asshole, if he came back he was a pussy. Her ambition had destroyed them. And so it fell to her to leave.

NOW YE KNOW WHO THE BOSSES ARE HERE NOW

an essay by J. MALCOLM GARCIA

T HIS YOUNG MAN sitting beside me, eyes tearing, balls of his feet bouncing ceaselessly off the pavement, tells me that he knew Paul Quinn for seven, eight years. Friends, so they were. Through school and driving tractors together and running bales in the summer.

He played soccer the night Paul died. Paul watched the game until halftime, left for something to eat, came back to pick his friend up. This young man, his feet still tapping the ground, eyes saucers of pain, tells me it doesn't go away, that sound. The sound of batons and metal pipes striking Paul and Paul screaming and then not screaming.

(The police say they have intelligence that my life is under threat.

I understand.

Don't use my name.

I'll use a letter. C.

Aye.

Take me back to that night.)

It's October 20, 2007. About 5:30 p.m. A good evening. Good enough, like. Not hot, not cold. C and Paul don't have plans after the game. Just spinning about, like. Shooting the craic. Driving the back roads of their Northern Ireland village, Cullyhanna. They decide to stop at Paul's house and get on his computer and mess about. Bored with that, they drive around Cullyhanna again.

Then Anthony, a friend, rings Paul. Anthony says some bulls is coming to his father's fucking farm this evening. He needs help cleaning a pen.

C and Paul mess about for another five minutes. Then decide, Fuck this, we have to help Anthony. His farm is near Castleblayney, just over the border in the Irish Republic, the "Free State." On the way, Paul has second thoughts. Take me home, he tells C. He can't be bothered. Fucking cows. C can't be bothered either. But it won't take long, C says. How long can it take?

(*I thought it was funny that Anthony called Paul.*

Why?

He would have called me, usually. I was closer to him. I thought to myself, He couldn't get through on my phone so that's why he called Paul.)

At the farm C and Paul park outside a shed where Anthony is to meet them. Still light out. Around ten to six, so it was. No one in sight. They stop, look around, pondering like.

A yellow lorrie stands down a ways. Bright yellow. C walks toward it. He's almost reached it when a man wearing a black mask, black jacket, black jeans, and black boots jumps out at him, shouting *You fucking scumbag bastards!*

C turns around, yells at Paul.

Go! Run, run, run!

Three more masked men come at C from his left. More are running out from behind hay bales. Another three, from other directions.

(*At first, I thought it was a joke, like.*

A prank?

Yeah, quite a joke, Anthony, yeah, good on ye.)

C shoves one of them away, but there are too many to fight off. Other men are on top of Paul. They drag C and Paul into the shed, hitting them with iron bars. Shouting, You bastards!

Three or four men stay on top of C until someone comes over and drags him into a pen. He sees Anthony tied up next to another one of their mates, Connor. On their knees, faces against the wall. Someone kneels on C again. Shouting, Shut it, shut it, shut it!

C can hear them bashing Paul about. He hears the *whoomp, whoomp* against his friend's body, hears Paul screaming, Stop, stop, fuck, fuck, stop, stop!

Then he stops screaming.

(*Just stopped, like. All of a sudden.*)

But they keep hitting him. Two minutes more, at least. Then they stop. The air still. The men breathing hard through their masks.

(*Did they say anything?*

Now ye know who the bosses are here now. Shouting, like. Now ye know!)

I am staying in a bed and breakfast in Crossmaglen, a small town fifteen minutes' drive from Cullyhanna.

In 1969, at the start of the Troubles, the police barracks here was attacked by the IRA. In 1971, British Army soldiers killed a Crossmaglen man who they wrongly thought was armed. The killing drove many young Catholics to join the fight. The community became much more insular and suspicious of outsiders. A characteristic it retains to this day.

With my long beard and ponytail, I stand out. People ask one another, Who's the hairy man walking about Crossmaglen and Cullyhanna?

The name sticks.

Hey, Harry, a man shouts to me one day, what about ye?

You enjoying your stay, are you, Harry? another man says.

What about Obama, Harry? Cheeky bastard, wha? declares a third.

But when I bring up the subject of the Paul Quinn killing, the good humor disappears and we quickly find something else to discuss.

However, if, at the end of the day, I meet someone alone in a pub or on the road or leaning on a fence post and considering the hazy distance across the field before them, when the evening hour has slowed and hesitates between light and dark and what lurks beneath the surface rises more easily, then I find people willing to talk about Paul.

Paul was a cheeky lad, so he was, Harry.

Good with his dukes. Wouldn't back down, don't you know. Not one to be pushed about, our Paul Quinn. He took a lot but didn't like someone with no authority telling him what to do. That was his downfall, aye.

Cullyhanna is naught but a church, a pub, and a convenience store. Everyone knew Paul. Everyone knows everybody. There's so-and-so's son. People look at their neighbor now and wonder, Was ye part of them that done him? People look at themselves and think, What could I have done to stop it?

Them boys who done Paul, they lured Anthony and that other boyo, Connor, to that shed by promising them some work. They broke Connor's ankle, so they done. Anthony cracked, then, made the call.

What would any of us have done had we been him?

Everyone keeps an eye on our Father Cullen. They tell the Quinn family, Father Cullen's talking to so and so. Maybe they done it. Maybe they're asking forgiveness. Father Cullen says our humanity has sunk to a new level.

What they done to him you wouldn't do to a dog. Beating him like that. Pipes and bats with nails in them. Breaking every bone in his body below the neck, so they done. The word got around. Young man battered to death. Just twenty-one. The savagery of it.

Sinn Féin says no republicans were involved. Ludicrous. They know that if another crowd did that to a Catholic boyo, the IRA would have stepped in and dealt with them, ceasefire or no ceasefire. But the IRA hasn't stepped in. No Sinn Féin counselor came to the Quinn house to pay their respects to a Catholic family that lost a son to murderers. Very strange. Normally they arrive quick like, if for no other reason than to get their picture taken for the newspapers.

Maybe they didn't mean to kill him. Maybe they meant to leave him in a wheelchair to look out a window for the rest of his wee life. A message to other young people born after the Troubles. Look at Paul Quinn and remember: respect the IRA. Whatever they planned, they beat our Paul to death, so they done.

There were good men in the IRA when the struggle was going on. It's the bad men that remain. They want to keep control. Like dogs killing sheep. Bolder and bolder. If they hadn't a killed Paul, they'd a killed others.

Kids today, the Troubles are forgotten history. It's something they read in a book. They don't remember it. Some asshole says he used to be somebody in the IRA, who the fuck are they, wha? Kids used to think, When we grow up we'll be one of the boys. But the new generation says, No we won't. Fuck the IRA.

It's created a void, so it has.

Paul was born in 1986 and raised on a farm in Cullyhanna, in County Armagh. By the 1990s, the South Armagh Brigade of the IRA had grown to about forty members. Thomas "Slab" Murphy, an alleged member of the IRA's Army Council, has been the organization's Armagh commander since the 1970s, according to British security personnel.

The South Armagh Brigade has not confined itself to paramilitary activities. Irish and British authorities accuse it of smuggling millions of dollars worth of gasoline and diesel north across the Irish border every year. As much as 50 percent of the vehicle fuel used in Northern Ireland has been estimated to have been obtained in this way. Gas is cheaper in Ireland proper.

Paul's parents, Stephen and Breege, were never involved with the IRA, they tell me. They would stop and listen to news reports about a pub bombing or attacks on the RUC and then get on with their day. Paul never called Breege mum. Just Breege. That was his way. He'd call and ask about dinner and pretend to be somebody else. Make up an accent, like. Every night before going to bed, he would shout Au revoir.

French for goodbye, you know, Breege explains.

He had a jolly way. He would always buy a chocolate and a drink and put change in the charity box in town. He'd help old folks carry their bags, so he would.

When Breege stood by the sink he'd come behind her and lift her up. He was just full of life and was all the time smiling. Even when she gave out a scolding, he'd smile.

He loved to hear drinking stories about his father. He would come home and tell Stephen what he'd heard and watch his face turn red. He enjoyed listening to old men talk to other old men. All those stories and the laughter. It never was serious talk.

He liked having his potatoes peeled for him.

Mommy's boyo, Breege says.

Paul worked on farms. He also drove lorries for smugglers. Sometimes he came home and the house filled with the smell of diesel.

Smuggling was always a way of life, Stephen says. When I was a wee thing, my father smuggled, and his father, and his father before him. Where there's a border, there's smuggling. Only way to make a living. Is it criminal? Then you'd have to call everyone a criminal. Everyone.

Stephen was fixing a wall with some other fellows the day Paul died. Looking at it more than fixing it, truth be told, Stephen says. Paul came home in a car belonging to a friend and stayed long enough to make a bacon sandwich. After he ate, he said he was going to pick someone up. Siphoned some diesel from a petrol tank near the driveway, maybe a gallon, and then drove off. Stephen watched him go and never saw him alive again.

Breege saw Paul for the last time the night before. She came home from an evening with friends and he was in the kitchen eating cereal. She said good night and went to bed.

Au revoir, Paul said.

Jim McAllister meets me at McNamee's Bakery, a few blocks away from my bed and breakfast.

Jim helped start the Quinn Support Group, a loosely knit organization of Cullyhanna and Crossmaglen families intent on maintaining pressure on the authorities to find Paul's killers. Jim and Stephen Quinn have known each other since the early 1960s, when they were both about sixteen or so. They met in a pub, something like that, Jim says.

As a young fellow, Jim had republican feelings. He was elected to the Northern Ireland Assembly as a Sinn Féin candidate in 1982. But over the years, he drifted away from the party, and he finally left it in 1996. He saw Sinn Féin becoming everything it had once despised—leaning away from its core beliefs to get votes.

A few years ago, a schoolgirl asked him, When was Bobby Sands shot? Bobby Sands died in the hunger strikes, Jim explained. He wasn't shot. That's when he knew his day was past. He remembered his grandparents talking about the 1916 uprising like it was clear in their minds, but it was history to Jim just as Jim and Bobby Sands were history to that girl. It's all relative. It depends what side of the years you're on, aye.

When Paul died, a friend rung him, Jim says. A young man been battered to death. He didn't know his name. Just that he was a Quinn. The county is full of Quinns. A moment later another man called and told him who it was.

The next morning he drove to the Quinn house. About twenty people were already there, and more were coming. When somebody dies in these parts, families gather around from all over to pay their respects. That's how we deal with death here, he says. They all talked about what happened. Not a wee beating, they agreed.

Paul had a reputation, of course. He fought. As a Sinn Féin counselor, Jim had dealt with anti-social behavior: boyos breaking windows, stealing, making a ruckus. That kind of thing. Years back some young lads, sixteen, seventeen years old, were in a gang called Hard Core. They'd assemble, drink beer, get loud. People were afraid. Jim asked to speak with them. Five or six lads showed up at his office one night. He told them they were scaring people. Those five or six boyos never came to notice again.

Two other lads, however, didn't meet with Jim. They continued to cause problems, and when he caught up with them they were made to wear placards: I'M A THIEF, something like that. Made to stand in a public place where everyone saw them. They never did anything after that. They became good men, so they did. Better to wear a placard than to be taken to a shed and killed, aye.

If it was smugglers who killed Paul, why would they want to bring attention to themselves? Jim says. Smugglers don't kill. If they have a problem with someone, they either hit them in their wallet, ignore them, or set them up to be caught by the police. They don't fight. No one has named specific smugglers as suspects. No one's come forward to accuse smugglers except for Sinn Féin.

Why's that, you think? Jim asks.

Paul would get involved in pub brawls, his father tells me, but he never talked about it. Nothing to tell. As far as he was concerned, once the fight was over, it was finished.

One time, however, he had a fight with Tomas McCabe. Tomas was the son of Frank McCabe, who police allege is an IRA man. Young McCabe would often get into rows with the other fellows. He lived in a political home and felt entitled to rule the roost, so he did, Stephen said.

The fight happened in Newry, a forty-minute drive from Cullyhanna. A car driven by Tomas blocked Paul's car outside a disco. They both got out, and Paul landed a punch. He wouldn't be bullied. A second boyo, one of Tomas's friends, told Paul he would see him shot.

Later that evening, Eileen McCabe, Tomas's mother, stopped outside a chippy where Paul was ordering food. Clad in only a nightgown, she threatened Paul with a hammer. You'll be found in a black bag, she told him.

About the same time, Paul had another fight: this one with Vincent Treanor, an alleged senior member of the IRA. Paul confronted Treanor after his sister Cathy accused Treanor of insulting her.

How long was this before he was killed? I ask.

Three weeks, maybe, Stephen tells me.

This man biting his nails to nubs sits across from me in a cluttered kitchen strewn with newspapers and dirty dishes.

He tells me to refer to him as an ex-IRA volunteer from Crossmaglen. He served in the organization from his mid-teens to his late forties. A farmer now, he fears the consequences of the IRA finding out he's spoken with a journalist.

Now ask your questions, he says.

If the man were younger, he would leave Northern Ireland. He loved it once because the people were all united, but he feels shame today. If it had been loyalists or Brits who killed Paul, he could stomach it. But not one of your own. The IRA takes anyone now. Before, they would cherry-pick. Before, a man could fight with an IRA man, have a bit of a pub row, and it was forgotten. Not now. The boys about today have recruited hoods, psychos, money-grabbers.

They're as bad now as the police were during the Troubles. Worse. In the old days, if the police stopped you, they'd shoot you. They didn't play by The Marquess of Queensberry rules, but they never battered you to bits.

The people in rural areas know what's going on. They watch who's moving what and where. Groups of men assembling would be noticed. Someone saw something when Paul was killed. They had to. But after thirty years of war, people know not to give the police information on IRA activities. The bodies of informers have been dumped in public places. Reason enough for the living to keep silent, aye.

Paul would have been just a wee thing during the 1994 ceasefire, the man says. Barely a teenager when the 1998 Good Friday Agreement was signed. A child of the peace process, so he was. Some peace, wha?

Had Paul survived, his beating would have been forgotten. It would have been considered housekeeping. An internal IRA thing. But he didn't survive, did he?

To know one of your own did this is soul-destroying.

* * *

A month after Paul's death, Ulster Unionist peer Lord John Laird asserted parliamentary privilege in the House of Lords to accuse Slab Murphy of approving Paul's killing. He said Murphy had ordered nationalists in the area to not cooperate with the police. Laird named Vincent Treanor as the man who planned the killing.

Both Murphy and Treanor denied any involvement.

In 2008, Northern Ireland's Independent Monitoring Commission issued a report attributing the murder to local disputes. Some IRA members, or former IRA members, may have been involved, the report said, without naming the assailants. But the IMC insisted that there was no evidence that IRA leadership was linked to the incident.

Some of the killers, the commission's report concluded, were "accustomed over a substantial period of time to exercising considerable local influence, collectively and individually. This would have led such people to expect what they would consider as appropriate respect from others, [including] being able to undertake their activities—including criminal ones—without interference. They would find it very difficult to accept any waning in this influence and respect."

Stephen Quinn and I stand in the St. Patrick's Church cemetery, beside Paul's grave. He lies buried next to a friend who drowned while he and Paul were on holiday in Greece. Just eighteen, both of them. Paul brought his clothes home afterward. Another friend buried nearby died by suicide.

IN LOVING MEMORY OF OUR DEAR SON AND BROTHER PAUL
SAVAGELY BEATEN TO DEATH 20 OCTOBER 2007 AGE 21

Stephen folds his hands and closes his eyes and tells Paul about his day. How he took his seven head of cattle to the market in Newry. It rained something awful. Gave them a good feed the night before, aye. Last supper. He gives a short laugh. He tells Paul to help him catch his killers and then pauses, his face a weather of hurt.

* * *

A nurse leads the Quinn family into the surgery room on the evening of October 20, 2007. They see the ventilator tube protruding from Paul's mouth. They see the swollen left side of his head. His right earlobe torn off. One of his front teeth cracked. Gray face beneath the bright ceiling lights. Eyes with no color, not completely closed. The rest of him covered in a sheet. Beaten so badly Breege is not allowed to put rosary beads in his hands. Still so young looking.

Paul's girlfriend, Emma Murphy, saw trouble coming three months before he died. Paul lived in Silverbridge at the time, a village near Newry. He told Emma the IRA didn't like him. Living on his own, he worried they'd come and get him. He decided to move back home.

Stephen Quinn remembers the night Paul returned. He came into the kitchen and Stephen asked him, as a joke, Are ye back home, aye?

I am, Paul said, and laughed a nervous laugh.

Before he came in, Stephen saw him outside the house in a car with three or four fellows. He didn't know if they were friends or not. He didn't ask.

I try to contact Anthony and Connor, but they won't talk.

I call Sinn Féin every day for three weeks, asking them to comment on the status of the Quinn investigation. I'm told someone will call me back, but they never do. Finally, a secretary says, We've got all your messages. Stop calling. There's no point for you to call anymore.

I call back anyway, but this time I leave a message for Slab Murphy. I never hear from him.

I call Vincent Treanor and leave a message with a woman I presume to be his wife. She's decidedly cool when I explain the purpose of my call. She takes my number, but I don't hear from him.

I call Patrick John Quinn, owner of the shed where Paul was killed and no relation to his family. A former IRA man, according to the police. The man who answers refuses to identify himself and tells me not to call the family again.

I call Frank McCabe, father of Tomas McCabe. His wife Eileen answers and I ask to speak to her husband. Just a minute, she says. I hear her call for him in the next room. She gets back on and asks, Who's calling? I tell her, and explain that I want to speak to him about the Quinn murder. He's not here, she says, and hangs up.

I call the press office of the Democratic Unionist Party. In 2007, Sinn Féin and the pro-British DUP entered into a power-sharing agreement to govern Northern Ireland. The DUP went into government with the republicans on the strict understanding that the IRA had ended all its militant activities. Proof of IRA involvement in Paul's murder would endanger the very existence of the administration. The DUP refuses to comment.

Finally, I call Peter John Caraher, a senior South Armagh republican listed by the Northern Ireland police as a veteran IRA member. I met him on a reporting trip in 1993, when he spoke to me about his son Fergal, who was shot dead in 1990 by a Royal Marine.

I can still see Peter John's wife handing me a framed photo of Fergal, her pale face lost in sorrow, her sunken eyes staring through me. Not a word exchanged between us. Just the silent offer of Fergal's photo. Surely, I thought, Peter John would understand the Quinns' need for answers.

Peter John remembers me and agrees to a meeting. On the day of our appointment, however, he changes his mind. He explains that he has the flu. He expects to be sick all day and the following day. And the day after that and the day after that.

Good luck, he says.

It took Stephen Quinn twelve months to visit the hulking red shed where Paul was beaten to death. He refused to look inside. He thought about the beating and the bastards who did it and was sickened looking at it.

I am quite convinced the IRA killed Paul, Pat McNamee tells me.

He cites the black military-style clothing the killers wore, the planning required to lure Paul to the shed, and the manner in which the shed was cleaned after the beating, leaving no weapons and little forensic evidence.

It's the modus operandi of the IRA, Pat says.

We are sitting at a long table in his Crossmaglen house, with pictures of his daughter and his grandchild looking out at us. Pat has a professorial air about him. Blue dress shirt, gray slacks, tie. Gray hair, trim goatee. An urban planner. But years before, he was a member of the IRA.

In 1978, he was jailed for kidnapping and possession of arms and ammunition. Four years later he was tried in a special criminal court in Dublin. He served six years in Portlaoise Prison. In 1996, he was elected to the Northern Ireland Forum for peace negotiations as a member of Sinn Féin.

As time went on, he began to disagree with the party's policies. Like Jim McAllister, he believed the real issues had been shoved aside to promote electoral success. He left Sinn Féin in 2005.

I knew Paul's family in the sense I'd know most families in the area, he tells me. In the IRA it was important for me to know who was who and where people lived. I would have seen him as a young fella knocking about. When I saw the pictures of him later, I remembered him. Quite a big lad. Bit of a terror. He did what young fellas do. He had a car. A bit of a racer.

He drove oil for people, Pat continues. He ran afoul of the IRA. When the republicans stopped their military activity, they occupied themselves by making money. Some members worked in legitimate ways. Some got into smuggling.

Paul was a competitor, he says.

They would have been at the shed an hour before Paul arrived, Pat says. Some of them would have watched the road. At least twenty others would have been waiting nearby. For that many people, the operation had to have been authorized by the IRA leadership in South Armagh.

Do him, they would have decided.

Easy enough.

Get a line on his mates.

Easy enough.

Get his mates to lure him in.

Easy enough.

Why not just shoot him? I ask.

That would have involved firearms. A violation of the ceasefire and the decommissioning of weapons.

So they beat him to death instead?

Yes, Pat says.

*   *   *

I consider a billboard that stands above a closed Sinn Féin office in Crossmaglen.

MURDER!

Beneath the word is the smiling face of Paul Quinn, striped shirt open at the collar. Short hair combed forward. A relaxed smile. The shape of his nose, the blue of his eyes that will be passed on to another Quinn.

PAUL QUINN REFUSED TO BE BULLIED
AND FOR THAT HE WAS BEATEN TO DEATH

The billboard has faded from the rain and sun and the days that have turned into weeks, months, years. No one has been charged. Perhaps someone will decide to talk to the police. For their peace of mind, if nothing else.

YOUR COMMUNITY IN THE GRIP OF MURDERERS
IS THIS THE "PEACE" YOU SIGNED UP FOR?

On my last night in Crossmaglen, Stephen Quinn picks me up for dinner.
One last story before you leave, he says.
A year or so before he died, Paul was driving down a road with a farmer, a good republican he worked for time and again.
Your man sees a picture of Bobby Sands and blows the car horn.
Why ye beep every time ye pass the wee picture of Bobby Sands? Paul asks the farmer.
To say hello to him, your man says.
Paul laughs. He doesn't have time for that.
The fighting's done.
The war is over.

Research support for this article was provided by the Investigative Fund at the Nation Institute.

STATISTICAL ABSTRACT FOR MY HOMETOWN, SPOKANE, WASHINGTON

by JESS WALTER

1. The population of Spokane, Washington is 203,268. It is the 104th biggest city in the United States.

2. Even before the recession, in 2008, 36,000 people in Spokane lived below the poverty line—a little more than 18 percent of the population. That's about the same as it was in Washington, DC at the time. The poverty rate was 12.5 percent in Seattle.

3. Spokane is sometimes called the biggest city between Seattle and Minneapolis, but this is only true if you ignore everything below Wyoming, including Salt Lake City, Denver, Phoenix, and at least four cities in Texas.

4. This is really just another way of saying nobody much lives in Montana or the Dakotas.

5. My grandfather arrived in Spokane in the 1930s, on a freight train he'd jumped near Fargo. Even he didn't want to live in the Dakotas.

6. On any given day in Spokane, Washington, there are more adult men per capita riding children's BMX bikes than in any other city in the world.

7. I've never been sure where these guys are going on those little bikes, their knees up around their ears as they pedal. They all wear hats—ballcaps in summer, stocking caps in winter. I've never been sure, either, whether the bikes belong to their kids or if they've stolen them. It may be that they just prefer BMX bikes to ten-speeds. Many of them have lost their driver's licenses after too many DUIs.

8. I was born in Spokane in 1965. Beginning in about 1978, when I was thirteen, I wanted to leave.

9. I'm still here.

10. In 2000 and 2001, the years I most desperately wanted to move out of Spokane, 2,632 illegal aliens were deported by the Spokane office of the U.S. Border Patrol. They were throwing people out of Spokane and I *still* couldn't leave.

11. In 1978, I had a BMX bike. It didn't have a chain guard, and since I favored bellbottom jeans, my pant legs were constantly getting snagged. This would cause me to pitch over the handlebars and into the street. My cousin Len stole that bike once, but he pretended he'd just borrowed it without my permission and eventually he gave it back. Later on it was stolen for good by an older guy in my neighborhood named Pete. I was in my front yard afterward, being lectured by my father for leaving my bike out unprotected, when I saw Pete go tooling past our house on the bike he'd just stolen from me. Stocking cap on his head, knees up around his ears. I was too scared to say anything. Fear has often overtaken me during such situations. I hated myself for that. Far more than I hated Pete.

12. In 1978, Spokane's biggest employer was Kaiser Aluminum. My dad worked there. Kaiser went belly-up in the 1990s, and all of the retirees, my dad included, lost a chunk of their pensions.

13. Now all of the biggest employers in Spokane are government entities. Technically, I haven't held a job since 1994. This does not make me unique in my hometown.

14. The poorest elementary school in the state of Washington is in Spokane. In fact, it's right behind my house. 98 percent of its students get free and reduced-price lunch. I sometimes think about the 2 percent who don't get free lunch. When I was a kid, we lived for two years on a ranch near Springdale, on the border of the Spokane Indian Reservation. My dad commuted sixty miles each way to the aluminum plant. On the third day of school, in 1974, a kid leaned over to me on the bus and said, "What's the deal, Richie, you gonna wear different clothes to school *every day*?" Because of my dad's job, my siblings and I were the only kids in school who didn't get free lunch *and* free breakfast. At home, we had Cream of Wheat. At school they had Sugar Pops.

15. Sugar Pops tasted way better than Cream of Wheat. In 1974, my dad got laid off from the aluminum plant and we *still* didn't qualify for free breakfast. You must have had to be really poor to get Sugar Pops.

16. Now they're called Corn Pops. Who in their right mind would rather eat Corn Pops than Sugar Pops?

17. While it's true that I don't technically have a job and that I live in a poor neighborhood, I don't mean to make myself sound poor. I do pretty well.

18. In Spokane it doesn't matter where you live, or how big your house is—you're never more than three blocks from a bad neighborhood. I've grown to like this. In a lot of cities, especially in Spokane's more affluent neighbors, Seattle and Portland, it can be easier to insulate yourself from poverty; you can live miles away from any poor people and start to believe that everyone is as well-off as you are.

19. They are not.

20. The median family income in Spokane, Washington is $51,000 a year. In Seattle, the median family income is $88,000 a year. Point: Seattle.

21. In Seattle, though, the median house price is $308,000. In Spokane it is $181,000.

22. Drivers in Spokane spend a total of 1.8 million hours a year stuck in traffic on the freeway. This is an average of five hours a year per person in the metropolitan region. In Seattle, they spend 72 million hours stuck on the freeway, an average of twenty-five hours per person in the region. That's an entire day. Suck on that, Seattle.

23. What would it take for you to willingly surrender an entire day of your life?

24. This used to be my list of reasons why I didn't like Spokane:

    - It is too poor, too white, and too uneducated.

    - There is not enough ethnic food.

    - It has a boring downtown and no art-house theater and is too conservative.

25. In the past few years, though, the downtown has been revitalized, the art scene is thriving, and the food has gotten increasingly better. There are twenty-nine Thai and Vietnamese restaurants listed in the yellow pages. The art-house theater

briefly reopened at a time when similar theaters were closing everywhere else. There are bike paths everywhere, and I keep meeting cool, progressive people. The city even went for Obama in '08—barely, but still.

26. For the most part, despite all that, Spokane is still poor, white, and uneducated.

27. My own neighborhood is among the poorest in the state. It has an inordinate number of halfway houses, shelters, group homes, and drug- and alcohol-rehab centers.

28. I remember back when I was a newspaper reporter, I covered a hearing filled with South Hill homeowners, men and women from old-money Spokane, vociferously complaining about a group home going into their neighborhood. They were worried about falling property values, rising crime, and "undesirables." An activist I spoke to called these people NIMBYs. It was the first time I'd heard the term. I thought he meant NAMBLA—the North American Man/Boy Love Association. That seemed a little harsh to me.

29. Bedraggled and beaten women, women carrying babies and followed by children, often walk past my house on their way to the shelters and group homes. Often they carry their belongings in ragged old suitcases. Sometimes in garbage sacks.

30. Poverty and crime are linked, of course. Spokane's crime rate is well above the national average, and ranks the city 114th among the four hundred largest American cities, just below Boston. There are about ten murders a year, and 1,100 violent crimes. There are almost 12,000 property crimes—theft and burglary, that sort of thing. One year, a police sergeant estimated that a thousand bikes had been reported stolen.

31. I believe it.

32. My wife looked out the window at two in the morning once and saw a guy riding a child's BMX bike while dragging another one behind him. He was having trouble doing this, and eventually he laid one bike down in the weeds. I called the police and crouched by the window all night, watching until they arrested him when he came back for the second bike. I felt great, like McGruff the Crime Dog.

33. Another time, before I was married, I had gone for a bike ride and was sitting on my stoop with my bike propped against the railing when a guy tried to steal it. He just climbed on and started riding away. With me sitting there. I chased

him down the block and grabbed the frame and he hopped off. "Sorry," he said, "I thought it was mine." What could I say? "Well… it isn't."

34. Another time, we hired a tree trimmer who showed up with three day laborers in the back of his pickup truck. One of them disappeared after only an hour of work. The tree trimmer didn't seem concerned; he said workers often wandered off if the work was too hard. It wasn't until the next day that I realized the day laborer had made his escape on my unlocked mountain bike. I'd paid only $25 for that one, at a pawn shop where I was looking, in vain, for my previous bike, which had also been stolen. Since pawn-shop bikes have almost always been stolen from somewhere, it seemed somehow fitting that it would be stolen again.

35. A friend's rare and expensive bike once went missing and showed up for sale on Craigslist. I drove with him to meet the seller. We made this elaborate plan that involved the two of us stealing the bike back, or confronting the thieves, or something like that. I just remember I was supposed to wait in the car until he gave me a signal. When we arrived at their house we discovered that the bike thieves were huge, all tatted up and shirtless. They were sitting on a couch on their porch, drinking malt liquor and smoking. I waited for the signal. A few minutes later my friend got back in the car. It wasn't his bike. He was disappointed. I was tremendously relieved.

36. The largest number of people I ever saw walking to one of the shelters in my neighborhood was five: a crying woman and her four children, all behind her, like ducklings. I smiled encouragingly at them. It was a hot day. I had the sprinkler on in my front yard and the last duckling stepped into the oscillating water and smiled at me. I don't know why the whole thing made me feel so crappy, but it did.

37. Once, when I was watching sports on TV, a guy pounded on our front door and started yelling, "Tiffany! Goddamn it, Tiffany! Get your ass down here!"

38. I went to the door. The guy was wearing torn jeans and no shirt and a ballcap. He seemed sketchy and twitchy, like a meth user. I said there was no one inside named Tiffany. He said, "I know this is a shelter for women and I know she's here." I insisted that it wasn't a shelter, that the place he was looking for was miles away, and that I was going to call the police if he didn't leave.

39. He said he was going to kick my ass. I tried to look tough, but I was terrified.

40. My lifetime record in fistfights is zero wins, four losses, and one draw. I used to claim the draw as a win, but my brother, who witnessed that fight, always made this face like, *Really?*

41. The shirtless guy looking for Tiffany swore colorfully at me. Then he climbed on a little kid's BMX bike and rode away, his knees hunched up around his ears.

42. Later, when I was sure he was gone, I went to the shelter and knocked on the front door. A woman's voice came from a nearby window. "Yes?" she said. I couldn't see her face. I told her what had happened. She thanked me. I left.

43. For days, I imagined the other things I could have said to that asshole. Or I imagined punching him. I felt like I'd not handled it well, although I can't imagine what I should have done differently.

44. After that I decided to volunteer at the shelter. I'd always seen kids playing behind the high fence, and I thought I could play with them or read to them. But I was told they only had a small number of male volunteers because having men around made so many of the women nervous.

45. Of the 36,000 people living in poverty in Spokane, most are children.

46. Right at the peak of my obnoxious and condescending loathing for my hometown, I rented a houseboat in Seattle for $900 a month so I could pretend I lived there. While staying on that boat, and hanging around Seattle, I had a conversation with someone about all that was wrong with Spokane. He said that it was too poor and too white and too uneducated and too unsophisticated, and as he spoke, I realized something: this guy hated Spokane because of people like me. *I* grew up poor, white, and unsophisticated. I was the first in my family to graduate from college. And worse, I had made the same complaints. Did I hate Spokane because I hated people like me? Did I hate it for not letting me forget my own upbringing? Then I had this even more sobering thought: Was I the kind of snob who hates a place because it's poor?

47. I think there are only two things you can do with your hometown: look for ways to make it better, or look for another place to live.

48. Last year I volunteered at the low-income school behind my house, tutoring kids

who needed help with reading. Most of the other tutors were retired, and it was sweet to watch the six-year-olds take these smiling seniors by the hands and drag them around the school, looking for a quiet place to read. One day I was helping this intense little eight-year-old, Dylan. We read a story together about a cave boy who was frightened by a wolf until the wolf saves his life and becomes his friend. Every time I showed up after that, Dylan had the wolf book out for me to read. I'd say, "You should get another book," and he'd say, "Why should I read another book when this one's so good?" Point: Dylan.

49. One day we talked about what scared us. After I told Dylan how I used to be afraid of the furnace in our basement, Dylan told me he was scared that his brother would kill him. I laughed at the commonalities of all people and told him that brothers just sometimes fight with each other, it wasn't anything to be afraid of, his brother loved him, and he said, "No, my brother really tried to kill me. He choked me and I passed out and my stepfather had to tear him off me. I was in the hospital. He still says he's gonna kill me one day." I reported this to the teacher, who said the boy's brother had indeed tried to kill him.

50. The Halloween before last, I glanced out the window and saw a woman making her way past the front of my house with a toddler in her arms. I grabbed the candy bowl, thinking they were trick-or-treating, and that's when I noticed a young man walking beside the woman. I noticed him because out of nowhere, he punched her. She swerved sideways but kept limping down the street. I dropped the candy and ran outside. "Hey!" I yelled. "Leave her alone!" Now I could see the woman was crying, carrying crutches in one hand and a three-year-old boy in the other. Her boyfriend, or whoever he was, was red with anger. He ignored me and kept yelling at her. "Your mom told me you were coming here! Now stop! I just wanna talk to you! You can't do this!" I stepped between them. "Leave her alone!" I said again; then I said, "Get outta here!" He balled his hands into fists and said, "That ain't happenin'." But during all of this he refused to look at me, as if I weren't even there. His eyes were red and bleary. I was terrified. I told him he just needed to go home. He wouldn't acknowledge me. He kept stepping to the side to get an angle on his girlfriend, and I kept stepping in front of him. At some point the woman handed me her crutches so she could get a better hold of her child. She was limping heavily. We air-danced down the

block this way, painfully slowly, silently: her, me, him. Eventually I said, "Look, I'm gonna call the cops and this is all gonna get worse." His face went white. Then he tensed up and took a short, compact swing. At himself. It sounded like a gunshot, the sound of his fist hitting his own face. It was loud enough that my neighbor, Mike, came outside. Mike is a big, strapping Vietnam veteran, about as tough and as reasonable a man as I know. The guy seemed worried by Mike, certainly more worried than he'd been by me. Mike and I stood on either side of the woman until her angry young boyfriend gave up and stalked off. Twice more he punched himself as he walked. He was sobbing. We waited until he was gone and then we escorted her to the shelter. All the way there, the little boy stared at me. I didn't know what to say. For some reason I asked if he was going trick-or-treating later that night. His mother looked at me like I was crazy.

51. At the shelter, I gave her back the crutches. The woman knocked on the door. It opened. Mike and I stayed on the street, because that's as close as we're supposed to get. Maybe as close as we want to get. A gentle hand took the woman's arm and she and her boy were led carefully inside.

THE GROVE

by NELLY REIFLER

HER OTHER CHEEK was pressed hard into the dirt. Her hair, pale yellow, had twigs and clumps of dried mud tangled in it.

From the edge of the clearing the rabbit contemplated the woman. Maybe someone would use the hair as a nest. He twitched his nose a few times and got a whiff of something. He hopped closer and pressed his head to her neck. Nothing. Her furless skin was cold against the membrane of his ear.

With his paw, the rabbit closed one of her eyes and then the other. He thought of his mother, whom he'd barely known. He had a few vague memories: her soft gray belly against his nose; a drizzle of shooting stars they'd watched together from a stump on the hill. She'd been snapped in two by a coyote not far from here. He'd seen it happen. After that, he'd almost starved. Then he'd met a lactating guinea pig that had escaped (or been freed) from a nearby elementary school. Both needing surrogates, they'd reached an agreement.

Meanwhile, in a sunny third-floor classroom, human children had held baby-doll bottles to the hungry mouths of a litter of abandoned guinea pig infants. Most of them had survived. This the rabbit knew.

The rabbit knew things.

Sometimes, in the warm weather, the rabbit went to the drive-in. He'd hop across the woods, down through the ravine, and into the scrubby semicircle behind the screen. There he would observe the painful transformations of werewolves and vampires, the exploding cars and boats and skyscrapers, the giant human faces mashed together in passionate kisses. The way that he knew things felt, to him, a little like the drive-in—except that the screen was inside his mind, somewhere near the front of his skull.

Sitting on his haunches by the woman, he closed his eyes. He was so close to her body that when he inhaled, his side touched her shoulder. On the screen within his mind he saw the clot break free of the narrow passageway of her blood vessel. For weeks it had been trapped there, like an empty bird's nest in a narrow stream. She had felt not quite right. A little woozy. Her blood had carried the clot to the base of her skull, where it lodged at the gates to her brain. She was walking in the woods when she collapsed. She fell in a moist grove of ferns, under some low sassafras and taller maple. She didn't know anything. For a brief moment, a picture had come to her. The rabbit saw what she had seen in that moment: a card with a picture of Santa Claus on it. The rabbit saw her last thought: *Oh God, I wish I believed in something*. Both the woman, at the time she collapsed, and the rabbit, now, were moved by the contradictory nature of her petition.

The woman, like most people, had a name: Jessamine. Jessamine's mother had told her she should see a doctor, just to make sure nothing was wrong. There was a man in her life, a man she lived with. Over breakfast, the man had said that Jessamine's mother was the problem—she was anxious and difficult. Jessamine had been feeling a little woozy, especially when lifting her arms over her head. She lifted her arms over her head often. The rabbit, breathing next to Jessamine's cold body, saw her driving to a studio each day, stretching other women out on equipment and instructing them to pull on handles and springs, to breathe and activate their cores. In warm weather she would eat lunch on a wooden deck off the back of the building. The rabbit saw her gazing across a fence into the yard of Tom and William, a couple on the next street over. Their son, small and brown with a Spanish name and indigenous ancestry (indigenous not to Massachusetts but to Guatemala), played on a plastic slide molded to look like a green dinosaur. That final day, out on the deck, she had felt queasy, too queasy to eat her wrap. She'd watched the boy and wondered if she were pregnant.

The rabbit had been abandoned by his surrogate guinea pig mother before he'd been ready to wean. Afterward he'd learned to survive on his own, making a kind of bitter artificial milk from dandelion sap and the powder scraped from chestnut shells left behind by squirrels. He forgave the guinea pig. No, he didn't even have to forgive her: he was never angry at her. Without her he would have died. She couldn't help her nature, which was fickle. The guinea pig was a restless being; the rabbit had known it. Even as a suckling bunny, he could taste her restlessness in her milk.

The rabbit knew: all fickle hearts beat against their mortal bounds.

And the rabbit could not help his nature. He was empathic, reasonable to a point that some might find pathological. If he found himself cowering in a damp hole with a coyote pacing nearby, he'd calm himself by thinking about the coyote. If a coyote comes across a hare and does not kill the hare, it is no longer a coyote. That's what a coyote does; not out of malice does it snap the neck of its prey. It was the coyote's nature that made it want to slaughter and eat the rabbit. These thoughts would help the rabbit through his dark moments in a hole. He'd imagine he was inside the coyote's very nature, and this caused him to become quite placid, to enter a meditative state, a state of something approaching grace.

Now the rabbit placed his forepaws on Jessamine's ribs. With a hop of his strong back legs, he climbed onto her chest. He rested his face on one of her breasts. It surprised him. He had expected it to have a congealed quality, like the rest of her flesh. But it was soft, and it brought to his mind a certain kind of algae he'd seen floating on the surface of the small pond between the drive-in and the border of the nature preserve. The rabbit knew things, but he did not know everything.

He closed his eyes and saw Jessamine five years earlier, in a classroom where a woman around her age was delivering a lecture about a book. With his whiskers pressed into Jessamine's shirt, the rabbit sensed that Jessamine found the instructor defensive. *Alice in Wonderland* was troublesome these days, the instructor said, slouching, and she joked about how hard it was to get funding for her studies. She was brittle. Out of the blue, she insisted that the author was not a pedophile. The rabbit saw the whole scene as if Jessamine were his vessel: her eyes portals, her ears antennae. Through the portals he looked, with Jessamine, at the instructor's belly protruding over her shabby black pants. *I'd rather teach people to activate their cores*, the rabbit saw Jessamine write in her notebook.

The rabbit knew that people couldn't help naming things: *core, Massachusetts, Jessamine, chaos.*

The rabbit, when young, had known he was lucky. He'd seen other infant creatures lose their mothers and die quickly: from hunger, from thirst, from cold or fear. One day in his early adolescence he had come across a baby fisher cat. It was lying on its side in a patch of brambles. The rabbit approached it with caution. It might have been small and weak, but it still had claws and teeth. When he got close enough to smell it he inhaled the sour odor of starvation, the beginning of a corpus digesting its own organs. The little fisher cat, upon seeing the rabbit, had struggled to right itself. Their eyes met. The fisher cat opened its mouth, bared its fangs, and exhaled a faint hiss. Then it toppled onto its side again. The rabbit did not move; even when the fisher cat fell, he did not break his gaze. He tried to warm the tiny predator with the light from his own eyes. He tried to feed it with feelings, extending peace toward it like a vine. Later he wondered whether it would have been more kind to feign terror at the baby's feeble show of menace.

Again and again, instinct broke the rabbit's heart.

Not long after the encounter with the fisher cat, he was drinking from the creek near the bottom of the ravine when another scent caught his attention. He stopped drinking and opened his nostrils. It was a scent he'd smelled before, but it had never had this effect on him. He felt consumed by need, a frenzied kind of need he couldn't place. It was coming from across the water, and before he could consider what he was doing he'd hopped onto one wet rock and then another, slipping once into the icy creek, getting his feet and belly soaked. All he knew was that he needed to make something, to put himself inside of something; he needed to relieve the desperate yearning. When he reached the other side he scrambled through brush and over a stone wall. The closer he got to the scent, the more he ached, the quicker his blood surged. Standing there, near a sumac sapling, was another rabbit, a small brown female. The scent was rising off of her. She was turning in circles, trying to nuzzle her own tail and emitting anxious noises. Her nose was twitching rapidly. He hurried to her; she smelled him and stopped her circles, awaiting him with her white cottontail raised. He got onto her back. And then in a rush, he understood what was happening.

He saw the world through the eyes of the brown female. He saw her nature, which was completely innocent. She knew nothing and had no thoughts. He saw that his instinct would cause him to give her a litter of babies, and that some of the babies would die, and that one would watch its mother die. His heart was beating fast; he could hear it, and it sounded like a convoy of trucks in the rain taking the curve out on the lethal highway. He wanted to be inside the little brown female more than he wanted to live. But he slid sideways off of her. She pushed against him, and he hopped away from her. She sniffed in his direction, her nostrils dilating. He turned and forced himself to head toward the stone wall. He looked back just once. She was moving in circles again.

Now the rabbit's whiskers brushed Jessamine's cold lips as he opened his eyes. On the screen within his skull he saw her on a sofa in a dormitory lounge, grappling with a boy's belt buckle. The rabbit watched Jessamine unbutton the boy's jeans and reach into the hot tent of his boxer shorts as she moved her mouth down from his navel. The boy moaned and clasped his hands on either side of her head. In the dark he told her she was beautiful and that he loved her.

She laughed. He removed his hands and asked her what was so funny. She couldn't stop laughing. The boy drew her up to his face and pushed his tongue into her mouth. She pulled away and sat up on the edge of the sofa. Through Jessamine's eyes, the rabbit saw that outside the lounge a loading dock protruded from the building. A dim fluorescent lamp on a steel stem hung over the loading dock. Beyond it the rabbit could see trees, an uneven black mass in the moonlight, and a small sign for the rear entrance to campus. Jessamine reached up under her shirt and fastened her bra, then adjusted her breasts to rest evenly inside the cups. The rabbit saw what Jessamine had remembered in that moment: the first time she had kissed a boy—which was seven years earlier, but felt like forever—and how she'd been certain she loved that first boy she'd kissed. She had kissed many boys between that first kiss and this night in the dormitory lounge. Kisses had become like handshakes, she sometimes felt, and blowjobs were like kisses. She had homework to do for her anthropology class. She already knew what she was going to write in her paper on the Guayaki Indians.

The rabbit saw a Guayaki Indian pounding the skull of his neighbor's nine-year-old daughter with a heavy stick.

The rabbit saw Jessamine at the age of six, touching her sleeping grandmother's hand in a blue bedroom where people danced on the television. He could feel how it had dawned on Jessamine, as she'd traced her grandmother's wrinkled knuckle, that she herself would draw a finite number of breaths. The time between then and now was so brief, the rabbit knew: no different from the time it takes for a horse chestnut to fall to the dirt.

The rabbit sniffed and opened his ears. A shrill new sound came arcing over the usual hum, over the friction of insect wings, the birds, the cars on the faraway road, the wind. He leapt from the human corpse and bounded into the brush. He watched, quivering, his heart shaking him with its tattoo, from behind a clump of skunk cabbage. The noise grew closer.

It was a pair of children, maybe not quite children. Siblings, the rabbit could tell. A male and a female. The older one, the brother, was taunting the sister, and the sister was punching at the brother's arm, pretending to be more angry than she really was. The rabbit smelled the sister's watermelon-flavored gum and bubble-gum-flavored lipgloss. He smelled the brother's frantic hormones, extruded along with oil from the surface of his skin. The rabbit knew he should retreat, but he found he had to watch. The children entered the clearing.

"What the fuck," said the brother, stopping short.

"Shut up!" The sister hit him again. Then she stopped, too. "Oh."

"Miss?" the brother said, taking a step toward Jessamine's body. "Miss, are you okay?"

The sister ran over to the corpse, knelt down, touched it, then hopped up and ran to the edge of the clearing. "She's *dead*," the sister said. She sank to the ground and began to shake. She heaved a jagged breath, expelled it, heaved another.

"Fuck," said the brother. The rabbit watched him force himself over to Jessamine's side. The brother knelt down like his sister had done, but he stayed there. He touched Jessamine's cold throat, finding the answer he already knew. He withdrew his hand. Trembling, the brother reached into Jessamine's pocket.

"Don't!" cried the sister. "Don't touch her."

"We need to know who she is. I just want to see if she has a wallet or phone or something."

"No. No." The sister was weeping now, convulsing. "Don't touch her. Call Dad. Call Dad." The sister shoved her hand into her own pocket and pulled out a small, lavender device. She tried pushing some buttons on it; her shaking made it impossible. "Please, Zachary, please. Just call Dad." She tried to stand up, but toppled sideways. She lay in the dirt, breathing rapidly.

"You're going to hyperventilate." The brother rose and walked away from the corpse. He stood over his sister.

"Oh God, oh God," the sister said over and over again. "That poor woman, that poor woman." She was rocking there on her side. Her brother sat down cross-legged on the dirt next to her. He placed his hand on her, first patting her shoulder, then stroking her hair. She began to breathe more steadily. "I don't want to be here,

Zach," she said. She handed him her telephone, then wrapped her arms around his body, pulling herself closer to him.

"I'm going to call the police," he said. "Okay, Emma? Then I'll call Dad." With one hand he kept stroking her, and with the other he pressed some buttons. The rabbit listened to him speaking in his deepest voice. The rabbit knew that the brother was trying hard not to cry, especially not on the phone with the 911 operator. He did sniffle once while he spoke to their father. The sister pressed her face into her brother's baggy brown pants while he made the phone calls.

When the brother was done, he slipped his sister's phone into his own pocket. He unwrapped her arms from his waist and lay down next to her. He hugged her then, and moved his face into the curve of her neck, where it was blanketed by her apple-scented hair. His sister clasped at his shirt. The brother wept, openly, wetly, into the warm, live flesh of his sister.

The rabbit's heartbeat slowed down to its regular rate. His mother had not known things, but her fur had been so warm and her milk had tasted like the dreams he'd dreamt inside her womb. The guinea pig that had saved him had traveled farther and farther north, constantly on the move, before she succumbed during a blizzard. Of her babies, one was still alive. The runt, it had been a favorite among the schoolchildren. A girl named Hayley had been the lucky one who got to take it home. She had given it a name, of course. Now it was old, and Hayley didn't pet it as much as she used to, but she did still put it on the pillow next to her for a little while every night.

CHEESUS CHRIST

by ETGAR KERET

HAVE YOU EVER WONDERED what word is most frequently uttered by people about to die a violent death? MIT carried out a comprehensive study of the question among heterogeneous communities in North America and discovered that the word is none other than *fuck*. 8 percent of those about to die say "What the fuck"; 6 percent say only "Fuck." Another 2.8 percent say "Fuck you," though in their case, of course, *you* is the last word, even if *fuck* overshadows it irrefutably. And what does Jeremy Kleinman say a minute before he checks out? He says, "Without cheese." Jeremy says that because he's ordering something in a cheeseburger restaurant called Cheesus Christ. They don't have plain hamburgers on the menu, so Jeremy, who keeps kosher, asks for a cheeseburger without cheese. The shift manager in the restaurant doesn't make a big deal out of it—lots of customers have asked her for cheeseburgers without cheese in the past. So many that she felt the need to write to the CEO of the Cheesus Christ chain, whose office is in Atlanta, and suggest that he add a plain hamburger to the menu. "A lot of people ask me for it, but at the moment, they have to order a cheeseburger without cheese, which is cagey and a little embarrassing," she confessed to him in one of a series of detailed emails. "It's embarrassing for me, and, if you don't mind my saying so, for the whole chain. It makes me feel like a technocrat, and for the customers, the chain comes off as an inflexible organization they have to trick in order to get what they want." The CEO never replied, and for her that was even more humiliating than all the times customers had asked her for cheeseburgers without cheese. When a dedicated employee turns to her employer with a problem, especially one that's related to her place of work, the least the employer should do is acknowledge her existence. The CEO could have written that it was being handled, or that while he appreciated her turning to him he unfortunately could not alter the menu, or a million other bullshit replies of that kind. But he didn't. He didn't write anything. And that made her feel like she was empty air. Just like that night in New Haven when her boyfriend Nick had started hitting on the waitress while she herself was sitting right next to him. She cried then, and Nick didn't even know why, and that same night she packed her things and left. Mutual friends called her a few weeks later and told her that Nick had killed himself. They didn't come right out and blame her for what happened, but there was something in the way they told her about it—something accusing. In any case, when the CEO of Cheesus Christ didn't answer her emails, it was that story with Nick that stopped her from quitting. Not that she thought the CEO would commit suicide when he heard that the shift manager of some crummy branch in the Northeast had quit, but still. It was a good decision, as it turned out, because the truth is that if the CEO *had* heard she'd quit because of him, he actually would have killed himself. The truth is that if the CEO had heard that the African white lion had become extinct because of illegal hunting, he would have killed himself. He would have killed himself even after hearing something much more trivial—for instance, that it was going to rain tomorrow. The CEO of the Cheesus Christ restaurant chain suffered from severe clinical depression. His colleagues knew that, but were careful not to spread the truth around, mostly because they respected his privacy but also because it would have instantly sent stock prices crashing. What does the stock market sell, after all, if not the unfounded hope of a rosy future? A suicidal CEO is not exactly the ideal ambassador for such an optimistic message. The CEO himself, who completely understood how problematic his emotional state was, both personally and publicly, had tried medication. That hadn't helped at all. The pills had been prescribed to him by a doctor from Iraq who had been granted refugee status in the U.S. after his family had been accidentally blown up by an F-16 trying to assassinate Saddam Hussein's sons. The doctor's wife, father, and two small sons were killed; only his older daughter, Suha, had survived. In an interview on CNN, the doctor said that despite his personal tragedy, he wasn't angry at the American people. The truth is that he was, of course. He was more than angry. He was boiling with rage at the American people. But he knew that if he wanted a green card, he had to lie about it. As he lied, he thought about his dead family and his living daughter. He lied because he believed that an American education would be good for her. How wrong he was. His daughter became pregnant at fifteen by some fat white-trash kid who was a year ahead of her at school and refused to acknowledge the baby. Due to some complications during birth, the baby was born retarded. In the States, as in most places in the world, when you're the fifteen-year-old single mother of a retarded child, your fate is sealed. There's probably some made-for-TV movie that claims that this isn't the case, that you can still find love and a career and who knows what else. But that's only a movie. In real life, the minute they told her that her baby was retarded, it was as if a GAME OVER sign in neon lights had begun to flash in the air above her head. Maybe if her father had told the truth on CNN, her fate would have been different. And if Nick hadn't hit on that bottle-blonde waitress, his situation and the shift manager's might have been much better too, and if the CEO of the Cheesus Christ chain had gotten the right medication, *his* situation could have been just great. And if that crazy man in the cheeseburger restaurant hadn't stabbed Jeremy Kleinman, Jeremy Kleinman's situation would be alive, which in most people's opinion is a lot better than dead, as he found himself about to be now. He didn't die right away. He gasped, and tried to say something, but the shift manager, who was holding his hand, told him not to speak, to save his strength. And so he didn't speak. He tried to save his strength. Tried, but couldn't. There's a theory, also out of MIT, I think, about the butterfly effect: a butterfly flutters its wings on a beach in Brazil and as a result a tornado starts up on the other side of the world. The tornado appears in the original example. They could have thought up a different example, in which the flutter of butterfly wings causes badly needed rain, say, but the scientists who developed the theory chose a tornado—and not because, like the CEO of Cheesus Christ, they were clinically depressed. They chose a tornado because scientists who specialize in probability know that the chance of something detrimental occurring is a thousand times greater than the chance of something beneficial happening. "Hold my hand," is what Jeremy Kleinman wanted to say to the shift manager as his life leaked out of him like chocolate milk out of a punctured carton. "Hold it and don't let go, whatever happens." But he didn't say that, because she'd asked him not to speak. He didn't say that because he didn't need to—she held his sweaty hand until he died. For a long time after, actually. She held his hand until the paramedics asked her if she was his wife. Three days later, she got an email from the CEO. The incident in her branch had made him decide to sell the chain and retire. That decision brought him far enough out of his depression to make him start answering his emails. He answered them from his laptop, sitting on a gorgeous beach in Brazil. In his long reply to her, he wrote that she was completely right. He would pass on her carefully reasoned request to the new CEO. As he pressed SEND, his finger touched the legs of a butterfly resting on the keyboard. The butterfly fluttered its wings. Somewhere on the other side of the world, evil winds began to blow.

Translated by Sondra Silverston

TAKE CARE OF THAT RAGE PROBLEM

by EDAN LEPUCKI

IT WAS POLICE BRUTALITY, her mother said. There's nothing more offensive to a man than a woman who used to be beautiful. They can see what they missed, and it stings them, and they seek retribution.

"But indecent exposure?" Molly asked. They were pulling out of the station parking lot. "How could you?"

"I didn't!" Gertrude cried. "I was itching, you know how itchy I get!"

Molly didn't answer, though yes, she knew this, her mother's issue. What she'd give not to.

"I didn't think anyone would see me. At that hour, the roads around there are deserted."

This was true. Her mother had been picked up after midnight on the east side. No one had been on that strip of Bonnie Brae but her, she said. Even the food vendors had gone home. And so, as she passed beneath a busted streetlight, she had slipped her hand beneath her waistband. No harm in a little relief.

"He called me dirty," her mother said. She meant the cop.

That day, someone in New York had planted a car bomb. It hadn't worked. The car had been smoking, witnesses said. Someone, some brave soul, had peered into the car's windows. He could have lost his face, Molly thought.

"How much you want to bet it's a white guy who planted it?" Sam had asked her a few hours before. They were on their computers, on opposite sides of the couch. "Only a white guy from the Midwest would have messed that one up."

That was when her mother had called from the police station. "She needs me to kill a spider," Molly had lied, putting on her flip-flops, and Sam had believed her. When she'd left he was still scrolling through the news stories.

Now it was after two in the morning, and Sam would know Molly hadn't been killing anything.

"What were you doing out this late, anyway?" she asked her mother.

They were on 3rd, where sewage work had whittled the road down to a single lane. Her mother was sitting up straight, two manicured fingers curled around the dry-cleaning hook, her gaze hard and focused on the stoplight. In the last few years, she'd had trouble keeping off the weight in her midsection—she complained about it all the time—and now her round belly protruded against the strap of her seat belt like a marsupial pouch.

Gertrude bobbed her chin, still looking straight ahead, and Molly realized her mother was embarrassed. She was trying to summon some dignity.

"It's green," Gertrude said, and Molly lifted her foot off the brake.

Molly hadn't spoken to her father in months, not since he'd moved to a bland one-bedroom apartment in West Hollywood. The divorce had been his decision. A whim, really. He wanted to be on his own, fancy-free, exploring the world and himself. Now he parked in an underground garage and, at night, alone, her mother blocked her front door with a dining room chair.

Sam and Molly had been living together for three days when her parents broke up. There were still unpacked boxes in every room. In the hallway, they'd stored a pallet's worth of toilet paper. Every time she passed it, Molly found herself hoping for some kind of natural disaster. It was sick, she knew. But she felt prepared. They had provisions.

Her mother had been hard to understand, that afternoon, on the phone—Gertrude was crying, and Sam was drilling shelves into the bedroom wall, cursing every few moments. "He's taking the credenza!" she said between sobs, while Sam swore. Molly had to wave at him to stop before she could coax the whole story out. And then, when the whole story *was* out—her father had left, he was taking the credenza, he was an asshole—she wished it weren't.

"He said he doesn't love me," her mother said. "He said I'm unlovable."

These words had choked her. Molly's father had always had a gift for erasing her mother down to a little nub. She recalled distinctly the time he'd told Gertrude she didn't have the body for the black leggings she'd been wearing all summer long. He'd said it during a dinner party, in front of their friends. It was true, the leggings were made for teenagers, but her mother had loved them. Afterward Gertrude had hid in the guest bedroom and sobbed, and Molly, aged thirteen, had delivered her a glass of Prosecco because she knew her mother wouldn't turn that down.

Moving in with Sam was not supposed to begin like this. Her parents were across town—they were supposed to be there together, in the old house, coping however they saw fit. Molly was busy! She was moving in with her boyfriend! In her mind, she and Sam were putting away their belongings. They were organizing their library, getting rid of duplicate books. They were cooking a simple meal and eating it on paper plates. They were learning to share a life. Molly had her own world to manage; how could she be expected to maintain anyone else's?

When her mother had calmed down and hung up, Molly took in the living room with its pillars of boxes, its random piles of papers and junk marring every surface. Sam had purchased an extension cord the day before, and now it lay uncoiled across the couch. She grabbed it and went to find him in the bedroom. "Why did you get this," she cried, "if you were just going to throw it down?"

Sam stood there, drill in hand, confused.

"You're fucking up this apartment for both of us!" she yelled.

He put a hand up, surrendering. "Geez, Moll, you all right? I'll put it away in a sec."

Molly shook her head. "I gotta go to the drug store," she said. She ran out of the room, cord still in her fist.

Later she learned that her father had wanted to tell Molly the news in person, together. "We're all adults here," he'd said when he called, finally, two days after she'd talked to Gertrude. Sam and Molly still hadn't unpacked most of the boxes, and only a single roll of toilet paper had been taken from the reserves; it looked like a squirrel had clawed at the packaging. "Gertie and I," her father said, "—we weren't right together. I don't think we ever respected each other." He'd signed a lease in secret, a month before. He was already in his new place. "It shouldn't have come as a surprise," he said.

After a long pause, he added, "I love you."

"I have to go," Molly replied. She felt bereft.

After she hung up, she sent her father an email. She had to send it from her phone, because they hadn't gotten their internet hooked up yet. *I'm hurt*, she wrote. *Don't contact me.* There was no subject line.

And that was it, their last communication. She ignored his phone calls and blocked his emails. Molly stayed angry at her father—it was a steady, headachey anger—but her mother was over it in a month. She was happier without Paul, she said. They were on good terms. Molly had apparently chosen sides for no reason, but she couldn't find a way to back down gracefully. The rage was lodged in her. It had taken up residence.

Sometimes she drove past her father's building, a big gray stucco box on a block with complicated parking restrictions, one street sign qualifying the next until you threw your hands up and drove away. Her father had moved to a place intolerant of strangers, she thought. Visitors, even. She supposed she had a vague hope of catching sight of him living his new life. He would be pathetic. He'd be alone. She imagined bringing eggs, and throwing them at him from her speeding car.

But she never saw him.

It turned out the car bomber was from Pakistan.

"You win," Sam said. He pulled out a five-dollar bill from his wallet and handed it to her.

Molly felt victorious as she took the money, and then appalled. She and her boyfriend made bets on terrorism.

He was reading her the story off the internet. The bomber had been on an airplane, headed to Dubai. He had failed in his mission, yes, but as he'd buckled himself in, he must have thought: *I'm free. I have my freedom.* Molly felt bad for him. He was going to be punished for something he didn't even get to do. And he had lost everything.

Had Sam won the bet, had the bomber been blonde, and fat, had he gone to Claim Jumper the night before, Molly knew she'd feel no such compassion. But this guy, he'd believed in something, however misguided it was. He was a victim of circumstance.

"They really need to work on that No-Fly list," Sam said as he shut his laptop.

Molly nodded. She hadn't told him about her mother's arrest. Instead, she'd said

Gertrude had needed company, that the reality of the divorce was beginning to dawn on her. Sam had put a tender hand on Molly's cheek and asked if she wanted some gelato. She wondered if she could tell him how she felt about the terrorist. But, no, there were limits to intimacy.

She *had* tried to talk to Sam, intermittently, about how she felt about her father. Sam's own parents had divorced when he was two, and he said their separation, their separate existences, was a relief. "Not to mention two Christmases, growing up," he'd added, to make her smile. When she tried to explain the feelings inside of her—the rage, the powerlessness—he'd rub her back and say something bland like, "Live and let live." Sam liked her dad. This made her even angrier.

She needed to change, she knew. She was being short with Sam for no good reason. She was learning to hurt his feelings in a way that made her uncomfortable. She recognized the behavior. Sometimes he would ask, "What can I do?" That same hand, on her back. Molly always told him, Nothing. There was nothing he could do.

But of course he wanted to do something. This is why she shouldn't have been totally surprised by what he said that evening, after closing his computer on the terrorist.

"Paul called me," he said.

"My dad called you?"

Sam nodded. He leaned across the couch to kiss her. He was a good kisser. "You can't be mad."

Molly, actually, was already mad. It was building in her chest. That old feeling.

"He wanted to know what he could do, to get you to forgive him," Sam was saying.

Molly stood up. Sam bit his lip.

"It's our Roman holiday," he said.

They had talked about going to Italy for almost as long as they'd been together. Molly had nursed a particular fantasy: the scooter rides, the wine, the olive oil that tasted like grass, the whistles from beautiful, dark-haired men in linen pants, the fourteen-year-old girls smoking cigarettes in the doorways of buildings older than Jesus. Sometimes she thought of it all as she fell asleep.

There was a more realistic plan, too, which she and Sam had hatched together—

smaller, economical hotels, and a rental car to drive to little villages, and flights in the off-season, so the tickets would be cheaper. Neither scenario was feasible right now, of course, but someday, they told themselves, cheaper would be doable.

When Sam told her the news, though, Molly hadn't thought of the plan or the fantasy. She became unhinged—really, that was what it was like. As if a great tornado had torn a door off within her. She yelled. She cursed. She may have called Sam a traitor, among other things.

"We leave in five weeks," he'd said.

Five weeks. The problem with that, Molly explained to her mother over the phone from behind the bathroom door, was that she couldn't find her passport, and even if she could, it wouldn't matter, because it had most definitely expired. Molly hadn't been out of the country for years. There'd been Paris, after high school, and later, Peru. She couldn't even remember the trip to Paris. In Peru she'd held a baby sloth in the jungle, eaten some ceviche that gave her a stomach parasite, and returned home five days early.

"Why don't you tell Sam you can't find it?" her mother said. "I'm sure he'll fix it."

Gertrude hadn't cared when Molly had told her about the tickets. "Just call your father already," she'd said. "I'm doing fine!"

"That's not the point," Molly had said. The thought of taking the tickets made her feel ill. She couldn't just accept his gift. She couldn't just forgive him.

Gertrude grunted, and Molly imagined her puttering through the rooms of the house: the dusty dining room, the living room with its curved ceilings, its built-in light fixture high on the wall, shaped like a snow hat. Molly had grown up in that house.

"How are you, anyway?" she asked her mother now. "Since the… thing?"

"I want to forget about it," her mother said. "I made an appointment with the doctor."

"More ointment. Good idea."

"You need to forget about it, too," her mother said.

"I never think of your vagina, if that's what you're worried about."

"You know what I mean. Your dad. He's only human."

"Well, so am I," Molly said.

It occurred to her that she should actually be mad at her mother. After all, Gertrude had allowed Molly to protect her and cheer her up for years. Not only allowed it, but expected it. By the time she was in high school, Molly had learned to hold her hand flat in front of her, aimed at her dad. It was a signal to him not to continue saying what he was about to say to his wife. Her mother had looked on at these exchanges without comment. She had condoned Molly's behavior, even encouraged it. And now, when it should have mattered most, her mother was waving away what she'd spent Molly's youth treating as a gift, or a right.

Molly knew this should make her angry. And it did, in theory. But in practice, she blamed her father.

"Mom?" Molly finally said.

"Hmm?"

"I could see myself staying put. Never going anywhere ever again."

"Don't say that, baby. It's not true."

"But I'm scared."

"No one will hijack the plane, baby. Don't worry."

The next day, Gertrude brought over the mail. Molly still used her childhood home as a permanent address. After her mother hugged both her and Sam, she said, "So what's going on with the expired passport?"

"What?" Sam said.

"Molly hasn't been anywhere in ages," Gertrude explained.

Sam was online in moments. "We can just push back the trip," he said. He ran a hand through his hair. He had already booked the hotels and the rental car, she could tell.

"Or look," he said, finding the right webpage. "It's easy to expedite—you've just got to get a new picture, and pay a fee."

"Am I really the only one upset by all this?" Molly asked.

To her surprise, her mother shook her head. "Paul shouldn't be trying to buy an apology from you."

"Thank you. That's exactly—"

"But," she continued, "you know that isn't how he sees it. There's nothing insidious about his behavior."

Sam nodded. "That's right. He did a shitty thing. But he's still your dad."

Her mother held up a tight fist, and released it, fingers fluttering. "Just let it go, honey. Take care of that rage problem before it eats you alive."

"It's not a problem," Molly said.

"Sure it isn't." Her mother flung herself on the couch. "You should follow my example. That cop pulled me over and accused me—me!—of masturbating behind the wheel."

Sam barked a laugh.

"He shined his flashlight into my eyes, made me put my hands on the hood of the car—"

Sam was wide-eyed. "Really?"

She nodded vigorously. "He kicked my legs apart like I was some criminal. Like I was some pervert. A desperate cougar."

"Mom—"

"You didn't tell him, dear?" her mother asked, sitting up. She had one eyebrow raised.

"You told me it was a secret." Molly felt her body clench.

"I did? Well, I didn't mean from *Sam*."

Sam had his eyes on her. He was smiling, but it was a careful look.

"I was trying to protect you," Molly said. "Not that it would make a difference." She looked right at her mother. "You wouldn't recognize that, right?"

Gertrude sighed. "I *forgave* that police officer, Molly. I lit a candle. I let it go." She held up her fist again, and released it. "And Paul left *me*, dear—not *you*."

"Anything else you want to tell me?" Sam asked.

Molly laughed. She gave up. "She *was* touching herself, just not sexually. She has an itchy vagina."

Her mother gasped. "Molly!"

"I can't be here," Molly said, and grabbed her purse before they could stop her.

The rage climbed as she got into her car and pulled into the street. She didn't even think, as she merged into the left-hand-turn lane without really looking, to turn on the radio. She would let it go. She would take care of her rage problem. She was halfway to her father's before she realized where she was going.

She'd left her cell phone at home, so no one knew where she was. She was tying a loop, and everyone else was out of it. She snagged a meter three blocks from her father's apartment.

From the sidewalk below his building, she looked up. Almost every balcony seemed to store a piece of exercise equipment, rusted and hulking. If not that, then some plants. Or a satellite dish. Molly wanted to feel disgust at these ugly objects, how they cluttered the view, mucked it up, but instead she found herself wondering which balcony belonged to her father. Did he take his coffee out there? The situation had to depress him. At the house, he used to step onto the back porch each morning like the lord of the manor and tally up the birds as they gossiped at the fountain. Now what did he tally? Russians? For a moment she felt sad for him. She shook off the feeling.

When Molly was nineteen, and home from college for Thanksgiving break, her father had told her that he had a little crush on the next-door neighbor, Cheryl.

"You won't act on it," Molly had said. Cheryl was in her thirties, and single.

"No!" her father had said.

"And you won't tell Mom."

Molly knew, that if she had not said this to her father, he would have revealed his crush—insignificant! Silly!—to her mother. Gertrude would have taken it hard.

Now, standing in front of her father's building, Molly wondered if her father *had* acted on his feelings for the neighbor. Cheryl had moved out less than a year after his confession, practically in the middle of the night, no forwarding address. Molly had never brought her up again.

It wasn't until she looked up her father's name—*her* name—in the directory and pressed CALL that she realized she had no plan. What if he wasn't home—what then? But in the next moment she heard his voice through the intercom, tinny and full of static.

"Hello?" he said in his usual distracted way. He sounded annoyed.

"It's me. It's Molly."

The annoyance disappeared. "I'll be right down." He paused. "Don't go anywhere."

Molly was about to ask where she might go, but the command made sense. She'd whisked herself away from his life with a two-line email. She was not the guilty party here, she reminded herself. She had not told her spouse of thirty-two years that she was unlovable and then taken her beloved credenza to some nondescript building on Sierra Bonita and called it a better life.

And then her father was through the door.

He hugged her before she could stop him. She left her arms at her sides, told herself to breathe. He pulled away.

"Your hair's so long!" he said.

"I just cut most of it off."

Her father laughed, as if this were a joke. "You have no idea how happy I am to see you."

He looked exactly the same. He was wearing a sweatshirt he'd gotten as a gift for donating to NPR fifteen years ago, and as usual, there was no shirt underneath. His jeans were three shades too light. He had on his penny loafers, pennies included.

Molly had never before felt so comforted by her father's terrible wardrobe. She felt herself unclench her fists. Let it go, she thought.

The lobby was mirrored. The residents had taken to dumping unwanted catalogues and coupons onto the floor by the mailboxes.

"Nice," Molly said.

"It's a shithole."

They stepped into the elevator. Her father pushed the button for the third floor, and Molly made a mental note to check the balconies on that level.

"I'm moving soon," he said.

"Are you getting remarried?"

"God, no." He squinted at her. "Did you really think I'd—"

"Are you gay?" She'd meant it as a joke, but she forgot to smile.

"I suppose I'm in the right neighborhood. But, no, I'm not. I bought a condo."

The doors opened on a long, carpeted hallway, a lighted exit sign shining like a beacon at the other end. Her father lived two doors down from the elevator, on the left side.

"Do you like your balcony?" she asked, as he fiddled with the lock.

"I don't have one." He nodded across the hallway. "Those units are pricier."

But you can afford flights to Italy, she thought. Two of them.

The apartment was more pathetic than she'd expected. There were sagging miniblinds and dark blue carpeting. Low, cottage-cheese ceilings. An Ikea-issued couch. In the galley kitchen, a plastic light fixture emitted a faint buzz. There was no place to eat meals, no table. He'd put up his vintage silent-movie poster, but its largeness dwarfed the space. He had hammered a nail into the wall by the front door, and as he hung his keys there, Molly felt a keen pity for him. She pushed it away.

He gestured for her to sit, and offered her a beer.

"Where's the credenza?" she asked.

Her father was already on his way to the fridge, and at her question, he turned around. His face was scrunched up, the color draining out of it. He looked like a baby about to cry.

"So you came to get a piece of furniture?" he said. "Is that all?"

"I was just curious."

"It's in the bedroom," he said. "You're welcome to catalogue the items in there as well."

Molly stayed put.

"It was my grandmother's," he said, returning with two bottles of Corona.

"But Mom loves it. You know that."

"It's a family heirloom." He handed her the beer. "And before you tell me I don't give a damn about family, let me ask you this, Molly. Are you here to argue with me?"

She gripped the neck of the bottle. "I don't know why I'm here," she said.

Her father smiled, and took a sip of his beer. "I'm still glad you came," he said.

They were silent for a moment.

"Mom was arrested last week," she said finally.

"Gertie was arrested?" He looked amused.

"It's not funny." She told him the story.

Her father was quiet. He took a long swig of beer, and then asked, "Does she have some kind of rash… down there?"

Molly nodded. "She's had it for, like, five years. Off and on."

"I had no idea," he said, but offhandedly.

Her father had no working knowledge of her mother's vagina. Of course he didn't. He couldn't be bothered. Molly felt an urge to stand up and scream, to pull the sad blinds off the window and choke her father with them. But just as suddenly as the feeling arrived, it departed.

"Ah, Gertie," her father said. He opened his eyes wide and fluttered his hands around his face. "Arrested!" he said, in a high, hysterical voice. His impression was impeccable, but all Molly could do was shake her head.

"Oh, don't take that away from me," he said. "It's all I have left." He grinned. He'd meant it as a joke, but it was also the saddest, truest thing in the world. It was all he had left.

"So," Molly said. "This is freedom."

He nodded.

"Are you happy?"

Molly had imagined his confession dozens of times: I've made a mistake, he'd say. I want my old life back. But now that his unhappiness was upon her, real and unassailable, she didn't think her heart could stand it.

Her father looked at her, his face solemn. But there, in his eyes, flashed a twinkle.

"I am happy," he said. "Right now, *right now*, I am."

They ended up ordering pizza. Molly could tell they were both making an effort to keep the conversation light, and as they ate he asked about her job, and her old friends; he never remembered their names, and so referred to them as the Jewish girl, the girl who had gotten that breast reduction, the girl with the rich parents. When he asked about Sam, Molly said things were pretty good.

Her father smiled. "You mad at him?"

She nodded.

"Don't let it fester," her father said. "Or in thirty years you'll end up like me."

"I can't take those tickets," she said.

"Sure you can. People can do whatever they want, Molly."

They finished their meal in comfortable silence. It was when she was putting the leftover slices of pizza into the fridge that she saw the email she'd sent him. It hung next to a save-the-date from a couple she didn't recognize.

She could only bring herself to read a little bit of it: *Dad Dont contact me.*

"Not even an apostrophe," her father said from the sink.

"Why is this up here?"

He held a plate aloft. "Because, whenever I considered groveling for your forgiveness, that email served as a reminder that you could be a real shit sometimes."

Molly breathed in sharply. "I can't believe you'd say that to me."

"I'm just trying to explain—"

"I don't *want* it," she cried. "Don't tell me. Don't explain anything else!"

The rage was there, in the room. She couldn't take it. She was through the front door, her father right behind her.

Right then, the door across the hall opened. A man about her age, in gym shorts and a Lakers shirt, stepped out.

"Kevin!" her father cried.

"Pauly, my man!"

Molly watched, dazed, as the two men shook hands, and Kevin slapped Paul on the back. This slap seemed to yank Paul from his reverie, and he turned to introduce this man to Molly.

"This is Kevin. We play poker together every Thursday night."

Kevin looked back and forth between them. "Paul, I didn't know you had a daughter."

Molly glanced at her father, who looked away.

"Yes, I do. Here she is."

No one said anything.

"When she was born," her father said. "I put the car seat in wrong—I guess it was wrong, because it unhooked on the ride home from Cedars. At a red light, it tipped over. Molly here, she started squalling. The strangest, most beautiful noise I'd ever heard."

"I bet," Kevin said.

"Her mother almost murdered me. She probably knew then I was a son of a bitch." Kevin laughed. Molly tried to smile.

"I really have to go," she heard herself say. She felt her feet moving, she was backing away from them, heading not to the elevator, but to that glowing exit sign. The stairs, she thought, the stairs will be faster. Kevin yelled goodbye as she rushed away.

She didn't need Italy. A tide had turned within her, she realized. Until all this, everything was fine, just fine. She was content with her office job, her morning jogs, with the occasional dinner party, with a cocktail served up, a lemon peel floating in its depths. If she wanted to feel moved, she merely had to walk around the neighborhood with Sam, holding hands, and imagine owning one of the modest homes. A front yard lined with rose bushes made her gasp. The tiny buds, and the ones unfurling like pencil shavings, and the ones in full bloom, their raided pollen hearts.

Before she'd left the house, Sam had copied the directions to the Passport Agency on a Post-it note and tucked it into her pocket. The necessary forms were waiting there, in a tray made of cardboard, just as Sam had said they would be.

She filled one out and knocked on the door marked RENEWAL. The door was blue, and like a door to a house, it had a peephole so that whoever stood on the other side could see who had come calling. Molly imagined a large living room behind this blue door, replete with rugs and armless reading chairs, an antique birdcage, maybe, and tea served on a silver tray. She considered how she might hold her face for the photograph.

Maybe the best thing would be to take herself to Italy. She still had the ticket. She could chill out for a while, get some perspective. She would call Sam from Rome.

A heavyset woman, in a uniform that matched the blue door, came out and said, "Passport?" Molly nodded and handed her the paperwork.

She was led into a small, uninteresting room: beige walls, no windows, a couple of card tables. The woman told her to stand before a white screen. It was just like getting your driver's license photo taken. The red lipstick she'd applied for the occasion suddenly felt pathetic. As if she'd mistaken this errand for Italy itself.

"Ready?" the woman said.

When the flash popped, Molly thought again of her mother, sitting in her car on the side of the road, the engine ticking to rest, the snarling police officer's flashlight shining in her face. Her body still itching, and her mind struggling to pretend that it wasn't. Her hand lifting to shield her eyes, and the cop's voice, gruff and without empathy. Like he was going to do something to her.

It had to have been awful. So much of everything was awful, wasn't it?

Molly watched the woman frown at her computer screen.

"We'll take it again, sweetie," she said. "Smile this time, okay? We don't want people turning you away at the border now, do we?"

Molly nodded. Then, shook her head.

This time, she showed her teeth.

STILL LOOKING

by JOHN HYDUK

CALL ME APPLICANT. First thing, there's no joy to being jobless. But come face-to-face with the nothingness, and one finds it's strangely sweet.

I worked at fifteen, when I lied about my age to flip burgers. Since then I've driven forklifts full of pine boards around a warehouse, loaded trucks, spun wrenches on an assembly line, wielded cutting torches and paint sprayers, dipped scaffolding into rust-proofing baths, and bent iron with fire and sweat. I've sold men's suits, tapped on an office keyboard, and sledgehammered old drywall like there was a better life waiting on the other side. I've spent thirty years in the octagon, moving from job to job like a man crossing a river ice floe to ice floe. The one thing I've never been, until now, is unemployed.

I got the news the day before Thanksgiving 2008. I'd been working receiving at a suburban big-box store, a job I'd washed up at after my gig at a building-supply center ended with the corporation in bankruptcy court. I figured I'd hunker down until something better surfaced, after I lost that building-supply job, and the truth is I swam to the first HELP WANTED sign I saw. I'd never been without a payroll number, and the prospect shook me. The big-box money was laughable—a bag of chips north of minimum wage. When we thumped our productivity numbers we got not raises but a pizza party. Retail is the last refuge of scoundrels.

Eight months later, with a dismal Christmas season looming, my leaving package was neatly stacked with a dozen others on my foreman's desk. He thanked me for my service, for my contribution. And don't you come back no more, no more.

But get past the shock and there's a giddy side. The world is mine, I told myself on the drive home, just waiting for reinvention. What do I want to be? One thing: I'm going to retain my dignity, whatever comes.

Two days in I get my first interview. This is going to be cake, I think.

I've got a 10:30 with the human-resources person at a paper company. The hiring office borders the main plant—Ms. Human Resources gives me directions over the phone. The whole complex takes up a good five acres of urban industrial park. I navigate an ice storm and skate into their parking lot with ten minutes to spare. The lot is full to bursting with rows of shiny SUVs and new pickups—I can't decide if that's a good omen or not. I'm dressed for a high-school ring dance— blazer and tie, shined shoes. Inside I find a roomful of shop-logo windbreakers and vacant stares. My competition.

Ms. Resources gives me the pitch between sniffles. Great heaving sniffles. Family-owned company, she snorts, real good people, and "We've never had a lay-off." She asks if I'm familiar with the business. Paper, right?

"Bingo cards," she says, twisting her tissue. Good times? I ask. "Never better," she says. They're dominant in the Mexican gaming market, which is exploding.

We dance: Will I work nights? Will I work days? Do I have reliable transportation? I say yes every time and add that I can drive a forklift and don't know how to spell *u-n-i-o-n*. She asks what my salary expectations might be. I decide to lowball it: no sense getting off on the wrong foot. I am yours for ten dollars per hour, I tell her.

She reacts as if I've asked to diddle her there on her desktop. We don't pay more than seven, she says.

Somewhere the Mexican gaming market is crying out. I tell her my salary requirements are flexible. Why not give me a chance, on a trial basis? They have an opening—they said so in the newspaper ad—and my resume says I can do the job. What, you're holding out for someone who can drive a forklift with more *flair*?

She's about to respond when one of the windbreakers from the waiting room sticks his head in. "Thank you *so... much*," he grins, and shuffles off. Ms. Resources leans in and whispers, "He worked for the same company for eighteen years and they let him go." Yeah, well, I'm heartbroken. Now about me…

Instead I say, "Tough times."

Something's died between us, though. She thanks me for my interest, and, oh yes, would I take a drug test? Here they take hair samples. I tell her for seven dollars per I'll shave my head. She promises to pass my application along. References must be checked, credentials weighed, entrails read by the light of a virgin moon. I'm not betting on hearing "Bingo!" anytime soon.

The state job center is a brick bunker near the Chevy plant. Inside the décor runs to scuffed concrete floors, security desks, and PARDON OUR DUST signs.

I'm visitor-tagged and pointed down a hall. In a cinder-block room, job orders hang from chipped Masonite clipboards. I pull down two that look promising and take a number—a counselor will be with me shortly. One job, a warehouse gig, asks that I apply online; the other—furniture assembly—requests a snail-mailed resume, or a faxed one.

Judy, my counselor du jour, is pumped. She's a plump woman with the thin smile of someone used to delivering bad news. Her cubicle is covered in snapshots of cats, kids, and tulips. "You've got everything you need here," Judy says, flipping through my CV. "These are both good companies, especially the furniture one." She suggests a tweak or two. "And the thing you want to do most is stay positive."

That will take some trying. I want to tell her my old job still tingles like an amputated limb. That I start awake in the wee hours thinking that I've overslept. That I move my car in the snow so that the neighbors will think I'm still working. That although I have nothing to be ashamed of—I know that—shame is exactly what I feel.

Judy would understand. She has nice eyes. Sympathetic. Or maybe it's the dust. But instead I tell her that Positive's my middle name.

I look back once after I hand in my visitor badge. Folks shuffle past the clipboards, slowly, like hair circling a drain. The security guard apologizes for the floor. "We're getting new carpet," he tells me. "Geez are we busy."

I spend the night fine-tuning my furniture credentials. When I'm finished I sound qualified to host the New Yankee Workshop. Make chairs? Hell, I invented 'em.

The next morning I drive to an all-night copy center with a fax service. 8 a.m. on a Saturday and there's a line. The guy ahead of me is just back from Cancún and wants his vacation snapshots blown up poster-size.

On the way home I catch a game show on NPR. The phone-in contestant is an unemployed Sunbelt accountant—she makes a plea for a job on the air ("Therese in Tempe! Call me!"). Her in-studio counterpart says he's a clerk in his son's video-game store. When the host presses, Dad fesses up: he was a consultant, and before that, well, he was an engineer at General Motors. I can picture the guy's long, slow fall down the mountain.

The accountant wins a cheese sampler and Dad gets the host's book. "Leave the wrapper on," the host cracks. "It'll be worth more on eBay."

More job postings.

ACTIVE ENTOMOLOGIST: U.S. ARMY MEDICAL CORPS. *Your knowledge of insects and their behavior can make a difference in the health and morale of our nation's defenders...*

NEEDED: FULL-TIME INDIAN NANNY. *We are looking for an experienced Indian nanny to care for our nine-month-old baby. Should speak Hindi/ English.*

TUTOR. *I need a Mandarin tutor to work with two children from an English-speaking home who want to become conversational in Chinese. They have studied Chinese for two years.*

I've seen hard times before—we all have. The Reagan Recession, the Bush Downturns, senior and junior editions. Dip, slowdown, rough patch—pick your poison. But this feels different. The old foot-in-the-door jobs are long gone, and there's a blue-collar backlog to fill what's left that puts the real-estate logjam to shame. Sweat laborers are the kids from the first marriage, and just about as welcome.

On a hunch I phone my old scaffolding job and inquire about the finishing line. We have machines for that now, the foreman snorts.

I remember reading somewhere that in plague times the desperate tied sacks of posies around their necks, trusting in something they couldn't see to save them from the Black Death. Posting on Monster.com is not that different, I think.

I spend my mornings playing liar's poker, casting resumes into the ether. I feel like a mail-order bride typing "I am a happy and smiling person" from a grim cold-water walk-up in Belarus.

I drive to an airport distribution center along Desolation Row and ask the guardhouse for the employment office. "You're looking at it," the cop yawns, then feeds a six-page application through my cracked window. "Fill it out over there," he says, pointing to a snow bank. It takes three minutes—I leave the motor running, which ticks off the guard—and I thank him when I'm done. "Have a good one," he says, and tucks my application on top of a pile as thick as a phone book, under a brick.

Hiring guy at a nursery asks about my tree experience. Been around them all my life, I say. He's requiring five years' documented work with shade trees now, not because it takes that much smarts to point a garden hose and slice burlap but because in this job market he can.

I apply for a food-service job—Jesus—and talk with the owner. Will I wear a smock? Yes. Will I wear a hairnet? Yes. Will I work in 45-degree temperatures for prolonged periods of time? Yes. Will I work in temperatures colder than 45 degrees? Yes. Can I lift seventy pounds? Yes. Can I lift seventy pounds repeatedly in temperatures colder than 45 degrees? Yes. Will I work for seven dollars per hour? Yes. Can I legally work in the U.S.? Yes. Can I speak any language other than English? No. Long pause. That's gonna be a problem, he sighs.

We are now in the part of the movie where the mayor is still telling the people it's safe to go in the water, even though the shark has been munching swimmers for half the picture. But I'm not panicking.

At night I rewrite my cover letters. Please find enclosed my resume listing previous employment back to 1980, including names, addresses, zip codes, and phone numbers for all my former employers. Also, a Tupperware of my famous salmon pappardelle. You might want to reheat that—or allow me. Say, did you get the roses?

Unemployment changes you. I find myself checking out other working people—clerks, stockboys, men and women I wouldn't have considered before. What've they got that I ain't got? Courage. And a job.

I'm no political scholar, so for me the Republican social plan has always seemed to boil down to *Are there no prisons? No workhouses?* I mention this because news arrives this morning of Ohio Senator George Voinovich's upcoming retirement. I am shocked: I didn't know we had a senior senator. Oh, I knew we had a nice suit filling the chair, but we never heard much from the guy. If you judge a pol in hard times by how much pork he hauled home, the V was strictly kosher.

Seems George wants to spend more time with his family. Maybe I'll use that— *Reason for leaving previous employment: Wanted to spend more time with my family.*

I'm half-listening to a talk show about all this when Rory on a car phone pipes in: "FDR actually prolonged the Depression; someday history will show that." Everybody in-studio agrees.

The next day I fetch my morning mail and find a shut-off notice from the gas company. It is 18 degrees outside, and dropping. I sprint to an ATM and take a cash advance on my last credit card, then head to the bill-paying counter at a convenience store. I tell the Hindu kid behind the register that an iceberg didn't mess up the *Titanic*'s maiden voyage; the real culprit was all those lifeboats. And history will show that.

The unemployed fall somewhere between the unborn and the undead. We get a lot of lip service when we're a concept, but when we get up close, most people turn and run.

Guy sitting next to me in the next personnel office sports a blue steelworker's local jacket and gray stubble. He says he hasn't worked the mills since '98 but the jacket's the warmest thing he owns. He's seen tough times before, but this is different. "Used to be, you lost a job in Michigan, you'd go to Florida where construction was booming. You got pink-slipped in California, you'd try Arizona or Nevada. Now it's bad everywhere."

I tell him everybody wants more customers, but no one wants employees.

"My brother-in-law called from Orlando," he says. "Before I could ask about the market down there he wanted to know if I had any room in my basement."

Guys like him and me, we're polar bears, watching the ice melt.

Best job I ever had? That's easy: a stint on the railroad when I was seventeen. I was underage—another story—so what I remember is filtered through the roar of teenage hormones. But I remember enough: the rail yard made the ground so dead that you swiveled your head to look at a wildflower poking through, because you knew damn sure it wouldn't be alive tomorrow. The air smelled like the Devil farting.

I was a car man's helper, repairing rolling stock, riding a tool car. Those crews worked together like five fingers on one hand. You wouldn't think a few skinny men could lift a locomotive, but I have seen it. The Earth turned, tugged along by men like us one wrench-pull at a time.

What I miss the most was that feeling I got riding home. I used to see them as a kid, working guys done for the day, stained with sweat, with raw knuckles. They knew they were working in the greatest country in the world, but they weren't assholes about it. And for a while I was one of them.

Five months in I get a callback. The warehouse is a grim cinder-block bunker circled by a razor-wire fence that would do any prison yard proud. Eighteen-wheelers squeeze through a mechanized gate. Tow-motors race out to unload them like clown cars at a circus.

It's dark and raining, but the building glows like a birthday cake. Through the open dock doors I can hear the shop radio blasting, and the crew inside ragging on each other, roaring like happy bears.

The lights are on. All is right with the world. People are working here.

LUGO IN NORMAL TIME

by KEVIN MOFFETT

L UGO AT HOME in a new pair of sweatpants. Unbidden, circling, waiting for
something to happen. Something often happens.

  This weekend he has his daughter. He's sipping brandy and following
her from room to room while she works on a project for school. She's supposed to
find a household item she can use to tell a story, so all morning Erica's been rooting
through the boxes in his closet, moving in long, loping strides and cracking open
the boxes in the hallway and in the kitchen. This is Lugo's house, his new house.
Actually it's an apartment, an old apartment with a carpet that smells like broth
and puppies and cheap disinfectant. The odor of a dozen forfeited security deposits.
Most of his things are still packed up from his move eight months ago. Extension
cords, Halloween appliqués, ornaments, a stack of old Louis L'Amour paperbacks
whose covers Erica studies, bemused, when she finds them in the hall.

  "How about those?" Lugo says.

  She opens *Under the Sweetwater Rim*. "'Death had come quickly and struck hard,'"
she reads, "'leaving the burned wagons, the stripped and naked bodies, unnaturally
white beneath the sun.' Wow. Are these yours?"

  "They were when I was about your age," Lugo says. "I was saving them."

  "Not for me, I hope."

  "No," Lugo says. "No, not for you."

  No, not for her. Not since three seconds ago, four seconds, five. He takes sips
from the edge of his drink. It's cold and warm and cold. It is a wading pool and he's
just tranquilly wetting his ankles.

*   *   *

In his bedroom, under the bed, she finds a shoebox full of family photographs organized by shape. "Me as a baby. Me in front of a chicken shop," she says, dialing through them. "Me in front of another chicken shop."

Lugo's picked up a crushed blue sock while she was pulling out the pictures. He underhands it into the closet.

"You were obsessed with the Popeyes sign," he reminds her. "Whenever we drove by it you'd chant *Popeye Popeye* until I pulled over and let you look."

"I don't remember."

She also liked street sweepers, bats, kangaroos, the sound of television static...

"Bring one of those photos to class with you. You could say, 'Once upon a time I was in love with the Popeyes sign.' It'd be a great story."

"You don't know the kids in my class," she says. "I mean, they'd *annihilate* me if I came in with something like that." She pushes the shoebox back under the bed with her bare foot. Her toenails are painted black, with a rim of tan-pink newness at the cuticle. When he asked her what the black polish meant she looked at him as if he'd asked what dancing, what the leaf of a tree meant. He remembers a song— "I wear black on the outside because black is how I feel on the inside." Maybe that's what it means.

Erica is fourteen years old. She has brought a to-do list with her and taped it to Lugo's refrigerator. This weekend she must finish two pages of geometry problems, start *The Member of the Wedding*, figure out feudalism, and go to a friend's birthday party. Back in the kitchen Lugo notices *Stay With Dad* written on the list, among her obligations.

Uneasy, he says, studying this. His daughter's not-easiness makes him uneasy.

"So you still haven't unpacked your things," Erica said when she arrived.

"I'm going to find a new place," Lugo said. "A few weeks ago I noticed a huge footprint on the bathroom ceiling. Right in the middle. How'd it get there? I think about that every time I'm on the toilet. It's horrible."

Erica was organizing her homework into discrete piles on the coffee table. "Do you remember anything about feudalism?" she asked.

*   *   *

At the kitchen table Lugo wraps a gift for Erica's friend. The box is small and light—when he picks it up it feels like there's nothing inside. This is the only reason he opens the box, to make sure it contains a present. It does: a peso tied through with string, a necklace.

He wraps the box in slow time. Often, when he's undertaking a task that requires particular care, he switches to slow time. He folds the paper over the box, he slices off a perfectly sized piece of tape. He centers the tape on the paper's edge and runs his finger over the top of it, making it invisible. In slow time each movement lasts twice as long, but each is twice as efficient, so wrapping the present doesn't take any longer than it would in normal time.

Finished, Lugo looks at the newspaper. Searching for the movie listings he finds an article about a prison escape in Illinois. A prisoner sealed himself inside a box underneath some packing peanuts and shipped himself to freedom. He jumped out of the mail truck. It's been two days and he's still at large. At large, Lugo repeats, treasuring the sound of it. Sometimes an expression like this is all it takes. He closes the newspaper, forgets what he was about to do. Then he remembers: he was about to fix himself another drink.

Erica walks into the kitchen holding a clear plastic baggie of hair. "This?"

"That," he says, "is a baggie of hair."

"Whose hair?"

"Your mother's. But we pretended it was yours. So." Erica turns away. He's boring her. "It's a good story." She walks into the hall with the hair. It's actually not a good story. "Don't you want to hear the story?"

"I can't bring a bag of hair to school, Dad," she calls back. "I have to go get ready for Adrienne's."

"Why can't you bring hair to school? Didn't you just ask me what it was?"

He hears nimble feet scurrying up the carpeted stairs. The door of the spare bedroom shutting lightly.

Earlier that day, when she dropped Erica off, his ex-wife Irene handed him a note. *Remember what we talked about*, it said. *Ease up on the scotch. Distract yourself (and her). Maybe take her to a movie.*

It was on the back of a recipe card for twice-baked potatoes. He flipped the card while climbing the stairs to his apartment with Erica, and he examined the recipe as he'd examined the note. Irene's messages to him lately weren't as clear as they used to be. They leaked static and forced Lugo to listen so closely he couldn't hear anything. Why write the note on a recipe card? Was she trying to impel him to make twice-baked potatoes?

He stands up and gets his brandy, a nod to Irene's request to ease up on the scotch. The brandy tastes how smoke and feet smell, agreeably disagreeable, and Lugo feels suddenly impatient for Christmas. Stringing popcorn and cranberries and mulling wine and all the other things they should have done and never did.

They treated time like it didn't mean anything, that was the main problem. They forgot how the past moves aside for the present, and the present moves aside for the future, and what that leaves you with is a ceaseless series of transitions. Ceaseless, one after the other, alignment to realignment. It's hard! How do people not drink? Drinking's actually the only thing to do about it. To hem all that jagged edging and make the intolerable tolerable. Now that he and Irene aren't together he's able to navigate all the transitions he has to.

Irene is a potter. It took her nearly ten years to establish herself, and it happened by accident when a gallery owner asked if she'd be insulted if she, the gallery owner, marketed Irene's box-shaped pots as funeral urns. Soon people from all over the world were mailing her the cremains of their loved ones.

She used to let Lugo destroy the pots she wasn't happy with. He'd put on an apron, load the pots onto a dolly, push them into the back yard, and use a hammer with an antler handle to crack them. Few things before or since have been as satisfying. The terra cotta shattered with a *plink* and Lugo would be left with shards to survey before he threw them into a garbage bag. What was wrong with these pots? he wondered. They always looked fine to him. He never asked.

After they realized they'd neglected to collect the hair from Erica's first haircut, Irene snipped some of her own hair and put it in a baggie. Why in the world were they saving hair? Did they think they were Mayans? He and Irene thought memories could be safely housed. That was another one of their problems.

Lugo gargles mouthwash until he can no longer stand it. He waits in fast time for Erica to come downstairs.

Driving to the party, he searches for something interesting to say. Last night he dreamed he was hiding in a barn from a tornado. Today he read about a man who mailed himself to freedom. He could ask a question, but his questions are too general (How's school? Life? Your mother?) or too needling (What are you thinking about? Why are you so quiet? Do you know you didn't used to be so quiet?). In front of them is a van with a license plate that says I BREW, which he points out to Erica. She nods without looking at it.

"I used to brew, you know," Lugo says. "Back then. When I brewed. You wouldn't remember."

"What are you talking about?"

"Just testing you. Making sure you're paying attention. You pass."

Erica opens the glove compartment and closes it. She wears a short dress with a cacophony of letters along the midriff. Her hair is tied into twin braids and pulled back. She looks pretty. At a red light he asks, "What do you want for Christmas? I think I'll do some shopping while you're at the party."

"I haven't really thought about it."

"Well, think about it. I want to get you what you want."

"Dad, it's June. I have like a billion things to do before Christmas." She opens the glove compartment again, closes it. "Light's green."

He drives slowly, stalling for time. He turns on the radio, cycles through the pre-programmed stations. All the songs are love songs. He turns it off.

"I'm gonna go through my things when I get home," he says. "I'll find something for your class."

"There's stuff at Mom's I can use. It's no big deal. I was just teasing you about the hair. Don't worry."

He laughs. He feels strange, as if caught in that brief gap between glimpsing himself in a mirror and recognizing the reflection. "I'm not worried," he says. "I've got my daughter for the weekend."

Erica's friend lives on the river in a big Victorian with a widow's walk on the third story. The garage door is open: Lugo can see a tool bench, and pegboard walls with neatly arrayed tools. Only some kind of asshole, he thinks, would keep tools so neatly arrayed. He leans over and kisses Erica on the cheek.

"I'll call in a few hours," she says, unlatching her seatbelt. "You'll be home, right?"

"Finding something for your class."

He watches her walk toward the house, up the stairs. A woman steps out onto the porch and waves to Lugo and Lugo waves back.

*   *   *

What is it about the sight of a woman waving? Lugo can't go home. He can't even think about it. He drives along the riverfront, past houses he and Irene and Erica used to point out and claim as theirs. On Saturdays they would wake up early and drive this way, looking for yard sales. "How much for all of it?" Lugo would ask, and the homeowners would smile or not smile while he appraised them, waiting longer and longer each time to say he was kidding.

He barely remembers the other woman. He met her at the playground inside the mall where he used to bring Erica on the weekend. The woman was with her nephew. She and Lugo sat on a bench and watched Erica and the boy pretend to be monsters. The woman was an elementary-school teacher, lonely. The sort of person who checks out books ten at a time from the library. Her plates at home were plastic, laminated over colorful drawings by her students. *Thanks for the great year, Ms. Something!* Her last name wasn't actually *Something*. Lugo can't remember her last name.

How much for all of it, he'd ask. And when he bought something, he'd ask the person selling it, "What's its story?" Just like Erica this morning. Even if it was just a belt, or an unopened picture frame. He wasn't looking for a story. He wanted them to acknowledge what they were getting rid of, to see it for the last time and perhaps feel a little regret while he handed them seventy-five cents...

Lugo drives and drives until it feels like exercise. After talking to a young woman in a booth at the mall, a woman who sold him perfume by rubbing different kinds on each wrist, asking in a woodwind voice, "So you like? They're imposters, based on designer perfumes. Can't smell the difference, right?" tilting her face close to his, and Lugo smelling something besides perfume, sweet invigorating mall smell, after buying two bottles of perfume and telling the young woman before she handed over the receipt, "You have a great voice," and her saying thanks, and him saying, "I mean, it's studio quality," and her saying yes, tearing the receipt from the register, and him, "How old are you?" and her, unblinking, hardening her jaw, "Off you go now. Enjoy your perfumes," after walking out past the playground, driving around, reenacting the exchange in his mind, remembering it away, Lugo finds himself in a bar. It's one of those places with news clippings and snapshots of patrons covering the walls.

"It's too beautiful to be outside today," the bartender says, pouring his drink.

She's the owner's wife, an older saturnine woman whose name Lugo can never recall.

"I can only stay for one. I have my daughter for the weekend."

The bartender drops a cardboard coaster in front of him, sets his drink atop it. "You remember Shandra, our youngest?"

"Your daughter," he says.

"Yep. We've been at it all week. Turns out last Tuesday she went and had both nipples pierced. You believe that? A stranger did it. She's nineteen, but goddamn. I said to her, 'Now why would you volunteer for that?' She says, 'A bunch of reasons.' And I say, 'One. Give me one good reason.' And she says, 'For increased pleasure, Mom.' For increased pleasure. Like she's reading it off a box."

Lugo studies the ice cubes, dissolving cavities of light, floating in his drink. "My daughter's at a birthday party."

"You could see the studs through her shirt. That's how I knew. But once they're eighteen, isn't much you can do. The cord is cut."

"Erica's just fourteen," he says. "I'm helping her with a project for school."

One drink. Lugo is gifted with willpower when he needs to be, but he rarely needs to be. He sips the drink in slow time—not too slow, he doesn't want the ice to melt—and thinks about Erica. When she was a baby, around the time of her obsession with the Popeyes sign, he, too, became obsessed: with the idea that he would die or go missing before Erica was old enough to remember him. The thought was enough to make his chest palpitate, lying in bed after a half-hour fight with Irene over something he did or failed to do, and he'd often get up to check on Erica. It would take years for her to begin remembering, he knew. He would lift her out of her crib and sit in the velour glider in the corner and rock himself to sleep to the sound of her sleeping.

"She's nineteen," the owner's wife says to a woman down the bar from Lugo, "but goddamn."

He takes a final sip, stands up, and starts to transition himself, mentally, home. Not to his new old apartment, he can't go there, but to his old old house, where Erica and Irene live. He needs to go there. Leaving the bar, turning the key in the ignition, driving five miles per hour below the speed limit, he tries to project casual concern. The last time he surprised Irene at home, it did not go well. She was entertaining a big group of friends, artists, some of whom Lugo had known, and she'd reluctantly invited him in and… it did not go well.

"We should really talk more often," he says to himself as he drives. It's a beautiful day. A few cloud wisps in an otherwise clear sky make the sky look clearer. "I think we can do better with Erica." No, too imperative. "What does Erica want for Christmas?" Close. "Is there anything Erica needs?" Closer.

He started bringing Erica to the indoor playground at the mall during the winter she learned to walk. They went early, before the stores opened, when it was just Lugo, Erica, and the mall-walkers swinging both arms in exaggerated crisscrosses to increase their heart rate. *Right behind you*, they would say, when approaching from behind. They said it in a singsong, drawing out the third syllable, to make it seem less repetitive.

This was before he met the woman who came to the playground with her nephew. The nephew was staying with her because his house was being tented and fumigated for termites. She'd driven him by the house to look at the tent, she said, but the boy couldn't see it. Literally could not see it. "It's as if the tent's not there," she said. This was when Lugo knew she was lonely.

Erica was a happy baby, predictable, easy. When she didn't like what was going on, she cried. When she did, she laughed. What she liked and didn't like always used to make sense to Lugo.

One year he called Popeyes corporate headquarters in Atlanta and told the customer-service woman how he and his daughter had to take the long way home from preschool so they could drive past the sign. He wanted a miniature replica of it to give to her for her birthday, but the woman said they didn't make them. Instead she sent a poster of an awestruck fat man biting into a piece of thigh meat. Beneath him it said, LOVE THAT CHICKEN FROM POPEYES!

A month later Erica no longer cared about the sign. He drove past it a half-dozen times. "It's your sign," he would say. She wouldn't even look at it! Maybe, he thought, she was just tired of that *particular* Popeyes sign. He drove across town to a different Popeyes, but she remained unmoved. What was the matter with her?

"It's your *sign*," he said. He unbuckled her from her car seat and brought her into the parking lot. "Look, there, just look at it."

He lifted her chin a little too roughly and she began crying. He tried to console her. "It's okay," he said. "We'll just have to find you something new to like."

Driving home that afternoon he felt terrible. He knew he'd meet every phase she went through—and what did he suppose her fixation on the sign was but a phase, temporary, brief, dear—with this kind of stubbornness. Better to go out of his way to avoid the sign. Better to stop keeping track.

At the window of the studio, behind the house, Lugo watches Irene edge a thin metal rib along a piece of greenware. Her back is to him. Her hair looks shorter than it did earlier in the day, and her apron is tied in a neat bow at her back—so neat that he imagines someone helped her with it, someone careful. She shapes the corners of the pot, then crouches down and levels her gaze. She'll go on shaping it for hours before glazing it and firing it in the kiln. Next to her sits a metal caddy with four unfired pots on it. They're the color of dry chocolate, box-shaped with contoured edges, large enough to accommodate the cremains of an adult human. The thought of ending up inside a piece of Irene's pottery makes Lugo's ears perspire.

He remembers Irene, four months pregnant, ruddy and self-contained, in a state of heightened appreciativeness. Cleaning the house room by room, throwing away anything, she said, that didn't make her happy. She went on long walks by herself. She came home with her pockets full of acorns, seedpods, nutshells, leaves, all sorts of tree trash, which she would arrange artfully on their bookshelves, along the mantel. When he asked why they were there, she said, "Because they're beautiful."

He knocks on the door. She doesn't look surprised, much less pleasantly surprised, when she opens it. Her chin is streaked with slip clay. She chews on what must be a tiny piece of gum; Lugo discerns it only because he knows she can't work without it.

"Where's Erica?" she says.

He explains that he dropped her off at Adrienne's party, then went Christmas shopping at the mall, where he bought a nice selection of perfume. "Do you have a minute?"

"No," she says, standing in the doorway. "I'm working. I have thirty orders to meet in the next two weeks. Why are you here?"

"I'm here to help," he says confidently. "With Erica." And he thinks: Perfect. Perfect in its timing and execution. Casual yet direct. Poised, concerned.

"You look half-cocked," she says. "You haven't shaved. You smell like a bar. You're wearing pajama bottoms."

"These?" Lugo fights the urge to look down. He watches Irene's cheeks pucker almost imperceptibly around the tiny piece of gum. "These are sweatpants. Never worn these to bed. Plus I'm not even close to drunk. I haven't had a drop of scotch at all today, so." He looks down at his sweatpants—it's clear to him they're sweatpants. "Sweatpants," he repeats.

"Listen." She steps back but not away from the door. "Every time we talk about Erica, it turns into a fight. I don't want to fight anymore. Erica's fine when she's with me. I can't imagine it's all that different with you."

"She's just been getting so," Lugo looks past her to the inside of the studio, "serious." He's searching for the rejects on their caddy, the pots she used to let him dispose of. "At least let me see what you've been working on."

"No."

How easily she dispenses that word! As if she's answering a mail-in survey about a minor appliance. Were you satisfied with our product?

The phone rings in the back of the studio. "That's the phone," she says.

"I know what a phone sounds like," Lugo says.

Irene leaves the door open while she answers it, so Lugo steps inside. "Yes," he hears her say. By her tone, instantly, unguardedly solicitous, he knows she's talking to Erica. "That's because he's standing right here." Next to the worktable are four sturdy-looking green boxes with typed labels: last name comma first name. These are the cremains. "Of course you're not in trouble," Irene says. Next to the boxes is the caddy with the rejected pots, alongside the hammer with the antler handle. What's wrong with them? He lifts one up, turns it over to see his last name, which Irene kept after they divorced—she'd already, in her words, *established herself* with it—etched on the bottom. He loves seeing it there. "I'll come do it myself," she says to Erica.

Lugo is studying a serrated scraper when she returns. Irene unties her apron and balls it up. "Erica's been trying to reach you for a half hour," she says. "I'm picking her up and bringing her home."

"No," Lugo says. "No, I'm going. She's mine this weekend."

She takes a deep, abiding breath. "Just so you know, Erica didn't want to stay with you. She says your apartment's filthy. She says you drink too much and say random things and don't take care of yourself. I made her go." She tosses her apron onto the counter. "Won't be long until I can't make her go anymore."

"All I know," he says, hesitating, steadying himself on the caddy, knocking one of the taller pots onto its side. It doesn't break, or if it does, it isn't audible. "Is that I'm doing everything I can."

This is not what Lugo wanted to say. It isn't true or germane and now Irene is looking at him with undisguised pity. Sort of a smile stuck through with wires. All I know, he wanted to say, followed by some singular insight. Something that only he could know.

"I'm going," she says. "Get home. We'll hash things out later in the week."

She slopes around Lugo. He wants to switch to slow time, but it's impossible with Irene. She's already started the car. She's backing out, she's miles away, she's gone. It has always been impossible.

He looks around the studio at all the artful disorder. In the back, over the slip machine, like a tub with an outboard motor, she has glued shards of old pots to the wall. He wants to pick up the pot she was so attentive to before, so carefully shaping, and let it drop to the ground. No, this is exactly what she wants him to do. It's why she left him alone in the studio. She wants him fully unhinged. Which is probably why she told him what Erica said. She wants him hopeless.

He won't break the pot she was working on, but he can at least push the dolly into the backyard and break up the reject pots. There are three of them. Identically shaped but finished with different glazes—brown, violet, green. The special hammer is right next to them, which is how he knows they're the rejects. He pushes the dolly carefully between rows of bamboo he planted years ago, along the footpath he cut, into a clearing he made…

The first pot he lifts and drops. It falls with a *crunk*, breaks into four or five large pieces. Unsatisfying. The next pot he decides to break by tapping the ball peen against the side, softly, then harder, a little harder, like cracking an egg. He does this to two sides before the pot collapses into shards.

The last pot is heavier and glazed violet, with a coral bead attached to the top. He lowers it to the ground and looks at it. He remembers the man in Illinois who mailed himself to freedom. If he told Erica about it on the way to the party, she would've probably thought *random, random, random*, but it wasn't random. It was… what was it?

It was integral.

This pot he wants to break with a single righteous blow of the hammer. He sets it on the ground, lifts the hammer, and strikes it once, hard. The force produces a cloud of what looks like smoke, but which Lugo can see, after the pot collapses, is ash. Ash and tiny fragments of bone, spilling out onto the grass. He looks at the mess and at the hammer. He can't breathe for a long time. His first impulse is to run away, his second is to cry, but he can't do either. He can only gather the cremains with his hands and attempt to sift them back into the smashed pot. Fruitless, of course, yet he tries anyway. The ashes are filled with sharp, spur-like pieces, shards of pot, shards of bone.

Lugo in normal time. All the promises and warnings and slowing down and speeding up and this is when it becomes clear. This is when he has his comeback for Irene, when he knows the thing that only he can know. He is in trouble.

A BRUTAL MURDER
IN A PUBLIC PLACE

by JOYCE CAROL OATES

A T GATE C33 of Newark International Airport, in a waiting area facing curved-glass windows and a heavily occluded sky beyond, a sudden frantic chirping!

Everyone looks around—upward—the frantic chirping continues—the bird—(if it is a bird)—is hidden from view.

A bird? Is that a—bird? Here? How—*here?*

In these rows of seats, strangers. There are three sets of ten seats each, with six plate-glass windows arrayed before each set: in all, eighteen windows between them and the runway outside and the overcast New Jersey sky.

Behind the seats, on the other side of the walkway, which is not wide, no more than a few yards, are more rows of seats arranged in the usual utilitarian way: back to back and, across a narrow aisle, facing other rows.

You might guess fifteen seats in each row. Ten such rows of seats at Gate C33.

This place of utter anonymity, impersonality.

This place of *randomness.*

Emptiness.

And suddenly—the tiny bird-chirping!

An improbable and heartrending little musical trill, like an old-fashioned music-box!

A sound to make you glance upward, smiling—in expectation of seeing—what?

Near the ceiling above the closest row of seats facing the window there appears to be a ledge of some kind, probably containing air-vents—(from my seat, about fifteen feet from the seats by the window, I am not able to see the front of the ledge)—and very likely the trapped little bird—(if it is a bird, it must be "trapped" for it to be in this place, and if it is between the ledge and the ceiling, it must be little)—is perched there. The seated travelers continue to look around, quizzical and bemused. A white-haired woman in a wheelchair squints upward with an expression of mild anxiety. A contingent of soldiers—mostly young, mostly male, mostly dark-skinned, in casual-camouflage uniforms like mud-splotched pajamas—squint upward, too, frowning as if the bird's chirping might be a warning or an alarm.

How is it possible, a bird *here?*

Though the chirping is fairly loud, rapid-fire and somewhere close by, no one has yet sighted the bird. A lanky young man with a backpack stands to squint toward the ceiling with the air of an alert bird-watcher, but the bird remains invisible.

Another possible place (I see now) in which the little bird might be hidden is in the leaves of a stunted little tree near the windows. This is a melancholy tree of no discernible species in a plastic planter meant to resemble a clay pot. At first you assume that the tree must be artificial; then, when you look more closely, you see to your surprise that the stunted little tree is a *living thing.* The tree is a well-intentioned "decorative touch" in Newark International Airport. Intended to soften the harsh utilitarian anonymity of the place. And intended, too, to soften the horror of *randomness*—of strangers gathered together to no purpose other than to depart from one another as swiftly and expeditiously as possible.

But the little tree has not fared well in this mostly fluorescent-lit environment. Coaxed out of a seed, nurtured into life, it is now a *thing* scarcely living: its large spade-shaped leaves no longer green but threaded with what looks like rust. Still, the little bird might yet be hidden among these leaves…

There is another tree, of the same indistinct species and in the same sort of plastic planter, about thirty feet away, at (unoccupied) Gate C34. Very likely, at other gates in the terminal, and in all the terminals of the airport, there are other trees similarly potted, of a near-identical type, height, and condition, their once-glossy green leaves grown shabby, desiccated. You can tell that these trees are *not artificial* because they are *shabby, desiccated.*

The *artificial* endures. The *living* wears out.

Invisibly, almost teasingly, the tiny chirping continues. Like tiny bits of glass being shaken together in a great fist. There is an announcement, then—a particularly shrill-voiced woman—and some of us who have been searching for the bird turn toward the speaker. When the announcement ends, the chirping has ceased.

Everyone turns back to their preoccupations of a moment before—desultory conversations, laptops and books, the high-perched TV news of far-flung and domestic tragedies that never ceases, whether anyone is watching or not. Even the soldiers who'd appeared vigilant a moment before have turned away. Even the lanky young man with the backpack is now hunched in his seat, speaking into a cell phone.

Am I the only traveler thinking—The little bird is still here somewhere, it could not have flown away without our seeing?

Stubbornly, I listen for it. Scarcely daring to breathe, I listen. As if its tiny heartbeat had aligned itself with my own, as if it is as aware of me as I am aware of it.

A *living thing. Somewhere close by, invisible.*

How loud and intrusive are the announcements! How grating, the human voice! It seems that, at Gate C33, an incoming flight has been delayed (weather, Chicago) and an outgoing flight has been delayed still more (weather, Minneapolis). For some time nothing else can be heard.

But at last, a few minutes later, the frantic little chirping resumes.

Already I am on my feet, restless and alert. I am annoyed and mildly anxious now that my flight has been delayed—(another forty minutes)—yet I am more intrigued by the mysterious little bird. It has drawn my attention. I know—you are advised not to leave your luggage unattended in this public place, but I intend only to walk—to stretch my legs—for a short distance.

It's probable that the bird entered the terminal through an opened door in this area when passengers boarded one of the smaller propeller planes, the ones that, when entered, after a walk across the tarmac, exude the cramped, claustrophobic air of a straining intestine. And yet—think of the odds against this! A luckless bird blown by the wind, unable to prevent itself from being sucked into the terminal through the opened door... Unless, confused by plate-glass reflections, the poor bird blundered through the opened doorway of its own volition.

And now, as I near the windows, there is a sudden blur of wings! Small wings! My vigilance has paid off—I am almost directly below the bird—it was hidden, as I'd surmised, between the ledge and the ceiling—it's a small sparrow—beating its wings madly, careening in the air—striking the row of plate-glass windows looking out onto the runway—making its way into a high, windowless corner of the waiting area. By this time everyone has glanced up again, and several people smile—why does the panicked fluttering of a small bird, trapped in such a place, provoke people to smile?

After a few minutes of wing-beating, chirping, blundering along the row of windows, the little bird—(it's a beautifully patterned sparrow)—has positioned itself back on the ledge, but near the outer edge, where it's visible. I have followed it here, to this relatively quiet space near the (unmanned, unlighted) Gate C34; beyond the window there is an empty runway, and close by is another stunted little potted tree—glamorous poster-ads for Costa Rica, Tampa Bay, Rio. Poor little bird! How did it get into this terrible place, and what can I do to help it?

Gazing up at the tiny, damp eyes, the tiny beak moving soundlessly, as if its terror has made it mute, my heart begins to beat rapidly, and my wings—(wings! Suddenly I realize what is sprouting from my shoulders)—and now I see a fattish woman standing about twelve feet below me and peering up, quizzical and curious rather than concerned—I am crying *Oh please help me! I am one of you! I don't know what this terrible thing is, what it is that has happened to me but I am a living thing, I am one of you*—

Unable to stop the agitation of my wings, I am flying about in terror—striking the ugly, unyielding ceiling—ricocheting against the windows and the ledge—there is a ventilator humming within, a ghastly grinding sound—in the midst of my terror another woman comes to observe, eating an apple—so acute is my eyesight, I can see saliva gleaming on this woman's lips—in her eyes a reflection of mild concern— so very mild, it's like a flickering candle seen at a distance; beyond this woman are rows of seats, most of which are occupied—there are soldiers in their bizarre jungle uniforms—some glance up frowning, or smiling—faint distracted smiles; a few have seen me, or the blurred beating of wings that I have become. *Help me! I want to go home! I don't belong here, I live in*—but my tiny trilling voice can't accommodate the words. *I am one of you—I am a living creature—help me out of this terrible place— I was a traveler like you—a human being like you—my flight to Chicago was delayed, and then—somehow—this, to which I can give no name—this curse! Please hear me! Please help me! I have done nothing to deserve this punishment—I am innocent—I cannot even remember my "sins"—my "crimes"—I may have believed that I was an extraordinary individual, but the fact is, I was utterly ordinary—I am utterly ordinary—I am blameless—it is a terrible injustice that I have been singled out like this—please, you must help me! Don't just smile inanely or look away, bored—help me! It is a mistake that I am here, trapped against plate-glass windows—flinging myself against plate-glass windows—so yearning to escape into the open air, to freedom, my tiny heart is near to bursting! Take me to my home—when they see me, they will recognize me—there are those who love me—they will know who I am—I must consume food at once, I am starving—my little sparrow-wings, my tiny organs, my heart, my teaspoon of blood must be nourished—I am so very cold, I am shivering convulsively—if I don't consume food—just a few crumbs—please, just a few crumbs—I will begin to die— my organs will shut down—my panicked, darting eyes will close over, and my vision will become occluded—my wings which I had believed would beat forever, will slow—not one of you is starving—not one of you is beginning to shut down, and die—you have no right to smile at the suffering of a bird in the final minutes of its life—you have no right to ignore me, for I am a very beautiful white-crowned sparrow with elaborately patterned wings of white and brown and black, with rust-colored curved feathers—I am more beautiful than any of you crude, wingless, earthbound creatures—I am as deserving of life as you!—more deserving than you!—I deserve better than this nightmare-curse: a random death among strangers—*

Except—am I going to be rescued? Has someone called for help, and help has come? Eagerly my eyes take in an unexpected sight below: two men in work uniforms—quick-striding, efficient, and seemingly well-practiced—are approaching at last. One has a stepladder and a small net with a three-foot handle; the other carries a wicked-looking broom.

LION'S JAWS

by JOE MENO

A GIRL I USED to know wanted to be eaten by a lion. It was all she could talk about: being eaten by a lion.

At first I thought it was all an act, but then I found out she wasn't joking. It was disturbing but also kind of attractive. Whenever somebody really wants something, even if it's crazy, it makes you think there's more going on there than there really is.

She was tall and a little too thin, with long, straight brown hair. There was a glow in her eyes, which were gray-blue. She was from Berlin. She wore a lot of torn-looking T-shirts made to look like dresses. She mostly listened to European dance music. I don't think I'm describing her right. She looked like she'd been exposed to a lot of things she shouldn't have been exposed to at a young age, like she was already a little bored with the world, which is maybe why she wanted to be eaten by a lion.

I used to think her father or uncle or some other male figure must have made her watch some inappropriate German movie when she was little, but I don't know if that's true. I don't how else she might have gotten the idea.

She didn't live in Berlin, back then, but there was something about her, the way she stood—her shoulders slanted, kind of aloof, her taste in clothes—that made it obvious where she came from.

I met this girl while she was living in Chicago. Her name was Opal. Whenever I ran into her, on the street, at openings, at parties, it always seemed like we got on very well.

We slept together once but it was not fun. She was too serious, or something. It was all knees and elbows. I think both of us felt bad afterward. We weren't even friends, and now there was no chance we would have any kind of remotely normal relationship. I don't know if I was reading too much into it. It didn't seem to bother her at all.

The next day I decided I didn't want to leave her place until we came to some kind of an agreement. At the very least, I thought, we should agree not to avoid each other— even though we were no good in bed together, we could at least be civil in public.

She said fine, when I said all this. I remember her sitting up in bed, smoking. She had a white T-shirt on but nothing else. I think I should mention that she didn't shave her pubic hair. It turned me on, I have to say. The hair was a lighter brown and made you think of an animal.

In the bed, which was just a mattress on the floor, the way she fit that cigarette to her lips and stared at the corner of the room made you think she thought you were an absolute idiot. It's something I've found most Europeans can do very well.

I kept trying to explain to her that I didn't want there to be any hard feelings. She sighed and said it didn't really matter to her either way: what happened had happened, and if she saw me in a crowded room, she wouldn't walk away. It was all well and good. Those were her exact words. Then she said she wasn't interested in discussing it any longer and would I please leave as she had things to do.

I couldn't let it go. I don't know why, really. I mean, it's not like we even ran into each other that often. It's just that, by then, there were four or five other girls who, if I saw one of them at a party, or at some bar, or sitting on the subway, one of us would end up leaving. We couldn't be in the same room together. I didn't think it said a lot about the kind of person you were, having to sneak around town like that. I was getting close to thirty and was trying on the idea of becoming more mature. I was reading more. I had gone out and bought a lot of shirts.

I offered to make her some eggs and she said okay, but without any kind of enthusiasm at all. She had put on a red kimono—this very exotic-looking robe—but it was too short for her. It made her legs look like daggers. I don't know why, but suddenly I thought I'd be an idiot not to try and get her back in bed.

I started frying an egg and making lewd comments to her. She was sitting at a tiny kitchen table, looking at a newspaper that was already a couple of days old. I told her I thought she ought to give me another chance. I explained that, that way, the next time she saw me, there wouldn't be any resentment. She didn't seem all that interested.

The egg, when I finished making it, looked like a large, runny eye. She ate it without looking up, taking very tiny bites. I was relieved because it gave me a little more time to think of how I was going to get her to sleep with me again.

I decided to be bold. I reached across the table and put my hand on her breast, right there. She didn't seem to care. So I pulled my hand back and sat there, trying to think of something else.

I'm no good at all when it comes to quick decisions. In a crisis, I'm not the kind of person you want to have around.

She finished her egg a lot sooner than I would have liked. She set her fork down in the middle of the plate, which seemed a little formal. Then she looked up. I'm busy today, she said. I'm supposed to be shooting my movie. I have to go to the zoo later.

What movie? I asked.

She got up and walked across the kitchen, to a small TV sitting on the counter next to the sink. Part of the TV was covered in tinfoil. She switched it on, then turned on the VCR next to it. I got the feeling I wasn't supposed to say anything while the movie was playing.

The movie was like a lot of films I had seen being shown in galleries at the time. It was mostly a kind of collage, inexpertly assembled, and it cut between all sorts of black-and-white nature-film clips and parts of various pornographic movies.

In one scene, a rhinoceros was trying to court another rhinoceros. A male tiger was attacking a female. A spider was devouring its mate. Then there was a clip of John Holmes or Ron Jeremy having intercourse with a faceless woman. The porno films were oversaturated—the men's skin looked bright orange, and the women seemed unnecessarily pink.

I asked her if it was finished, her movie. She said she had some scenes of her own she had to shoot.
    Of what? I asked.
    I need to find a lion.

What for? I asked.
    It's for the final scene. There's a gallery show in a couple months, and my movie's going to be part of it. That's why it's important I get to the zoo today.
    It seemed like she was flirting with me. She was sitting across from me at the table again, and she had her feet in my lap now. Her toes were long; the nails looked like they'd been painted red some time before, but all that was left were tiny red scratches. I could look up the long avenues of her legs and see everything in between. I'm not trying to be coarse here. I just think it describes how unclear it was, what was going on between the two of us. I had no idea what she was thinking.

Do you want to help? she asked me.
    I didn't have anything better to do, and I told her so. It seemed like the best way to get her back in bed.

Wunderbar, she said.

Wunderbar, I said.

Marvelous, she said, and pressed her feet harder into my lap.

She brought her film equipment to the zoo. Her film equipment was a child's video camera manufactured somewhere in Russia. She said it was perfect for the kind of movie she was trying to make.

It's more authentic, she said.

What's your movie supposed to be about? I asked.

The annihilation of our species through sex.

Wow, I said.

I know, she said. It's very complicated.

It doesn't seem all that complicated, I said.

It's like animals. They have no illusions about sex. We're the only animals who try to kid ourselves. It's not supposed to be about enjoyment, she said, leaning against the railing. It's about submission to something other than yourself.

The lions weren't cooperating. They were all sleeping in the sun, on the rocks. It wasn't very dramatic. She wanted to get a shot of the male doing something savage to the female. Preferably intercourse, she said. She said she had searched for hours through all sorts of nature films, and couldn't find any clips of a male lion trying to mate with a female. She said it was part of a dream she'd had.

Do you want to hear about my dream? she asked. I've had it since I was a very little girl in Berlin.

Okay, I said.

In the dream, I'm still a girl. Back in Germany.

I'm at the zoo. The one I went to when I was a child.

The lion's cage is open. I walk inside. The lion is sleeping. I open his jaws and climb in between them. It's like a room in there, like a cave. I fit without him having to eat me. And then I am inside his stomach.

He eats you?

He does, but not with his teeth. I'm inside his stomach and I know this is where

I'm meant to be. Don't you think that's lovely? It's what I think of when someone says I love you. To find that place. That's what love is, to me.

Well, I said. Maybe you don't understand the word.

To be devoured by something. To give yourself over in totality. No one in America does this.

There are laws against it, I said, trying to be funny.

I'm being serious. Everyone in this country is afraid to give in. It's pitiful. No one here can give themselves over to anything. That's why all of you are bad in bed.

I think this country has some definite problems, I said. But which one doesn't?

I'm just telling you what your problem is, she said.

Okay, I said. I appreciate it. Really.

The lions in the exhibit were still sleeping. I looked at them and thought they had the right idea.

So what about the movie? I asked. Are you going to film the lions or not?

No. They're too docile. They look like the kind of lions that watch television, she said.

Then she turned, looking along the ground for something. She walked off into the grass, toward the pond, which was inhabited by hundreds of flamingos.

Here, she said. She was walking back. She had picked up a rock. It was about the size of her fist.

I told her it seemed like a bad idea to throw a rock at the lions. It seemed like they were getting along pretty well without our interference, I said.

Opal didn't listen. She was maybe twenty-eight. Twenty-nine. She could have been older than me, but I never asked. She was used to doing what she wanted, is what I mean to say.

She looked around to be sure we weren't being watched, and then she threw the rock. It landed right beside the male without much of a sound. The lion didn't move. It looked just like a piece of furniture. Opal sighed, leaning against the railing again.

I'm going home, she said.

All right. Let's go, I said.

No. You're not coming.

No?

No.

You don't need any help with your equipment?

No.

And so I watched her go.

I didn't see Opal for a few weeks after that. I didn't have her number, and even if I had, I don't know if I would have called. I wanted to meet a girl who was a little more fun, outgoing. Someone who would wake up one Sunday and decide to put her hair in pigtails, that kind of thing. I had a friend with a girlfriend like that. When she'd come over in overalls, her hair in pigtails, it always made me feel jealous.

So I didn't see the girl for a while. I know you're not supposed to refer to women as girls anymore, but it's a bad habit. I'm working on it, believe me. It just makes things seem more fun, like you're still young, like you're not wasting your time night after night looking for the right one. I was just looking for someone I thought I could understand, and who would understand me. It hadn't happened yet.

I got a call from her, the girl Opal, a couple weeks later. She got my number from a guy named Carl. Carl made paintings protesting the war. They featured tanks rolling over babies. I didn't think it was very subtle, what he was doing, but he was making a living at it and I wasn't.

Hello, the girl said, on the phone.

Hi, I said.

Funny to hear from you, she said, even though she was the one who had called.

Yes, I said.

I heard you had a car, she said.

I do. I definitely do.

I was wondering if I could borrow it.

I don't think that's going to be a possibility, I said. I was just trying to give her a hard time.

I have a license, the girl said.

That's a different story, then.

I had a car, but my boyfriend took it.

What boyfriend? I asked.

Hans, she said. He's in Texas now. He's starting a band.

This is all very interesting, I said, but what about the car?

I need it for my film.

The one about the lion?

Yes, she said. I found a place that has a lion.

You did.

It's in Indiana. But I can't get there by the train.

We can go, I said. I can take you.

Would you want to?

I would, I said. Where's it at? A zoo?

Yes, she said. The lion was in a circus and then it ate a boy's arm and then it got put in this zoo in Indiana.

Really? I asked.

Really, she said.

We took my car. It was a Plymouth. I had bought it used after my first book came out. The book had not done well. In the only review I got, the person used the word *unsubstantial*. I was thinking I was probably going to have to do other things with my life from now on.

The book I had written was about a man who sold hand cream door to door. Not that that matters now. I had several hundred copies of it piled all over my apartment. My editor had felt bad for me, and sent me all the books she could before they were destroyed. I was actually a little sick of looking at them.

We drove in silence for most of the way. My radio had been stolen, and the sounds the car made were less than ideal. At some point we passed an Amish family riding in a horse-drawn buggy.

We have those back home, she said. They're Dutch, mostly.

The farmland stretched out in all directions. I thought, this is a part of America almost no one ever sees. I thought it would make a great book, but then I remembered I had given up on writing.

We found the zoo without too much trouble. The problem was that it looked like it had been closed for years. There was graffiti all over the walls, and different kinds of automotive parts strewn around the entrance. But the front gate was open. We found a zookeeper who said people kept leaving their garbage in the parking lot. For some reason or another everyone in town had given up on the idea of a zoo. They'd decided that what they really needed was a junkyard.

I followed the girl past broken-down exhibit after broken-down exhibit. The elephants were all missing their tusks. There was a peacock whose feathers had been stolen and a pair of chimpanzees in dirty children's dresses. The zookeeper explained that the chimps had found the dresses in the trash and had grown very attached to them.

The lion enclosure was typical, rocks and grass, all of it surrounded by a moat. In the moat was a white refrigerator that someone had dumped there. Most of the moat was dried up, anyway. I asked how come the lion didn't jump out, and the zookeeper said they made sure not to feed it too much protein.

Unbelievably, the lion looked to be in pretty good health. His coat was golden, and his mane, which was very long, looked regal. I could tell Opal was pretty happy. I told her I thought he'd be perfect for the movie. She said she thought so, too.

Can we go in there with him? she asked the zookeeper.

Oh, no, he said. We don't do that. Only when the vet comes around, he said. And he only comes once a month.

But we came all this way to film him. I don't think it will look good if he's so far away.

I wish I could help you, the zookeeper said.

I noticed then that the zookeeper was maybe only sixteen or seventeen. He had a mountain range of acne all along his narrow jawline.

To be honest, the zookeeper said, I don't think I even have the keys for this exhibit.

The lion was licking his enormous front paws.

And besides, I don't want to get in trouble, the zookeeper said. This is a pretty good job and all.

The girl, Opal, didn't seem to be listening.

What kind of movie are you making? the zookeeper asked.

It's an art film, the girl said. It's about love.

Oh, he said, nodding, like he had heard about the movie already. Well, this is about as close as we're allowed to get.

The girl opened her bag and pulled out her video camera. The lion didn't seem to mind. I looked around and noticed the camel in the exhibit directly across the way. It had its head poked out over the railing and was eating from a garbage bag filled with metal.

What's his name? I asked, pointing at the camel.

Ulysses, the zookeeper said. He killed somebody, too. At a birthday party. This place, it's like a maximum-security prison for deranged animals.

The bad camel was just standing there, eating tin cans like it was the most natural thing in the world.

Can I touch him? I asked.

Sure. He's just like a horse, the zookeeper said.

I walked over and put a hand out. His muzzle was wet and firm.

The zookeeper gave me a handful of sheared tin and asked if I wanted to feed it to the camel.

Is this what camels are supposed to eat? I asked.

Not normally. But this one likes it.

I held the tin out and the camel clamped his long jaws down over it, snatching it gracefully from my hands.

Wow, I said. It's hungry.

From across the way, the lion let out a magnificent roar. The zookeeper and I turned around. The girl, Opal, had climbed over the railing of the exhibit and was kneeling in the dried-up moat, filming the lion from only a few feet away. The zookeeper ran over, shouting at her, but Opal didn't respond. She didn't look scared at all. In fact, it seemed like the lion was actually afraid of her. It was crouched up in one corner of the enclosure, roaring. It sounded like an airplane falling from the sky, low and rumbly.

What are you doing? the zookeeper shouted. Climb back out! Hurry!

But Opal didn't seem to hear. She kept inching closer, holding the camera to her right eye. It occurred to me then that I didn't know anything about this girl. It felt like another sign that I wasn't taking the important things in my life very seriously.

The girl put the camera down. The lion kept roaring. The zookeeper had run off, looking for the keys.

Listen to me, the girl was saying. Listen to me.

The lion kept crouching there, its heavy jaws opening and closing in panic.

Listen to me, she was saying, and then she was kneeling there, right before it. Please, she said, like a plea. Please. Do it. Do it. Do it. Please.

The lion was looking down at the girl. It roared again, flicking its tail back and forth, and then it became quiet. The girl kept speaking to it, trying to get it to attack her. Her voice sounded very timid, very lovely. Finally the lion just sat down, turning away from where the girl Opal was kneeling. It faced the corner of the exhibit and began to lick its front paws.

By then the zookeeper was back with the keys and had gotten the exhibit open. He ran in and grabbed Opal under her arm and dragged her out while the lion cleaned its paws, ignoring the sound of her angry shouts.

Back in the car, Opal was inconsolable.

Are you okay? I asked, without expecting an answer.

She had her video camera in her lap and was holding one hand over her eyes.

We drove past the same farms, past the same fields, the car shaking from the wind. Opal was sitting in the bucket seat, staring out the window, not saying a word, silently sobbing. When we got to the end of Indiana, I realized I had no idea what to say to her. I didn't think we'd be seeing each other again. Even though she was sitting a few inches away, she was somewhere else now, beyond me, and the devastated look on her face told me that whatever kind of relationship we'd had, it was definitely over now.

In the end, I did see the girl, Opal, three more times: once at a record store, once at a party, and once while waiting for the bus. Each time we both pretended like we didn't see each other. It bothered me, but not enough to get me to say something.

I started dating my friend's ex-girlfriend, the one with pigtails. Once she found out I liked them, she started doing it every day, putting her hair like that. It got old. We ended up fighting a lot. One night we went to an art opening for my friend

Carl. He had more paintings with tanks and babies. Now there were dogs under the tank treads, too. I was walking around the gallery, trying to think how I was going to break up with the pigtail girl, when I stumbled into a little room where people's films were being projected. One of them was of the lion. I recognized it right away. There was the nearly abandoned zoo, and the zookeeper's nervous shadow, and a flash of the girl Opal's fingers. From the angle of the camera, crouched down low, the lion looked like a statue, like something from a play, or a storybook maybe. It was magnificent, even in its panic. It looked like it was older than the idea of God. You could hear the audio of the girl from Berlin trying to talk to it, trying to convince it to eat her. The editing was pretty jumpy. But it was like you could feel the girl's heart breaking right there, the dream not happening. For once I felt like I finally understood somebody else. The girl was absolutely right. It was the reason I had been unhappy. I had never given myself over to anything like that. It was one of the most beautiful things I'd ever seen but no one else seemed to be watching.

THE PURSUIT OF ORDINARINESS IN KENYAN WRITING:

AN INTRODUCTION TO THIS ISSUE'S FIVE NEW STORIES FROM KENYAN WRITERS

by BINYAVANGA WAINAINA
AND KEGURO MACHARIA

CONTEMPORARY KENYAN ARTISTS are obsessed with ordinariness. The word comes up in news commentary, political speeches, and literary criticism. These days, it even has a name: *Wanjiku*. What would Wanjiku say about this or that? What are we doing about Wanjiku? What does Wanjiku want? Nobody admits to being Wanjiku—she always lives somewhere else.

Yet ordinariness has more aspects than one figure could ever contain.

In Yvonne Owuor's "Weight of Whispers," the protagonist has a PhD in diplomacy and a master's in geophysics. In Muthoni Garland's *Halfway Between Dundori and Nairobi*, the most successful character is a poorly educated black woman who is a mistress to a seventy-year-old white man. In the memoir of one of this essay's authors, Binyavanga Wainaina, ordinariness is having a Kenyan father and a Ugandan mother with deep ties to Rwanda, living as an undocumented worker in South Africa, and belonging to a cosmopolitan family spread across Africa, Asia, and Europe. In Parselelo Kantai's "You Wreck Her," ordinariness is a young woman shuttling between being a hustling sex worker in Nairobi and an international model in Europe. And in Judy Kibinge's short film "Killer Necklace," ordinariness is a different kind of Nairobi hustle—a game in which a female domestic servant pretends to belong to the upper-middle class she serves while her impoverished boyfriend pretends to be the upwardly mobile man she craves.

In striving to find the new ordinary Kenyan, these authors inch away from the allegorical paradigm established by Ngugi wa Thiong'o, the dominant voice of Kenyan literary production. In works including *The River Between* and *A Grain of*

Wheat, Ngugi voiced the discontent and utopian hopes of peasants and urban workers for whom the promise of independence from the British in 1963 remained unrealized. Throughout the 1970s, he attempted to represent the common Kenyan. But Ngugi went into exile in the early 1980s, after being proclaimed a dissident by former president Daniel arap Moi's government. He became a figure with whom younger writers could identify, insofar as they shared his political critiques, but who was also removed from the everyday. His works felt iconic, but not present.

Instead, in the 1980s, the romance of Nairobi's hard streets captured many of our imaginations. We read Meja Mwangi's blaxploitationish *Going Down River Road*, John Kiriamiti's *My Life in Crime*, and Charles Mangua's *Son of Woman*, about a gangster who was the son of a whore. In the vast, growing offshoots of Nairobi City, people were mingling, creating, breakdancing, fighting, and speaking Sheng—a new Kenyan language that mixed Swahili with English. We found all this exciting. The moment that the airwaves were liberated, the first literary movement was Sheng-based hip-hop. We trusted this sound—it spoke to us, about our alienation from truth and about a place called Babylon, which was evil, and uncreative, and uncool. Some of us recognized that we were a part of it.

Writers were taking in these new influences even as we suffered from a state-imposed writer's block. In her poem "A Gifted Almost Fifty," Sitawa Namwalie marvels that, as she approaches fifty, she is writing "angry young poetry" that should have been "used up at twenty." Explaining this phenomenon, she indicts the Moi regime, which lasted from 1978 until 2002. His was a government "that did not allow vocalization." Sitawa speaks for a generation of writers and artists muzzled through the '80s and '90s, exiled materially and psychically. It is only now that writers are reclaiming that time.

In fact, if one word describes contemporary Kenyan writing, it must be *convergence*. Silenced and invisible writers from the Moi years are being published alongside writers born in that same period. And the writing is multi-lingual, shifting from English to Kiswahili to Sheng, and exploring the resources offered by ethnic languages. Read Potash, one of Kenya's leading young online writers, and you'll find Shakespeare rubbing against Sheng (*"lenga* that *storo"*—kill that story), and Cicero juxtaposed against the wisdom of street hustlers.

The journey abroad, meanwhile, once a marker of elite status, has been transformed by the global economy into a marker of labor. The resulting cultural promiscuities flavor Kenyan writing with restless, shifting registers: we have come to enjoy the simple, shocking pleasure of writing and reading our prose in English with dialogue in Kiswahili or Sheng. It's not uncommon to find an American expression rendered in British spelling. Nor is it uncommon to have writing travel across virtual and geographical borders. This essay, for instance, has been written on planes and trains, in Maryland and New York, in the U.S. and Canada, and been read by friends and colleagues in DC and Nairobi and Illinois.

In a very profound way, we are only now discovering the Kenya we have been sharing over the past thirty years. That discovery is taking place in fits and starts, marked by first-person narratives that straddle fiction and autobiography. The memoir is as popular in contemporary writing as fiction. Voices long unused are learning to speak. And stories long untold are now being written. If we found ourselves ideologically scrambled after 1989, when the fall of the Berlin Wall made the world seem smaller and more confusing, leaving us with fewer ideological choices, we also created our own unique spaces, shaped, but not determined, by the socio-political air around us.

To be "ordinary" has come to mean many things. Writers in their mid-thirties are only now writing about the high-school life of twenty years ago. Others have seized on *matatus*, college drinking games, bars and churches, and childhoods in the spanking new suburbs of Nairobi in the 1970s. Our most viral video concerns Makmende, a superhero out of the urban legends of '90s Nairobi kids. Supposedly his name (it means "A hero" in Sheng) was born out of a scrap of Clint Eastwood dialogue—"Make my day." Kenyan truth is as invented as it is real.

We chose the writers included here because they embody that spirit of innovation and play. Richard Onyango's story, recorded by Onyango in paintings and captured by Binyavanga Wainaina in prose taken from recorded interviews, offers a rich, singular portrait of the Kenyan artist. It also features a character found in our other four selections—the trickster-hustler figure, who moves from Billy Kahora's downtown Nairobi to Annette Majanja's peri-urban boarding school to Wainaina's own story of a journey from Njoro to Nakuru.

These selections also represent experiments in feeling. Yvonne Owuor's account of loss and mourning breaks through a literary numbness that suffused the Moi years—we are now writing down what it means to feel and not to feel. And in telling these stories, we are creating new possibilities, connecting with each other in new ways.

In our youth, we came to invest a lot in the project of school: our national school system once provided a common set of codes and sensibilities, a flattish-seeming ground, a merit system that was more coherent and comprehensive than any other national insitution we knew. Many of us are still looking for that feeling again—for the old friendships, the discovery of each other in boarding-school dorms, the drama of our differences, the suspended world that often seemed fair and equal. It did not exist outside the gates, at the time, but perhaps it can be found now.

The Last Game
SERIAL IX D3M-Vol II

Richard
Malindi Kenya 2000

THE LIFE AND TIMES
OF RICHARD ONYANGO

by RICHARD ONYANGO

WITH PAINTINGS BY THE AUTHOR

MY NAME IS Richard Onyango. I was born on the second day of the second month of 1960 in Kisii, which is a district in south Nyanza. Soon after my birth my father got a transfer to the Tana River District, where he found a job with the National Irrigation Board. He was a water-supply technician. He helped to refine the drinking water for the company.

In 1961, the country was still developing. Tana River was still bush, and that year there were floods.

We lived next to the police station, and in front of our house was a road to Mombasa, through Malindi. At the time the town was called Hola. Now it is called Galole, after the people there insisted on the change. Hola was the place where eleven Mau Mau were beaten to death at a concentration camp set up by the British in the 1950s. The story spread all over the world, and Hola became famous.

The only cars we saw were the government Land Rovers and my father's tractors. There was also a Lister machine that my father used to pump water to the big storage tanks around the area. My father's working place was just next to our house.

Family friends who came to visit would sometimes leave their Land Rovers in front of the door, and I would go down under them to see the differential, the gear box, and I thought that this was a very fantastic machine. One day a family friend came to visit us, and I stayed under his car until he was ready to leave. He got in and the car started and began to move back, and I slid out. I was in a lot of trouble. My father beat me.

Another thing I was interested in was the bus: there was only one bus, and when we wanted to go for holidays and visit my grandmother we had to travel by bus.

We could not travel without it, and also this same bus came to Hola with bread and books and so many things from town. When the bus came, everybody came to watch.

This bus was a Tana River Bus Company bus, and the owner of this bus was named Mohammed Lalji. It was the only one with 67 PASSENGERS written on its side, so people in the village thought the name of the bus was *Passenga*. Everybody was always waiting for the *Passenga*.

This is how I started drawing buses.

One day, when we were coming back from Christmas holidays in 1965, we got stuck in Malindi. The roads were closed; there was too much rain. So I walked around in Malindi town, and at the petrol station I saw my father's Land Rover, which he had gotten for work.

I went to my father and told him, "But father, I have seen your Land Rover at the petrol station."

When we went back to the petrol station we found one of his employees, who was transporting spare parts from Nairobi. He was stranded there because he wanted to go to Hola but did not know the situation of the road. We got in with him and made our way to Garsen.

When we reached Garsen we were told again that the roads were impassable. After a while we got to a place where the water from upcountry was roaring like a lion, past us and into the ocean. We stepped out to see if there was a narrow route through the new river, but the Land Rover roared forward, and we were stuck in the water. We spent four days there, and even today I wish, like I wished then, that I had had a camera, or a video camera, to take pictures of this time when Kenya was still a bush.

Four days, we stayed in that Land Rover like it was our house. In my mind, from this time, I was drawing Land Rovers. Fortunately my father had carried food; we had UHT milk and bread and tea. We also had fruit.

Every night we could hear the animals in the bush, and the insects. It rained and rained, and water was screaming past us. We heard lions and elephants and hyenas. I made a picture of this, then. I admired the Land Rover, from this time. It is such a tough machine. Later I bought one in the same model and color. I have eleven Land Rovers in my garage, for the orphanage I am building.

There were some giant machines in Hola. I used to follow my father as he repaired those big Lister machines. At some point giant cranes came to Hola to lift storage tanks, to dig wells. The tractors used to come by our home when they were being washed. There were so many machines here in the middle of the wild bush, thanks to the government's Hola Irrigation Scheme. There were welding machines, pump machines, and cutting machines. There was a plane for spraying insecticide on the farms.

There were nomads in Hola, too. The Galla, the Orma, and the Somalis. They were afraid of the machines at first.

They used to bring milk for us, and I watched them going to the marketplace every week. Our house was in a very good place. The Mombasa–Malindi road passed just outside our door, so I saw every new thing that came into town. The road brought people from the desert and the bush, from Garissa and North Eastern Province, and from Mombasa it brought modern people and machines. There was a lot of security for us, because there were bandits who came from the North, called *shiftas*. When you heard the siren from the police station, it meant shiftas were terrorizing the area.

All the educated people, the ones working in the government and in the schools and at the Irrigation Scheme, were from upcountry: Kambas, Luos, and Kikuyus. The local Pokomo did part-time work and unskilled labor.

The government built a school here called Mau Mau Memorial School. The trenches people had dug at the detention camp in the 1950s were still there. There were stories about Mau Mau ghosts, but I was not interested in these.

I was interested in the machines, and the developing place. It was changing fast—there were new things coming and the old things were disappearing. I wanted to become a truck driver. I did not know that God had other plans for me.

Recently, one of the machines, one of the very big machines of Hola, was sold by tender. It is a big crane that can lift very big loads, even containers. I bid for it. So it is mine. I like it because it was one of the first machines to arrive in Hola. It is still there. I am trying to make a plan to transport it to my place in Lamu.

Real life started when I went to secondary school. You know, my father really wanted me to become a District Commissioner or a Provincial Commissioner. He really admired the way the District Commissioner was carried by Land Rover to his office, a few meters away, and then carried in a Land Rover back home. He had a uniform, and guards.

When I told my father I wanted to be a truck driver, he was very angry. So I went to secondary school in Mombasa, in 1976. This is when I got full independence from my parents. I went to Tudor Day Secondary School. I had no guardian, no relatives in Mombasa to live with. So I suggested to my father that a friend and I would rent a room together.

We bought a small stove and utensils and a table for doing homework. I was sixteen years old. We had to walk eight kilometers to school. I was always late, and always in trouble because of this. It took me two hours to get to class—Nyali

Bridge was always congested, so you could not move fast. I was always worried that we would be attacked—there was a notorious gang called Congo By Force, who liked to sodomize boys. They lived in a place called Kongowea.

My father gave me three hundred Kenyan shillings every month. This was very little money. Bread was KSh 1.50—so a loaf of bread a day would have cost me forty-five shillings a month.

I was always starving by the 17th. My father sent the money with the bus conductor from Hola, four hundred kilometers away, so on the 5th of every month I would go to the bus station to collect my allowance.

The road was bad, so sometimes I would wait for days, coming every day to the station to wait for the bus to arrive. Slowly, I started to use my drawing skills. I would watch matatus at the stage, make a drawing of them, and sell them for twenty shillings to the matatu drivers. With that I would buy bread, one egg, paraffin, one onion, a small amount of *unga*.

Once I drew a Tana River Bus Company bus, and the conductor was amazed. He took the painting to the owner of the bus company, Mohammed Lalji. Bwana Lalji was very excited when he saw the paintings. "Please bring the boy to me if you see him again," he said.

That bus was called Peponi. I still like to paint Peponi, because it gave me my first recognition.

When I next met the bus conductor, he told me the boss wanted to see me. I told him, okay, when I go home on holiday, I will stop in Malindi, while the bus is being serviced.

So when I got to Malindi, I went to see the man. He was very happy to meet me. He wanted to know if I had eaten. Then he told me, "From today, you should not pay. You are staff." He called the bus conductor, whose name was Safari.

Even today, since that time, I do not pay to go on Tana River Bus Company buses.

So I continued to paint buses, not knowing how famous I was becoming. I painted a Coast Bus—not knowing that the paintings got to the owner of Coast Bus too. So they were looking for me and did not know how to find me.

But one day, I happened to be in the Coast Bus office. And at the reception area, I saw my painting on the wall! I went to the woman cutting tickets and told her that I had painted the picture. She smiled and looked surprised.

"Oh," she said, "please stay right here. Don't move, because I will get into trouble if you do. Mr. Mirza has been looking for you. He has been here several times wanting to know if we have found you."

So they took me to Kingorani, where he was.

"You are Richard?" he asked me.

"Yes," I told him.

"You must be crazy, because what I forgot to put on my bus, you put on my bus, which means you are more intelligent than me."

What he meant was that I had changed some of the fittings and decoration in my painting. I always thought never to make something like it is, but to make it how I think it should be.

Mr. Mirza took me in his new Peugeot 504 to an Indian hotel. The food was terrible—everything tasted of *pilipili*, and I was suffering. Then Mr. Mirza took me to his workshop. He told me he wanted a very good picture showing the day service and the night service of Coast Bus.

"What kind of idea do you have?" I asked.

"Oh, the idea is yours—you are the artist," he told me. "You decide what to do."

I started to think how to make one picture with both day and night. I decided to make a kind of forest with two windows on one side and two windows on the other side. One side was night, one side was day. I painted one bus going, and one bus coming. In the background was the booking office, and Nairobi very far away.

I took the picture to Mr. Mirza, who was amazed. He gave me three thousand shillings! I had never seen money like that in my life.

I bought my first pair of jeans and a new shirt. Mr. Mirza also told me to come to him whenever I thought of a new design. He told me that if I wanted to go to Nairobi, or to any other place in Kenya, to come to him and get an FOC.

"What is FOC?" I asked.

"Free of Charge."

By this time, I was really hating school. I was not progressing. I was developing an interest in music, though, so I decided to leave school, and my choice then was between art and music. I chose music, because it seemed to offer a lot of money and a good life.

I started following the Kombo Boys Club. They were a *mtaa* band in Kisauni. They played *mbaazi*. Their instruments were very old—they played in local coconut-wine places. So I painted their instruments to make them look new and nice, so their instruments would have full authority.

I started to learn to play the drum set.

There was a famous band around in those days called Bahari Boys Band. They played in a local club that was full of prostitutes, next to Nyali Bridge. The band-master heard about an exciting new drummer, and he came to visit me secretly and asked me to visit them sometime.

So I visited them, and saw their new, good instruments. I left the Kombo Boys without even saying goodbye.

Bahari Boys Band began to play in the big beach hotels and the big nightclubs in town. It was while I was playing, for the first time, in a beach hotel that I met Drosie.

Her real name was Suzy, Dr. Suzy; Drosie was a nickname given to her by her mother.

When I arrived at the hotel, the Bahari Boys were already there. The band-master introduced me to the hotel manager. I was very nervous. I had never been to a place like this. There were lights everywhere, and the drum set was brand new. I was surprised to see, here in Kenya, a place like the films of America. It had plants and trees and beautiful buildings, and it smelled like flowers. But I soon became comfortable with it. I kept all this in my heart.

We wore smart red shirts and cream trousers. We arranged the stage, and then we had dinner in a private room. After dinner, the band said, Okay, we want to get high. Eh? I said. High?

Kaya, they said. We want to smoke kaya. You don't know kaya?

So we went to the beach, and I inhaled, *hmmmmm...* And then again, *hmmmm.* Then they took it from me, saying, Don't smoke too much if this is your first time.

Five minutes later I started trembling with excitement. I was seeing so many new things around me. But I got to the drum set and started playing. I could feel, at first, that my timing was off. But soon I was inside the music, and it was wonderful.

It was nearly midnight when I saw her. A woman, wearing a cream dress and shoes. She had a unique figure, because she was very big and strong, and she looked at me... she had very fierce eyes. Wow, I said to myself, who is this? She was smiling at me and admiring me, so I added some more beats just to make her happy. Then she stood and came toward the stage, and I thought she was going to the toilet—but she stopped at the stage and gave me one hundred shillings. One hundred shillings!

Later, as her table was leaving—she was with her sister and parents—she turned back to look at me and smiled and her mouth said goodbye.

Some days later, we were playing in a local *mnazi* bar. Mnazi is taken from the coconut tree, from the place where the fruit is being fed by a tube. They crack that area so instead of the water feeding the fruit, it drips inside a container. The more it stays, the more sour it is.

Anyway, we were singing "Jambo Bwana." After we played, a waiter came up to me and told me that somebody wanted to buy us a drink.

Who? I asked.

That madam over there.

I stood to go and thank her. My heart was beating. It was my first time talking to a white lady. I was respecting her very much; it was as if I was going to see a queen. She looked very expensive.

I introduced myself as Richard Onyango, and she said that she was Suzy, a doctor. She said she was interested in African music, so she'd come to hear us perform again. I told her we performed here on weekdays.

She left, but gave a message to a waiter saying she wanted to buy me lunch. It was going to be my first time having lunch in a tourist hotel. Nyali Beach Hotel was the biggest and best hotel in Mombasa.

All the waiters were Africans, and I was the only African in the dining room. I was very shy, and there were many glasses and spoons and forks and knives. I was feeling a bit sick, too, because there were all these giant insects on the table. I was feeling sick imagining these giant pink insects being eaten by white people. I managed to eat a bit of rice and chicken, but I could not finish because I did not know how to behave in front of white people.

So after that meal, she asked me, When do you get off days?

Thursdays, I told her.

Okay. On Thursday next week I will invite you to have dinner in Bamburi Beach Hotel, not Nyali this time.

I was worried. I wondered if maybe she was somebody's wife. A millionaire's wife, and when he finds out she is inviting an African to a hotel I will be killed. I knew white men could kill somebody with a gun, just like they would kill a bird or an antelope. So I was very afraid.

But she kept asking me if I would come. And eventually I said yes.

Because we work at night, I was used to sleeping late. But that Thursday I woke up very early in the morning. I washed the house. I spent the afternoon ironing. I scrubbed myself extra, put on Youth Hair pomade, and combed up my Afro. And I put on my best clothes with my crocodile shoes—those pointy shoes and a pleated pair of trousers. I did not like bell bottoms, bell bottoms were for young boys, and I was trying to pretend I was mature. This madam was a senior woman, and I wanted also to look like a senior man.

I was twenty years old.

That night I was late for dinner. When I arrived she looked at her golden watch and I said Sorry, madam, I am late because of the taxi. She said nothing. She was holding a novel in one hand, and a business magazine was on the table. She ordered a drink for me. And we sat.

We had nothing to say. My family were very godly people. My father would not give you a light for a cigarette. He would say, "I am a born-again Christian, and that is not of God." My mother had cautioned me not to move around with women, because if you want to be a good person you must wait until you are grown up.

I had never been with a woman.

I ate a little chicken. I did not eat much. I was afraid.

I did not tell her why I was late. I did not tell her that the watchman had not let me in. He'd said, No, you are a black person, and you are not staying in this hotel. I told him I had an appointment with a very senior person. If you let me in, I told him, it is good for you. If you don't, you will see what will happen.

After a while, Dr. Suzy stood up and disappeared. I sat there for a long time. I was afraid to stay and did not want to go. Eventually a waiter came to me and told me I was to go to Room 220.

Where is 220?

He took me in the lift, to the door.

I knocked. She opened.

Ohhh!

She was wearing a nightdress. It was cream colored, and transparent. She had cream-colored panties, but her top was naked! I felt like I was seeing my mother naked. This was very bad. So I picked up a magazine and was pretending my eyes were in the magazine. I did not want to look in her direction.

She asked me, "Do you want a drink? Or to use the bath? Feel free."

"Nonono." I didn't even look at her. "I am okay."

She came near me. She wanted to tell me something, but maybe she did not know how to start it. I was sitting on the sofa, like this, my back was to her. She came up behind me, and her face was at my cheek, and I felt like a revolver was blowing near me. I wanted to jump.

I said, "You know, I am surprised, you know... erm... I have never had such a life before..."

And she said, "I just like Africans. You are very handsome."

And I said, "But now... no, no, no... me, I cannot get into that situation. It is an abomination."

She was furious.

I heard *Pap!* and she held my trousers and my shirt, and she lifted me and threw me onto the bed and fell on top of me. I tried to push out, but she was very strong. I could not move at all.

So I said to myself, She will kill me if I do not accept what is coming. I said, "What do you want? I have accepted!"

Then she acted like a lion. Her eyes were red and storming, and she was sweating and breathing heavily. I think her blood pressure was very high.

It was a terrifying thing. I had never seen anything like this. I was wet from her sweat, but soon she cooled down and put on the fan.

I found I was very sleepy. So we slept.

In the morning, I found all my clothes were torn. My trousers had no buttons left. So she went to the gift shop and bought me pajama trousers and a big shirt with African pictures.

Then she told me, "I want to take you to my house. I did not trust you very much, but now I feel you should be in my house."

"Why? Why do you want me in your house?"

"You will see, you will see."

All the time I knew her, Drosie had very few words. So I kept asking questions, all the way to the car park. There were a few cars there, and I wondered to myself what car she drove. I said, It's that 504 there, but it was not. The Range Rover? No. The Toyota on the other side? No.

Then I saw her stop in front of the Mercedes.

I was very shocked. I had always thought that a Mercedes Benz was only for top government ministers. I had never expected to sit inside a Mercedes.

And it was a very big one. I opened the door, and the smell of velvet and leather greeted my nose. She had decorated the dashboard with flowers. And when I sat, everything was soooo soft. It smelled very good.

She drove us away from the hotel, and soon we reached the gate of her house, in Nyali. There was a sign saying BEWARE OF DOG. Then the gate opened and she welcomed me in.

It was a big house. Three bedrooms, a big dining room, two kinds of sofa sets. She had a watchman and one maid, called Monica. I was still wearing the pajama pants and shirt when Drosie introduced me to Monica. Monica did not look happy that I was in the house with Madam.

Drosie went straight to the bathroom. Then she came back abruptly and said Okay, okay, come, come… This is the toilet this is the bathroom this is my bedroom this is the other bedroom this is the library this is my office this is the kitchen… You know, she took me around, and after that she told me she had an appointment briefly and she would be back in the evening and she left me in the house with Monica and she went away.

In those days I really admired the music machine called Kenwood. You know, those big speakers really amazed me. You would think the singer is inside the speaker, it's so clear. You could hear every instrument. Those machines were very nice.

So I asked Monica, Please can you operate this for me, I don't know how to operate this. Maybe I looked stupid to her, but we learn through mistakes. So she started the music for me, and I was listening, and when she went away I closed my eyes to look for the beats and I was playing the drum set on the table with my fingers when she came back in. I quickly changed to doing something else. I was pretending, because I didn't want her to know who I was.

Drosie came back very late in the evening. She was tired, so she said, Okay, today we can't go out for a dinner, just eat something here, you can have whatever you want. And then she went to the bedroom and went to sleep. I couldn't go in the bedroom, because I respected her, so I just remained on the sofa set and slept there like that.

At midnight she came and found me sleeping on the sofa, and she grabbed me. You stupid boy! she said. Why are you sleeping here? I told you, you are free in my house!

And then we went back to her bed and she didn't care about me anymore.

She liked me. I don't know what she saw in me, but we started staying together just like that. We stayed there for a good two weeks, and then we went on a safari in the National Park. It was my first time visiting the Safari Park and the Hotel Intercontinental.

But now I was missing my band boys. It was a career that I was just beginning, and stopping that is like snatching water from a very thirsty person. I knew that Drosie would not want me to go, though, so I thought of a trick that would make it possible. I told her that I wanted to go and visit my brother in Hola. She didn't answer. We were having dinner. I waited for an answer, yes or no. She didn't answer.

I waited for another five minutes, ten minutes. Then I repeated the question. She did not answer. As if she hadn't heard anything.

I took courage, and I faced her. *I would like to visit my brother in Hola.*

Then she looked at me and asked, "The band boys?"

"No, no, no! My real brother—I told you that my real brother is staying in Hola."

"When do you want to go?"

I said tomorrow.

"I will take you."

I said, No, no. You can't go there, you know—the roads are very bad.

"Okay, I will take you to the bus stage."

She dropped me at the stage, and she made sure I got inside the bus. I wanted to get off, but my heart was afraid. Maybe she is hidden somewhere, waiting for me to get out? So I stayed on the bus for ten kilometers before I got off and switched to the right one.

I met the boys. "Oh, Richard, you met a *muzungu*, you abandoned us... because you've got a muzungu now you don't want to know about us anymore... you didn't even say goodbye..." And I told them Oh, if you only knew, I lied to come here because I was in custody. You didn't know that? But anyway I am here right now, so what is the program?

And then they told me today they were going to Salambo Club. I said Okay, I am with you. So we started rehearsals together and in the evening the time came to play.

I started feeling guilty. I didn't like to speak lies. But I thought I would be happy because of this lie.

Meanwhile, Drosie didn't believe that I gone to Hola. Okay, she said, before I go to sleep what I have to do is to go find out where the band boys are and if he is with them. She asked the watchman, "Where are the band boys today?"

"They are at Salambo," he told her.

"Where is Salambo?"

"Salambo is on Kilindini Road. When you are coming from Kilindini, you will see Salambo there."

So she got into that big Mercedes. But as she was coming to Salambo, her fuel ran out. She had to wait for somebody to help her, and then she came.

By then I was playing the drums. There were so many people there—the girls were dancing around the drums, cheering and making noise, and I was singing and doing my thing. At some point I turned my face, like this, and I saw the very big face of Drosie. Very big eyes, very red eyes, and you know I was stunned, *ghafla*— and my drum sticks fell down and I had to pick them up them very quickly. I tried to smile, which did not succeed.

She was sweating very furiously, but she respected me and didn't interrupt my playing. She went to the counter and I knew something was going to happen here.

She was holding her dress strongly, very strongly. As if she was holding something very tough. I think she was practicing how she was going to make a grip on me.

After the end of the number, we stopped for a moment to start another one, but I just kept on playing, *kiti-cha kiti-cha kiti-cha cha cha kiti-ti-ti-ti... kiti-cha-cha-cha...* I was doing so while waiting for the next number, to get the timing. But a very tough hand grabbed my back and pulled me. The floor was slippery, and I felt that I was going to fall down. The buttons tore from my shirt, and so to get a better grip she grabbed my belt very strongly.

She didn't care if you were in her way or not. People made way for her, and I was dragged outside. The stairs came very suddenly.

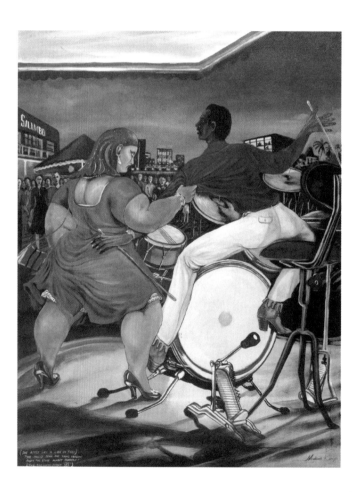

We went outside and she opened the door of the car and she did not say any-thing. She just kept quiet.

I thought Okay, I am a man, she cannot just pull me out, and I pretended as if I wanted to jump away. But she looked at my face with very big eyes and then looked at the seat. She looked at my face again and then looked back at the seat. She did it three times, as if she was saying Get inside. Don't be stupid. Get inside.

She never said this with her mouth, only with the eyes. I thought Okay, I might be ashamed here, but if she beats me in front of my friends it's going to be a big-ger shame, so I said Okay, okay, okay, and I got inside and banged the door and she went round to the driver's seat and never spoke until we reached her home, and then she just went into her office and started typing.

I went into the bathroom to take a bath. When I was putting on the soap, I felt there was some pain. Her fingernails had cut me in my chest, and I had to nurse myself.

Afterward I went to her in the office. She never cared to look at me. I asked her Do you need coffee do you need something do you need anything, but she just shook her head and never looked at me. I went to the bed and I slept until it was almost midnight. She never came.

I went to her again and said Oh, it's late, you have to sleep now, you have to rest. Tomorrow you have got a lot of things to do. She didn't reply, and I went and faced the wall.

After some minutes, I heard footsteps coming. Okay, *haiya*, now she is coming, what is going to happen.

But she just went past and dropped her head into the bed very heavily, and after a long time, when I came to bed, she put her arms around my waist.

I had been with Drosie for eleven months when her father came from England. At the end of the tenth month, she told me that her father was a very, very, very aggressive man, but don't worry she will handle it. Then, the day before her father was coming from England, she said Okay, you know my father is coming, and tomorrow we have to go to the airport to pick him up, so be ready.

I chose my best clothes, because I didn't want the father to see me like just any other person living with his daughter. I wanted to look as if I was of the same class, so I had to be very intelligent, very bright, very polite, so as to impress the family.

When her father arrived they hugged one another, happiness, Aha, this is Richard Onyango, my boyfriend, and I saw the father's expression change very quickly but he didn't say anything. We got into the Benz and we went off. Drosie had arranged an apartment for them, a place where they usually stayed when they were in Kenya. But she invited them to her Nyali house for dinner that night.

So they came, and the father wouldn't eat. He was drinking, you know, drinking wine and whisky, and when she moved toward him he went away. He comes back, he goes, he comes back. They were talking and moving like that. You know the British people.

When it felt as if the father wanted to burst, I went to the library, to give them their time. It was like he was just waiting for me to leave—as soon as I was gone he burst out with Shit, Drosie, you think you can just have this beach boy in your house to be your boyfriend, this is the most terrible thing I have ever seen in my life… He grabbed Drosie but he didn't know what to do with her. Then Drosie's mother, who was there too, she decided to say Okay, I am sorry our daughter has never told you even one time that she has a boyfriend, but now that she has decided to have one, why should you interfere? You know she feels that she can love an African man. You think she is a child, but you can't control her.

And ehh, he respected!

He just left, without saying goodbye. I just heard the bang of the car door, and the mother had to rush out.

From that day Drosie turned gloomy. She felt pressure, you know. She stopped going to work, and spent most times sleeping. Her eyes were swollen, as if she had been crying for a whole night. I tried to comfort her by telling her Okay, don't worry, if you want me to leave I can leave, don't worry.

I don't have any problem with you, she told me. You don't have to interfere. It is my problem.

And one day she surprised me. She took out a key and gave it to me, and she told me that she would not like me to suffer, in case she dies.

And I asked her, "You want to commit suicide?"

"No, no, no," she said. "I said in *case* I die. Take this key so that you can survive... it's the key for the safe, for something important."

I was young. I didn't know the meaning of all that, so I just took the key and put it back on the keychain she had taken it from. It was on the same ring as the car keys.

That night she didn't come to sleep for a very long time. She was in the office, making calculations.

And you know what?

In all the time I stayed with her, I didn't dare to ask what kind of job she was doing. I knew she was Doctor Drosie. I suspected she was doing something to do with gemstones. Tanzanite, rubies, from Voi and Tanzania. I heard some queer names I had never heard of, difficult names of jewelry material, which she used when she mingled with Indians and with the Kalasingas and with some of the European people. She was always in the office of the Provincial Commissioner. She would have to sign this thing and that thing for these shipments, but I couldn't ask her to tell me anything more, of course. She never talked about it.

I had very terrible dreams that night. Me and Drosie were on top of a hill, and there were two angels coming at us in slow motion. The front of the hill was full of stones, and I was trying to tell Drosie, Let's run, those people are coming to pick us up, but she could not run because there were a lot of stones. So I was trying to pull her away, I was pulling my bed sheet as I was pulling her.

And you know, she felt it. She woke up and asked me, What's wrong? Why are you pulling me?

I slept again. This time the angels had picked her up, and they were flying with her. I was struggling to hold her down, but she slipped slowly, slowly, until she was taken away.

The next morning, to my surprise, she woke up very bright and happy, not normal like every day she had been gloomy. She had a very bright face, she was smiling, she was happy. I told her that I had had very terrible dreams, and that

I didn't want her to go anywhere alone, so everywhere you go we shall be together. And she told me, all right, whatever you like, and we went for breakfast at the Manor Hotel.

Then she surprised me again. Every time she looked at me, she smiled and swung her hair.

"Okay, what is the problem?" I asked her.

"I have a story," she told me.

Now the story is like this. One day there was a man coming from the city. This man was passing through a big garbage pit, and there was a street boy, a *chokora*, who passed near, collecting things from the pit. This man did not have a child, and he said, Okay, this street boy has nothing to eat and yet I have a lot of food. Why can't I take this boy to my house and make him be my son? I have a good house, I have good clothes, why should you stay here? From today, you're my son—from today, I am your father. And they both were happy. But one day, to his surprise, as the man was coming from work, he saw somebody dressed like his son in the pit again. At first he thought, My son can't be there, because my son has everything. But the boy's clothes looked like his son's clothes, and when he reached the place he found that it was his boy. And he said, I thought you were coming here because of problems. You don't have any problem, but you're still coming here. So what is the big problem?

She was describing the Salambo night like a parable, or like a saying, because she picked me from the band thinking that I was doing that because I was starving, because I was looking for somewhere to earn my living. Yet I had my living.

I said Oh, Madam, I am very sorry, in fact I have been waiting since that day to fix something about that, because you only kept quiet, you never said anything about me speaking lies, and I promise you from this day onward I will never say lies—not to you or to anybody else. It's the end of me speaking lies, because I feel a lot of shame.

And then she said, It's me who caused you to lie. Because you know what, before this man met this boy, he had grown up in the pit. The pit was his home and his family. The pit collection was his father, his mother... so that is his home. When he was adopted by this man he was put in custody, and he missed his home. So I made a mistake in coming to take you out of something that allowed me to find you at all.

So I said Okay, let's forgive one another. When we got back home it was lunchtime, so we took lunch and she told me, I am feeling very bad and I want to rest, but I have an appointment at three o'clock. Please try to wake me up in case I don't wake up. She went to bed and I lay down next to her, and I started slumbering, and looking at her, and waiting for the time, and slumbering, and looking at her.

I saw her looking at the time and I saw angels pulling her, whenever I closed my eyes I saw angels, until at five minutes before three I woke her up. She stayed still for some time, and then she got up and went to the bathroom. I said, What is it, are you dizzy or something?

No, she said, and then she went. I just heard the car revving outside and she was disappearing, and that was the last time I saw Doctor Drosie alive.

That afternoon I received a telephone call—there were no mobile phones then—I received a telephone call telling me that Dr. Suzy is in Pandya Hospital, please can you come there?

I tried to ask many questions, but they didn't even answer, they just said, You come. So I found myself at the gate only to discover that I didn't have shoes on my feet, I was being pricked by the stones, the *kokoto*, and I went for my shoes and it was four o'clock and every bus that was coming was full because people were coming from work, and though I got the bus to Mwembe Tayari, from Mwembe Tayari I found that the bus would delay me, so I took a taxi only to discover that I had forgotten my wallet, and so I left my watch with the taxi driver. I took the license plate number of the car and then I went to the hospital, and when I reached it I said Okay, I want to see Dr. Drosie.

Oh, Dr. Drosie… Who is Drosie… Suzy… oh, Suzy? Go to Emergency.

When I got to the emergency room I found five Indian doctors coming out with one African doctor, and I saw somebody lying on a bed, but covered. You know, I didn't believe it. They tried to stop me, but they couldn't. I reached the bed and I lifted the sheet, and it was her. Half-opened mouth and half-opened eyes and it shocked me that Drosie was dead.

They told me something like cardial attack… cardial arrest. So I remained there, standing, and then they asked So who are you.

I said, Okay, I am the husband. And they started looking at me like, You, the husband?

I said yes.

So what do you want to do? they said.

I said, Okay, the parents are here, they were to travel next week… but how did she come here?

Oh, they told me, she was brought here by a policeman named Joseph Kariuki, from Central Police Station.

So I went to the Central Police Station to find out what had happened, and they directed me back to Nyali. So, you know, imagine, I passed through Nyali on my way to the hospital without even seeing the Mercedes on the side of the road. The officers had parked it there. So I went, and I saw the Mercedes, and Joseph Kariuki came then, and I said I was waiting for you because I was told that you took Drosie to the hospital.

Ah! You are Richard? This lady came, and we saw the car going as if… So we tried to help her, and she was suffering, I don't know… how is she?

I couldn't say the truth. If I had, then they wouldn't allow me to take the car, because they may think that I have come to steal it. So I said that she was okay.

I didn't know how to drive very well. But when Drosie was tired, she liked to teach me how to drive, so I made it to the apartment, the private apartment where her parents were staying. They were just coming from the beach, it was getting late now, and eh, when they saw me, they were surprised. They asked, So where is Drosie?

I said Oh, Drosie, you know, Drosie is in Pandya…

What is Pandya?

Pandya Hospital.

They didn't want to ask any more questions, so we just went there. I waited on a bench, in the lobby. I just heard the mother crying in there, and then the father came out and took the Mercedes and left us there for maybe half an hour. Then he came back and collected us and he dropped me at Drosie's house. He told me they would come back tomorrow.

Monica asked me what was happening, where is Madam, and I said What do you think is happening.

Drosie's father came here very quickly, she said, and then he took something away in his bag.

Aha, is that why he came here? He took something in the bag? I went to look then, and I found the safe was gone. So, okay, I told Monica I was sorry, but Madam has left us.

Left us gone to Europe?

No, Madam is dead.

Then oooh, she made a lot of noise, until the watchman came because maybe he thought I was raping her. You know, she made a lot of noise, Oh help me, the neighbors could hear. But I just remained there till the morning. And when Drosie's parents came, saying We are sorry Drosie kept you here, but now you can go where you like, they gave me seven thousand shillings. It was a lot of money. And they told me, Okay, you have twenty-four hours, and I said Okay, what is the plan, and they told me they were going to fly her back to England. Okay, I would like to be there the day of the flight. Okay, they said. It will be in four or five days.

So every day I go to the mortuary. And when it came to the day, so many friends, about eighteen, came to escort her to the airport. When the plane was climbing in the clouds it came to me to understand the meaning of the dream, the angels carrying Drosie climbing into the clouds—it was the plane, carrying the casket into the clouds.

For a long time after that I was like a chokora. Even when the band boys saw me, they didn't understand who I was. I just, I couldn't take a bath, I couldn't change my clothes, I looked as if I couldn't do anything. I just remained mentally disturbed for a very long time.

Eventually I went back to Hola. And you know, I never finished school, so my parents, they took me back to form three in Mau Mau Memorial Secondary School. This was in '82. I was now grown up, but in '82 I went back to form three, and then in '83 I did my form four, and then in '84 I went back to Malindi, to Mohammed Lalji of Tana River Bus Company. I was looking for a job, and he employed me as a bus inspector. I worked with Tana River Bus for three years, traveling from Mombasa to Garissa, Garsen to Lamu. After that I left, and I started driving personal vehicles.

At some point, though, I had gone six months without a job. I became very desperate. I couldn't pay my house rent, and I started starving. I would go to the bus stage, to find my old friends and colleagues, and they would give me five shilling or ten shillings, and I would get something to eat.

But one day I felt sure I was going to starve. I had gone to the stage, but I hadn't found any money. So when I was just about to go, at sunset, I prayed. I said, Oh my God, thanks very much, you have sustained me for six months without a job, and I have been eating and I have never slept with hunger, but today for the first time I am going to sleep with hunger, because I have nothing to eat. But I thank you for sustaining me these six months without a job.

That night, when I passed the Tana Hotel, the hotel of the owners of the buses, I saw somebody I knew inside. So I said, Okay, I know this man. He had worked in Darsaa, near Garsen, giving me mail bags when I was an inspector. His name was Mohammed Bashril. It was getting late now, it was almost 6:30, and I said, Why don't I go and ask him if he can help me? Then I went to him, and I said, Mohammed, *salaam alekum*, I lost a job, I am suffering, please can you just give me a job in your office, only a cleaning job…

He told me Okay, wait, and he took a telephone and he called somebody named Feisal Osman. Feisal is a carpenter, and he asked him, Feisal, are you all right? Is my furniture ready? You know on Saturday, there is a wedding, don't let me down, the furniture must be very quickly ready by Saturday, *ehe, ehe*… Now, listen, there is a friend of mine here, his name is Richard Onyango, he is an artist—those Italians of yours, are they still here? Can you introduce him to them? *Ehe*, what time? Eight o'clock? Tomorrow? To come there? In your office?

Okay, he told me, tomorrow eight o'clock go to see Feisal Osman. Go with your samples to show him.

And then oh great god, Mohammed gave me fifty shillings. I felt that my prayers had come to reality.

The next day I went to Feisal with my paintings. Feisal, he was a very pensive man, he nods, Move it like that, move it like that, okay, I like this, I take this, I take this, these Italian people are coming on Thursday, come back after they are here.

When he met with the Italians and showed them my pictures, the Italians went crazy. We want this man right now, *right now*. When I came back in he started quarrelling with me, saying Where were you, where were you? And then right away we took a taxi to meet the Italian guy, Mr. Sarenko.

This was in 1990, in August. I remember the day, the 16th. And Mr. Sarenko said, today is the 16th, and on the 26th, you have to finish thirteen paintings of this size. He gave me three thousand shillings—three thousand shillings for me and two thousand more for materials. And oh God, the house rent that I had not paid for six months was fifteen hundred shillings. So the first thing I did was I went and paid that fifteen hundred. I paid the house rent for the six months I had missed and I started painting and painting. The first group of paintings was buses, the second group was lorries, and the last group was cars. When I finished the first bunch, I sent them to him.

I started the second group, but I felt too tired to paint anymore. And somebody told me, Okay, you have to eat *miraa*, if you eat miraa you can work day and night. So that's how I started to chew miraa, and I finished the second lot.

When I was done with everything I went back to Mr. Sarenko. He said, Okay, now I want you to paint on canvas. He told Feisal to make 160-centimeter-by-120-centimeter frames for me, and to buy some canvas and some paint, show him the studio show him where he will work, if he wants he can stay here and if he likes he can even sleep in my bedroom.

He valued me in a way that I couldn't believe. I just slept in the studio, and when he found me like that he gave me a room somewhere, a very good room.

In 1992, he took me to Italy for an exhibition. I went again in '93, and then I went to Paris. Since then I have had almost thirty exhibitions of my paintings. The last time, I was in Monaco. Ehh, this is my life.

I found that my customers are divided into different groups: those who only like the paintings of Drosie, those who only like the paintings of the Land Rover adventures, and those who only like the buses and the trucks. And every one of them said that this is what you can do best.

My interest is very wide. I am interested in fashion design, in machinery, in personal experiences. I am interested in traveling. I am interested in so many things that can help create my work. I can make sculptures, I can make models, I can design furniture, I can furnish a house. I like to tame animals. I very much like orphaned children; I would like to bring up a good African generation. I have been building an orphanage for a long time—it will be the best.

I want to fulfill every one of these interests. Somebody told me, Okay, artists should paint what they like and not what other people like, but I found that difficult. I found that selfish, because I must force you to like what I like. So as an artist, I am trying to be fair to myself. People ask me why I like to paint Drosie. I tell them that I just painted her until clients felt that that is the best thing I can do, so by the time I wanted to paint something else they would say No, you paint just Drosie. It was only when, alongside of Drosie, I started to paint things like the bus, the Land Rover, that some people saw that and said Okay, now I think you can paint good Land Rovers, so they want paintings of Land Rovers only.

Drosie was so unique. She was my first lady, and maybe she influenced me to see the big ladies first, before the other ones. There is this lady called Deborah Teighlor, the biggest lady in the world—she is a wonderful lady, she is a kind lady, and I have seen a documentary about her. According to her, she has never felt the goodness of living, because she has never met a man to love her. She has never moved around, or rather she moves with difficulties, for example if she is on a plane she can't go to the toilet, she must be fitted with something special for traveling. You know, I would like her to feel like any other person, and to enjoy life like any other woman.

And this is the next project I am making—about the Biggest Ladies in the World, including Deborah Teighlor of California.

BOONOONOONOOS

by BINYAVANGA WAINAINA

IT IS FRIDAY.

Eunice and Milka, sixteen and fifteen, are form-three students at Larmudiac Secondary school—a series of long dark wooden buildings that sit deep in a thick plot of soft kikuyu grass in front of the Mau Forest, one of the coldest places to live in Kenya.

It is five-thirty in the morning. There are already lines of girls washing in buckets at the end of their dorm. Form-four girls, cheeks burnt black with cold, have been up all night studying for exams.

The air is cold and foggy and smells of cow shit and charcoal irons and foaming Imperial Leather soap. When Eunice and Milka walk outside the cold squeezes them immediately, like two women holding the ends of a wet blanket and squeezing. For a moment it is hard to breathe. The throat is seized. Then heat and air bursts out of them, they puff warm air out from their bellies—it licks their noses, their cheeks.

They tiptoe slowly past the school security guard, a cantankerous old Kikuyu and Dorobo man, Josphat, who is paid thirty shillings by the school for each girl he catches sneaking out. Josphat is wearing a khaki overcoat from the 1950s. He is asleep, and so this is the best time to sneak out of school. Usually Josphat is up all night smoking *bhang*. During the day, he likes to sit outside the gate near the bus stop, sewing patches on his overcoat. The coat smells of old milk and old smoke.

When he catches girls sneaking out, he is usually satisfied with asking them to let him touch their breasts and put a finger into their panties. The finger lasts a few seconds. Then he'll frown and say, "Moto Sana." That is his nickname, Moto Sana.

Josphat was a tracker of Mau Maus in the 1950s, and talks of his days of glory as Sergeant Meeks's right-hand man. He met Idi Amin twice, while they were hunting down Mau Maus. He sells very good *bhang* to students, and is popular for his stories— of tramping through the Aberdare forests, of elephants and the day Dedan was caught, of strange white men like Lord Egerton, whom he once worked for, and who would not allow any women onto the grounds of his castle, a few kilometers away.

The girls start to breathe harder and shuffle faster. Wet, frosted grass slurps and slaps against their heels. A boy streaks past them, coming from the senior girl's dorm, buttoning his trousers and carrying books self-consciously. Maina. His jaw is working, like most *miraa* chewers'. He smells like strangled cigarettes, Big G chewing gum, and stale plant juice. He is a school legend—he can drink a whole tin of *changaa*, can study all night for three nights in a row if he chews *miraa*. He winks at them, and Milka winks back. Eunice looks at the grass and hides her eyes.

They walk past the history teacher's house. The girls can hear morning mood music on his general-service radio. Startling basses and the sound of old American railroads: *NORTH! To Alaska! North to HUNT for GOLD*. Mr. Simiyu is singing along. He likes to talk about his days studying in Manitoba.

They giggle.

Dark is unraveling quickly. They shuffle past the last guard post, past the little line of whitewashed stones, the large school sign, and into the small trading center on the main road to Mau Narok. Only a few miles from the roadless woods and wheat farms of Maasailand and the giant mountains of the Mau Forest.

They have known each other since they were in primary school in Njoro DEB, five or so kilometers away. They were in the same class for seven years, but did not once speak to each other until they found themselves in the same dorm on the first day of school at Larmudiac Secondary.

Eunice is the shy one. Sharp bones at the top of her cheeks push her face forward. She has wide round eyes surrounded by what she calls her Rings of Satan, circles of darker skin that give her a feverish look.

Milka is short, round, and hard, with round hard breasts and a round yellow face. One of her front teeth is cracked and has a small streak of brown.

When she was nine, she cut off the legs of a school chicken and let it stumble and whirl like a dervish in the school playground, spraying gouts of blood. The headmaster, Mr. Gachohi, whipped her in front of the whole school with a long swaying stick cut from the tender new branch of a caterpillar tree. After three or four strokes aimed at her back and legs, Milka took off running, twisting in between pupils and laughing. The prefects caught her before she got to the gate. She was brought back to the playground, held down, and whipped harder.

On the main road, three barefoot young men are unloading huge donkeyloads of giant carrots, brought in from guarded plots deep in the illegal regions of the Mau Forest. Mountains of washed carrots steam by the side of the road, waiting for a morning lorry.

Milka and Eunice walk past the carrots. The young men barely glance at them, even though they have lived deep in the forest for months. These carrots are the result. Their hair is long and wild. When the madams of the Nakuru market have paid them in cash, tonight, that hair will be cut, and beer and new clothes will be bought, and they will dance all night in the Gituamba Day and Night Club in Nakuru.

Boyi, all of ten years old and impervious to the cold, runs across the road in a torn T-shirt, bare feet, and navy-blue school shorts. He carries a red flask, two enamel cups, and ten chapatis wrapped in newspaper for the lorry men. He does this every day. They pay him to deliver tea and run errands and sleep in the back of the lorries, making sure no thieves sneak in and steal wheat. It is his plan, in a year or two, to be a turnboy—attached to a driver and adventuring all over the Rift Valley, wherever the lorry is called to work. He knows every lorry, every lorry driver, every license plate of every vehicle that passes by. He knows every car that took part in last year's Safari Rally. He stops when he sees Eunice.

"Sasa?"

"Fit." Eunice points to the three ringworms on his head. "You're going to be rich."

Boyi laughs and hands them a chapati before he runs off. The chapati, as big as the head of a metal drum, is still hot. They tear it into two and chew.

"Isn't he—"

"Josphat's son? Yeah, I knew his mum. She had a kiosk in Ndarugu. They had three acres in Ndeffo, but Josphat drank it all when she died."

"Call him back—maybe he can get us some."

"Some what?"

"Some *bhangi*."

"Ai, Milka… With which money, now?"

They sit and wait for the first matatu. To their left are three more lorries, laden with seed, parked in the small gulley of hard-packed earth between the road and the short line of shops. As soon as the dew is dry they will head into Maasailand, followed by a tractor in case they get stuck in the mud.

That first night of boarding school, the first time they spoke to each other, a freezing Larmudiac night, three thousand meters above sea level, the senior boys came into the dorms to visit their "wives." Eunice lay frozen in her bed, in the dark, as she heard the giggles, the protests, the moans, the springs. A hand of wind slapped a door against a wall somewhere in the distance. The forest leaned over them, then leaned back with the swelling, surround-sound chorus of crickets. A cassette player was playing Boney M.'s "Rivers of Babylon." Eunice turned and faced the wall.

And then she felt a hand on her shoulder. The hand lifted her blanket, and a wet, hot tongue ran across her fingers. She almost laughed out loud when she heard the boy's voice, forced down into his belly to sound deep, whispering, "Baby, you are my brown girl in the ring…"

But then the hand grabbed at her crotch and squeezed. She shot up and turned, rubbing the saliva off her fingers with her pillow. The boy's eyes were frightened, and standing next to him was Milka. She grabbed his ear and twisted, laughing.

"*Kihii. Gasia.* Come back when you've been circumcised."

He staggered back and ran. Milka climbed into the bed.

She was singing the Boney M. song. Where she did not know the words, she made them up.

"*Kitanda whiskey, blabbin' is the way of si si si… and how can we play the love song in a straaange land…*"

Eunice kept her body very still. She tried to keep solemn, but could not. Her chest started to shake with laughter. Milka wriggled and nestled in. Then she started talking.

"George Oduor—you know that guy from Plant Breeding Station? Who does private tuition for CPE? He was telling me Ugandans are bringing red mercury here.

People are making millions selling it to the Americans. It is for nuclear. Twenty thousand for one suitcase. It's wet, and you can see it in the dark, shining bright red."

Milka's cold hands slipped under her nightie and grabbed her breasts. Eunice gasped slowly. Her feet were very cold, and she reached them back to tangle with Milka's. Soon they were warming each other up, and they slept.

Women in large sweaters and marked cheeks—some marked with black coldburn, others with three thin parallel cuts from an old past—are unpacking produce to sell. They haggle with their morning customers, mostly owners of the nearby rickety teashops and restaurants. A tractor driver and two Masai men spill out of one of the shops, talking loudly and laughing, and climb up on an old Massey Ferguson, the two Masais sitting on each ear above the giant wheels. Metal teapots sit by the side of the road, gushing on charcoal stoves next to giant crisp *mandazis*. The first matatus are fuming up the street, some coughing, touts bellowing and rubbing hands. Eunice and Milka stay hidden in the courtyard of a wholesale shop, drinking tea and waiting for the right time to make their way to Milka's home. Waiting for her mum to leave to go to the market in Nakuru.

When she was thirteen, in standard seven, three months before sitting for the Certificate of Primary Education exams, Milka became famous in Njoro DEB primary school for moving out of her childhood home to live with Efantus Mungai Patel as his girlfriend. Mungai was seventeen then, and famous in Njoro himself. He had smooth skin, soft Somali hair, and could do something with one eye that made him look like Steve Austin of *The Six Million Dollar Man*.

His father, a Masai from Ngong, was a Christian Religious Education teacher at Njoro Girls Secondary. His mother was the great-granddaughter of Patel Bao, whose father came to Njoro from Gujarat in the 1930s and started a sawmill. The original Patel Bao had a Bajuni wife, from Pate Island, but she fled to Kitale with a red-haired Scot called Rapeseed and their two daughters. After that Patel Bao famously paid forty goats to marry Sofia Kotut, the daughter of one of the first families of the Nandi nation to become Christian. Mama Sofia opened a supermarket in Nakuru before she inherited her father's farm. It was on that farm, three generations later, that Mungai was born.

Mungai was famous even in Nakuru. He had his own pickup and a fleet of carrier pigeons and four hunting dogs, and he paid his own rent for a "cube" in Ndarugu. The cube was decorated with posters of Khadija Adams, Miss Kenya 1984, Pam Ewing of *Dallas*, and Björn Waldegård, the Safari Rally champion. In those days, Mungai was a golf caddy on weekends at the Njoro golf club, where he supplied college lecturers and senior management people with girls and bhangi. He'd dropped out of school in form three. His parents did not talk to him.

One day, near the main matatu terminal to Nakuru, thirteen-year-old Milka jabbed seventeen-year-old Mungai's forearm with a blue Bic pen. He screamed while blood trailed down his arm. That evening, after school, he caught up with her at the Njoro River bridge, near the Plant Breeding Station. He dragged her down to the patch of thick grass where young men washed cars on Sundays. With one hand around her hair, he proceeded to beat her up while students cheered from the bridge above. Eunice stood and watched, thrilled. Everybody scattered when they saw two Administration policemen running down the road, rifles on their shoulders.

After that first night together, Eunice and Milka became friends. They would sneak out of school and walk all the way to the gate of Egerton Agricultural College to use the phone booth. Call random numbers and breathe into the phone and start laughing. Once, a man picked up, and barked "*Nani*" in a deep, hard, cigarette-and-beer voice.

Milka was quiet for a moment, and then she said, "Mary Wanjiru."

Eunice tried to grab the phone, but Milka hung on.

"What do you like, Mary?" His voice was slurry.

"*Napenda wewe.*"

His laughter growled.

"*He babe. Haunijui.*"

They kept talking, and talking, and soon, in self-defense, in the small voice of a girl, Milka turned to English. "No. I am mashure. I am very mashure."

He said something to her, and she laughed shyly. As they walked back to school, Eunice leaned to the side and bumped Milka on the shoulder. "Mm? *Uliniuthi…* what's his name?"

"Evans Ogutu. He is a soldier."

* * *

Eunice and Milka walk up the road. They sing. And laugh.

"Hot banana with the morning sun! Daylight come, me and Anna go home. Hey! Dibeday, dibeday dibedaaaayo…"

A Mau Narok matatu stops for them. Milka grabs the forearm of the tout and whispers something in his ear. He laughs and lets them on for free. And they enter the world of The Gambler, the driver in a Stetson hat, Kenny Rogers knowing when to walk away and knowing when to run.

They stop just before Njoro town and walk the two kilometers to Milka's house, sliding on the muddy road. The main building is a simple wood cabin, built out of two layers of off-cut wood painted black, stuffed with cardboard and sealed from the cold with thick sheets of plastic. There are a few other scattered buildings—a pigsty, a milking shed, and a separate cabin for her three circumcised brothers.

Peter Ole Matu, Milka's father, sees them and smiles as he shoos his sheep into a paddock. He heads toward them jauntily, three dogs following behind, a menthol cigarette in his mouth—from where they are, it looks like his whiskers are foaming.

Milka's mother is from a fierce Kikuyu squatter family back in Molo. She can hit a fleeing dog, a drunk husband, or a running child at a distance with whatever is within reach. Her grandmother, who died in 1970, was a Mau Mau enforcer. Two days after independence, in 1963, she flayed a young sub-chief in front of everybody, flayed him with a whip on a patch of ground near the Molo junction.

Eunice gets along well with Milka's mother. She fusses over Eunice, and knits for her. Eunice is the first friend Milka has brought home—the first female friend she has had. Eunice does not know this. She often spends the night at Milka's; they sleep in the same bed. She cooks with Mama Milka sometimes, while Milka steams and sulks and spends the night in her brother's room listening to reggae and smoking.

Peter is smiling. "Hey girls, ah? You missed your mother. She left an hour ago…"

He winks. They laugh. He has clear, yellow-brown eyes, common among some Kalenjins. He is medium height, with a lean, whippy body and a large moustache, already graying and yellow at its tips from tobacco. There is a big gap between his front teeth, which lends some warmth to his smile. His hands are as flat and dry as old chapatis.

"Sasa, Eunice? What has my daughter been planning for you?"

"Nothing."

Her chin points down, and left, and her foot starts to draw pictures. She still cannot understand how or why Milka's father is so nice.

"We… we… came to get money for School Activity Fund," Milka says.

His eyes crinkle, and turn to Milka. "Ai. More money? What is this activity fund?" Milka shrugs.

The day Milka got whipped in front of the school, her father paid the school a visit and beat up the headmaster, who fled to the chief's office.

As a boy Peter Ole Matu wandered into a Masai *boma* in Tipis one night, crying and wearing a torn blue shirt and nothing else. He had a faded red toy car in his pocket. He was not yet five years old. He spoke Kipsigis, which made him Kalenjin. They assumed him to be a victim of one of the Masai–Kipsigis clashes in the forest.

The family adopted him. His adoptive father, a land-and-cattle wealthy man, a prominent elder, sent him and a sickly stepsister to school. The old man had some contempt for the ways of the white man, and did not enroll his own children in the colonial schools. They had something to inherit, after all.

Peter eventually got a diploma in agriculture from Egerton College, the same year Eunice's father graduated. He worked for the Artificial Insemination Department of the Ministry of Agriculture for ten years before quitting to farm and plan a career in local politics, with his stepfather as a sponsor.

He is going to run for councilor in 1982.

They stay indoors, where it is dark and smoky and comfortable, and drink milky tea that Milka's father makes for them. They eat thick chunks of bread with Blue Band.

"Ha," he says, "I know how you students like loaf! I used to eat a whole one alone when school closed. Slowly, chewing each bite slowly. But we did not have Blue Band—sometimes I would put sour cream on it."

He puts on the radio for the 8 a.m. news. They listen in silence. Immediately after the news, Milka looks straight at her father.

"Dad. I need the money. They sent us home to get it. They said you did not respond to their letter."

He looks at Eunice, sheepishly. "*Huyu ni mangaa sana,*" he says. Then he stands, disappears into his room, and comes back with a sheaf of notes.

"I have given you some extra, for loaf and Blue Band and a soda before you both go back to school. And you go straight back, eh? Girls get pregnant from just wind blowing in this place, you know."

"You don't think he will tell your mum?"

They are walking fast, back to the main road.

Milka laughs. "Oh, no. Mathe is like a ninja with money. He will never say anything."

Peter watches Milka walk away. He sits and puts on his gumboots and a thick sweater as shrapnels of thoughtlets tiptoe behind his sinuses. He kicks the back of the boots firmly against the table leg, stands, and walks outside. He decides not to worry.

He can remember his own mother firmly. A ring of harsh pink flowers on a pale blue enamel cup. Wet flesh slaps his forehead, a little node of memory bursts, milk streams, and he is dozing gently in and out of oblivion, inside a bus, a bright bright green sweater scratching him, a faint gray road pulling away.

One day, after college, he was posted for a few months in Kipkelion. He was standing behind a grade cow. Two small legs were poking out of it, and he was ready to help pull the calf out. An old, thin man, the milker, stood behind him with a bucket of hot water and a blade of grass in his mouth. He was missing some of his teeth. The man had put the bucket down when the cow started to kick and wail, and rubbed the animal's neck, first whistling something from the side of his mouth, then singing softly, something in Kalenjin. As he sang, spurts and sprays flooded Peter's mind, tributaries of his first language, and Peter started to sing the same song. Since then, his Kalenjin has grown. He even made a short speech without notes, in Kipsigis, at a farmers' retreat a few years ago.

Whenever Milka looks at him, from those hard round eyes, he is weak. It has always been that way. He does not know why. No one else feels so essential.

*　　*　　*

They walk to the railway lines and pay five shillings each for a hot comb, done by one of the freelance railway women who plait and comb on a patch of grass between two straight lines of old stone railways housing. Then they change their clothes behind a forgotten train carriage and take a matatu to Nakuru.

They agreed to meet him at 7 p.m., at Tipsy restaurant. It is bright with fluorescent light and smells of India. They order. They do not talk when the food arrives. They shovel in the masala chips, the sausages, the Cokes. Both wearing new midi dresses, matching earrings, their hair oiled and hot-combed, rollered and fluffed up. Milka has cut her eyebrows and drawn a new line to replace them. They both have lipstick on.

Every few minutes Eunice looks at her friend, lifts her eyebrow, and says, "Eh?"— then watches Milka's new thin, high semicircles respond involuntarily. It makes Eunice burst out laughing.

Two men dressed like Abroad sit at the table next to them. One an Indian, one probably a Luo. Yes—he is called Washington. They both have Afros, and open shirts, and fat, high shoes and wide-bottomed jeans. They have stretched themselves out slouchily, their legs sprawled and comfortable. Eunice and Milka fidget next to them, suddenly stiff and shy.

Washington sits back and speaks in London television hiccups.

"So tha( )'s the story. Take it or leave it, brover. And I have somefink else for you. Read i( ) la( )er."

The girls burst out laughing. Washington is quiet for a moment, and Milka turns and glares at him. He stands, walks toward the table, brushes past them, smelling good, and lopes toward the urinal without looking at the girls. When he walks back, he wrinkles his nose at them. Immediately Eunice can smell paraffin, cheap soap, polyester, and small towns in her clothes.

Evans walks in a few minutes before seven.

He drives a brown Citroën that droops back like a tortoise. It is parked next to an old stone wall at the back of the Rift Valley Sports Club. They both sit in the back while Evans argues and jokes with the street kids who are trying to wash the car. Inside, it smells of hot nylon. The seats are a yellow-orange velvet and so deep and soft it is hard to find a way to sit.

Milka tries to sit up straight, but that makes her feel too schoolgirlish, so she leans back, letting her body fall into the nauseous cloud of soft Citroën sponge, and turns to look at Eunice, who is sitting up straight and still and looking out the window, her ringed eyes saying nothing. When Eunice turns to face her, eyes cool, Milka is suddenly shy.

"*Let me tell you of a feeling…*" she sings, "*that is spreading through the land…*"

Eunice giggles. "*It will give you good vibrations. It will help you understand. Boonoonoonoos, that's boonoononoos.*"

Over the past two weeks, both of them have taken turns talking to Evans on the telephone. When he sat next to them this evening, he looked carefully at them both, eyes warm and teasing. "So who is who?" he said.

"That is for you to find out," said Milka. They had decided that he would pick the one he wanted.

When he walks back to the car he does not come to her side. Instead he pulls Eunice's door open and asks her to sit in front. He takes her hand. Eunice's face is still. She does not look at Milka. When she moves Evans leans in and looms over Milka, his smile wide, his scratchy voice like short-wave. "Back left is for VIPs," he says.

They are at a party. In Section 58. A smart, small house, next to a long row of identical smart-looking houses. There are other women here—older women, with Afro wigs or raffia plaits, and a lot of makeup. Laughing and dancing, and touching the men in ways that makes Eunice uncomfortable. She has managed to finish the bottle of Kingfisher cider she asked for. Milka is quiet, and looking down into her glass of Cinzano Bianco. They both have a picture, in their heads, of a woman in a long, sequined dress, sitting in a piano bar lit by the lights of skyscraper teeth. She has a fluted glass in front of her, and a cigarette with a filter. Underneath her it reads, *Cinzano Bianco!*

"How is it?" Eunice asks.

Milka looks at her, and they giggle. They are sitting on a half-sawn-off log. There are seven or eight other logs like this. On the wall are two giant framed parallelograms made out of colored strings and small nails. By the large window facing the veranda there is a large silver music system, several layers mounted on top of each other.

Evans and his army friends are standing at the door to the kitchen, laughing loudly and talking. Faces slick and gleaming with excitement. He is very tall, muscular—and light-skinned, which was a surprise. All the men have uncomfortably short hair, and they are all fit. Their clothes, even now, are ironed and tucked in. Evans's jeans have been ironed, and the line shows. His pink and green shirt is unbuttoned, and he wears a gold chain. He has hair on his chest, another surprise, and large, very dark lips, charcoal and ashy like a heavy smoker's.

Bhangi-lips, whispered Milka, eyes shining, when he went to piss at Tipsy. Eunice watched him stride past Washington's table, and saw Washington's eyes try, then fail, to meet Evans's. Evans didn't even notice him. Eunice kicked Milka's ankle under the table. Milka turned and caught Washington's eyes, and winked.

Later they are standing outside, smoking a seed-ridden joint, as the men light a fire for the meat. Faces in and out; Evans's teeth, as he laughs up and loud. Milka is jabbing at her waist with three hard fingers.

"*Wewe*. Ah. Pslp. *We acha*," she whispers hotly.

She moves a little away from Eunice and tries to compose herself, bending down and covering her head with her arms, eyes shut tight; inside she is burning silver and rust.

Evans is beating a piece of firewood with an axe. She can hear the saliva sluicing back, over, and then under his tongue as he pulls in air; then a hiccup as he reaches the back of his throat; and then a cough, as he lurches forward suddenly and breaks into laughter. Meat falls onto the flame and starts to smell immediately, and a laughing group of people make their way to the fire.

Then his arms are around her waist, and a warm, wet snail moans between the cables of her neck. She is looking at the tips of the inner tubes of his nose above her; they are glowing, red and wounded. She moves her water-heavy head from side to side, thick sheets of starlight rolling quickly all across the sky, then settling back into small, mean glares.

She pushes him away, and bursts into the living room.

President Moi is mouthing something on the television screen. It makes Milka want to salute. She tries to move, and stumbles, and hears her breath slap hotly against her cleavage. She hears Eunice laughing, standing with two tall men by the silver stereo. Her words cartwheel across the room and spin back and settle thickly under her tongue.

"*Papapa papapapapapaaaa. Papapapaaaa.*"

Milka's legs jolt forward. She grabs Eunice's hand. They have danced to this song so many times in the dorm. As if she has left herself, Milka sees her limbs lurch to the center of the living room, her skirt bursting with color and soft wind between her legs. Little bowls of living-room light are spinning gently around her as she turns, arms around Eunice's waist. She can name each of her organs, which sit spinning inside her like hot rocks peeping out of a creamy pool that reaches out to lap and lick.

The trumpets slow down. Flared skirt-sounds ripple, then fold, and then stand still. They both stop.

Milka leans forward and says into Eunice's ear, "*Umelewa*, baby."

They jump to the side and face the guys and the older women standing at the stereo. They bend up and down. Strumpets in military formation, leaning down, bending up, leaning down, fingers pretending to play the trumpet as they bend and rise.

Eunice's face is right there, her eyes burning. Eunice's nails are cutting into her wrist. Tears streaming. Eunice's mouth is screaming in her ear.

"Are you? Are you my girlfriend?"

Something clutters and Milka is on the ground, her leg tangled with a fallen chair. Glass screams; beer foams and hisses on the floor and snakes its way around a heap of fallen goat ribs.

There is silence, and she can hear Evans outside saying, "What?"

Then they are running down the straight low road into Nakuru town proper. The men follow, shouting, Hey, hey, but eventually they turn back to their party. The girls stop, and pant.

The night is bright, the moon is fat, and they walk and talk all the twenty kilometers back to Njoro.

URBAN ZONING

by BILLY KAHORA

OUTSIDE ON TOM MBOYA STREET, Kandle realized that he was truly in the Zone. The Zone was the calm, breathless place he found himself in after drinking for a minimum of three days straight. He had slept for less than fifteen hours, in strategic naps, had eaten just enough to avoid going crazy, and had drunk enough water to make a cow go belly-up. The two-hour baths of Hell's Gate hot-spring heat had also helped.

Kandle had discovered the Zone when he was seventeen. He had swapped vices by taking up alcohol after the pleasures of casual sex had waned. In a city–village rumor circuit full of outlandish tales of ministers' sons who drove Benzes with trunks full of cash, of a character called Jimmy X who was unbeaten in about five hundred bar fights going back to the late '80s; in a place where sixty-year-old tycoons bedded teenagers and kept their panties as souvenirs; in a town where the daughter of one of Kenya's richest businessmen held parties that were so exclusive that Janet Jackson had flown down for her birthday—Kandle, self-styled master of The Art of Seventy-Two-Hour Drinking, had achieved a footnote.

In many of the younger watering holes in Nairobi's CBD, he was now an icon. Respected in Buruburu, in Westlands, in Kile, in Loresho and Ridgeways, one of the last men standing in alcohol-related accidents and suicides. He had different names in different postal codes. In Zanze he was the Small-Package Millionaire. His crew was credited with bringing back life to the City Centre. In Buru he was simply Kan. In the Hurlingham area he was known as The Candle. In a few years, the generation of his kid brother Giant Rat would usurp his legendary status, but now it was his time.

The threat of rain had turned Tom Mboya Street into a bedlam of blaring car horns, screaming hawkers, screeching matatus, and shouting policemen. People argued over parking spaces and haggled over underwear. Thunder rumbled and drowned it all. A wet wind blew, announcing a surreptitious seven-minute drenching, but everybody ran as if a heavy downpour threatened. Even that was enough to create a five-hour traffic jam into the night. The calm and the wise walked into the bars, knowing it would take hours to get home anyway.

Zanze patrons walking into Kenya Cinema Plaza shouted jeers at Kandle because he was going in the opposite direction, out into the weather. Few could tell he had been drinking since noon. Kandle was not only a master at achieving the Zone, he was excellent at hiding it. The copious amount of alcohol in his blood had turned his light-brown skin brighter, yellow and numb and characterless like a three-month-old baby's. The half bottle of Insto eyedrops he had used in the bathroom had started to take effect. He had learned over time that the sun was an absolute no-no when it came to achieving a smooth transition to the Zone. Thankfully, there was very little sunshine left outside, and he felt great.

"Step into the p.m. Live the art of seventy-two hours. I'm easy like Sunday morning," he muttered toward the friendly insults. A philosopher of the Kenyan calendar, Kandle associated all months of the year with different colors and hues in his head. August he saw as bright yellow, a time when the year had turned a corner; responsibilities would be left behind or pushed to the next January, a white month. March was purple-blue. December was red. The yellow haze of August would be better if he was to be fired from his job at Eagle Bank that evening.

Kandle had tried to convert many of his friends to the pleasures of the Zone, with disastrous results. Kevo, his best friend, had once made a deep cut into his palm on the dawn of a green Easter morning in Naivasha after they had been drinking for almost a week. He had been trying to impress the crew and nearly bled to death. They had had to cut their holiday short and drive to Nairobi when his hand had swollen up with infection days later. Kandle's cousin Alan had died two years ago trying to do the fifty-kilometer Thika–Nairobi highway in fifteen minutes. Susan, once the late Alan's girlfriend, then Kandle's, and now having something with Kevo, stopped trying to get into the Zone when she realized she couldn't resist stripping in public after the seventy-two-hour treatment. After almost being raped at a house party she had gone into a suicidal depression for weeks and emerged with razor cuts all over her body and twenty kilograms off her once-attractive frame. Every month she did her Big Cry for Alan, then invariably slept with Kandle till he tired of her and she moved on to Kevo. The Zone was clearly not for those who lacked restraint.

Stripping in public, cutting one's palm, thinking you were Knight Rider—these were, to Kandle, examples of letting the Bad Zone overwhelm you. One had to keep the alcohol levels intact to stay in the Good Zone, where one was allowed all the wishful thinking in one's miserable life. The Bad Zone was the place of all fears, worries, hatreds, and anxieties.

Starting off toward Harambee Avenue, Kandle wobbled suddenly, halting the crazy laughter in his chest. Looking around, he felt the standard paranoia of the Zone start to come on. Walking in downtown Nairobi at rush hour was an art even when sober. Drunk, it was like playing rugby in a moving bus on a *murram* country road. Kandle forced himself back into the Good Zone by going back to Lenana School in his mind. Best of all, he went back to rugby-memory land, to the Mother of All Rugby Fields, Stirlings, the field where he had played with an abandoned joy. He had been the fastest player on the pitch, a hundred meters in twelve seconds easy, ducking and weaving, avoiding the clueless masses, the thumbless hoi polloi, and going for the girl watching from the sidelines. In his mind's eye the girl was always the same: the Limara advert girl. Thin and slender. Dark because he was light, slightly taller than him. The field was next to the school's dairy farm, so there were dung-beetle helicopters in the air to avoid and mines of cow-dung to evade.

He could almost smell the Limara girl and glory a few steps away when a Friesian cow appeared in the try box. It chewed cud with its eye firmly on him, unblinking, and as Kandle tried to get back into the Good Zone he saw the whole world reflected in that large eye. The girl faded away. Kandle put the ball down, walked over to the cow, patted her, and with his touch noticed that she was not Friesian but a white cow with some black spots, rather than the other way around. The black spot that came over her back was a map of Kenya. She was a goddamn Zebu. All this time she never stopped chewing. With the ball in the try box he took his five points.

Coming back to, he realized he was at the end of Tom Mboya Street. A fat woman came at him from the corner of Harambee Avenue, and just when she imagined that their shoulders would crash into each other Kandle twitched and the woman found empty space. Kandle grimaced as she smiled at him fleetingly, at his suit. At the corner, his heightened sense of smell (from the alcohol) detected a small, disgusting whiff of sweat, of day-old used tea bags. He stopped, carefully inched up against the wall, calculated where the nearest supermarket was, cupped his palm in front of his mouth, and breathed lightly. He was grateful to smell the toothpaste he had swallowed in the Zanze toilets. The whiff of sweat was not his. That was when Kevo came up to him.

"Fucking African," Kandle said. "What time is it?"

"Sorry we were late, man. Here's everything. Susan's upstairs. We just got in and Onyi told us you'd left."

"I'm starting to lose that loving feeling for you guys," Kandle said, taking the heavy brown envelope from Kevo, who began doing a little jig right there on the street, for no sane reason, jumping side to side with both feet held together. Passersby watched with amusement.

"Everything else was sent to Personnel," Kevo said, still breathless. "So good luck."

"Were you kids fucking? That's why you were late?" Kandle grinned, seeing that the envelope held everything he needed.

Kevo smiled back. "See you in a bit."

As they were parting ways, Kevo shouted to him.

"Hey, by the way, Jamo died last weekend. Crashed and burned. They were coming from a rave in some barn. Taking Dagoretti Corner at 8 a.m. at 160—they met a *mjengo* truck coming from Kawangware. Don't even know why they were going in that direction. Motherfucker was from Karen."

"Which Jamo?"

"Jamo Karen."

Kandle rolled his eyes. "There are about five Jamo Karens."

"Jamo Breweries. Dad used to be G.M."

"Don't think I know him."

"You do. We were at his place a month ago. Big bash. You disappeared with his sis. Susan was mad."

"Ha," Kandle said.

"Anyway, service in Karen. Burial in Muranga. Hear there are some wicked places out there. Change of scene. We could check out Danny and the Thika crew. You know Thika chicks, man."

"I'll think about it."

"You look good, baby," Kevo said, and waved him off.

Kandle suddenly realized that he had forgotten his bag. It meant he was missing his deep-brown stylish cardigan, his collared white shirt, his grey checked pants, his tie. He should have asked Kevo to pick it up for him. Feeling tired, he almost went under again.

Since childhood, Kandle had always hated physical contact. This feeling became especially extreme when he'd been drinking. It had been worsened by an incident in high school—boarding school. One morning he'd woken up groggily, thinking it was time for pre-dawn rugby practice, and noticed that his pajamas were down around his knees. He was hard. There were figures in the dark, already in half-states of readiness, preparing for the twelve-kilometer morning run. Nobody seemed to notice him. He yanked his smelly shorts on, and while his head cleared he remembered something. Clutching hands, a dark face. He never found out who had woken him up that morning, and after that he couldn't help feeling a murderous rage when he looked at the faces in the scrum around him, thinking one of them had abused him.

Over the next few months, during practices, he looked for something in the smiling, straining boyish faces, for a look of recognition—he couldn't even say the word *homosexual* at the time. With that incident he came to look at rugby askance, to look at Lenana's traditions with a deep, abiding hatred. Then one day he stopped liking the feeling of fitness, the great camaraderie of the field, and started feeling filled with hate when even the most innocent of tacklers brushed by him. He took to cruelty, taking his hand to those in junior classes. He focused on his schoolwork, became supercilious and, maybe because of that, ever cleverer, dismissive of everyone apart from two others who he felt had intellects superior to his. He became cruel and cold. His mouth folded into a snarl.

In spite of a natural quickness, he'd never succeeded in becoming a great rugby player. Rugby, he discovered, was not for those who abhorred contact. You could never really play well if you hated getting close. Same with life and the street, in the city—you needed to be natural with those close to you. As he went up Harambee Avenue, he realized he was well into the Bad Zone. Looking at his reflection in shop windows, he felt like smashing his own face in. And then, like a jack-in-the-box that never went away, his father's dark visage appeared in his mind's eye, as ugly as sin. He wondered whether the man was really his father.

After completing third form he had dropped rugby and effaced the memory of those clutching hands on his balls with a concentrated horniness. He became a regular visitor to Riruta, looking for peri-urban pussy. One day, during the school holidays when he was still in form three, he had walked into his room and found Atieno, the maid, trying on his jeans. They were only halfway up, her dress lifted and exposing her thighs. The rest of those holidays were spent on top of Atieno. He would never forget her cries of "Maiyo! Maiyo! Maiyo!" carrying throughout the house. God! God! God! After that he approached sex with a manic single-mindedness. It wasn't hard. Girls considered him cute. When he came back home again in December, Atieno wasn't there; instead there was an older, motherly Kikuyu woman, ugly as sin. His father took him aside and informed him that he would be getting circumcised in a week's time. He also handed him some condoms.

"Let's have no more babies," was all he said after that.

On Harambee Avenue, three girls wearing some kind of airline uniform came toward him in a swish of dresses, laughing easily. He ignored their faces and watched their hips. One of the girls looked boldly at him, and then, perhaps for the first time that day, a half-stagger made him realize how drunk he actually was, though it would have been hard for anyone apart from his father to tell.

And so the Bad Zone passed on. He quickly fished into his jacket pocket and came out with a small bottle of Smirnoff Red Label vodka, swigged, and returned fully to the Good Zone. Ahead of him was Eagle Bank. He smiled to himself. He forced himself to calm down and breathe in. The usually friendly night watchman, Ochieng, was frosty.

"You are being waited for," he said in Kiswahili, shaking his head at the absurdity of youth.

Inside he was met by the manager's secretary, Mrs. Maina, a dark, busty, and jolly woman. She too was all business today.

"You are late, Kandle," she said. "We have to wait for the others to reconvene."

This was the first time she had ever spoken to him in English. She had lost that loving Kikuyu feeling for him.

Kandle, who knew how to ingratiate himself with women of a certain age, had once brought Mrs. Maina bananas and cow innards mixed with fried *nundu*, cow hump, for her birthday. She had told him later that they were the tastiest things she had ever eaten, better than all the cards she'd received for her birthday. Even the manager, Guka, coming out of his office and trying some, commented that he wished his wife could cook like that.

Mrs. Maina blurted out another few words as Kandle waited outside the manager's office. She sounded overcome with exasperation.

"What? What do you want? Do you think you're too good for the bank?"

"No. I don't want much. I think I want to become a chef."

She couldn't help it. They both laughed. Kandle excused himself and went to the bathroom.

When he was alone he removed a white envelope from his jacket pocket and counted the money inside again. Sixty thousand shillings, which he planned to hand over to the accountant to pay for the furniture loan he had taken out before he went on leave. Back in the bank, Mrs. Maina told him that the committee was ready, and Kandle was ushered into Guka's office.

There was a huge bank balance sheet in the center of the desk. Guka Wambugu, the branch manager, was scowling at the figures. The man was dressed like a gentleman farmer, in his perennial tweed jacket with patches at the elbow and a dull, metallic-gray sweater underneath, over a brown tie and a white shirt. All he needed were gumboots to complete the picture. Kandle noticed that the old fool wore scuffed Bata Prefect shoes. Bata Mshenzi. Shenzi type. Kandle held down the laughter that threatened to burst out of his chest.

Some room had been created on each side of the desk for the rest of the committee. Mr. Ocuotho, the branch accountant, sat on Guka's right, looking dapper and subservient as usual, his face thin and defined, just shy of fifty and optional retirement. He was famous in the branch for suits that hung on his shoulders like they would on a coat hanger. He was a cost-cutter, the man who stalked the bank floors like a secretary bird, imagining the day he would have his own branch to run. He had once been the most senior accountant at the largest Eagle branch in

Kenya, and had been demoted to the smaller Harambee branch only after a series of frauds occurred under his watch. As a result, though he was here representing the bank's management, he was partly sympathetic to the boy in front of him. He had been in the same position, albeit at a managerial level.

Next to Ocuotho, at the far-right corner of the desk, was a bald-headed man, Mr. Malasi, from Head Office Personnel. He was wearing designer non-prescription spectacles. Kandle thought he recognized him from somewhere. At the far left, representing the union and, in theory, Kandle, was the shop steward, Mr. Kimani, a young-looking, lanky, forty-year-old man with curly hair and long, thin hands that he cracked and flexed continually. He also happened to be Kandle's immediate boss. He was the man behind the year-long deals in the department. On Kimani's right was a younger man, the deputy shop steward at the branch, Mr. Koigi, a rounded youth with a round belly and hips that belied his industry. He had had an accident as a child, and was given to tilting his head to the right like a small bird at the most unlikely moments. Like Kandle, he had worked at the bank for a year, and was considered a rising star. He was also Kandle's drinking buddy.

There was a seat right in front of the desk for Kandle. Just as he was lowering himself into it, sirens blared, and everyone in the room turned to watch the presidential motorcade sweep past, out on the street. The man, done for the day, heading home to the State House. Kandle grinned, and remembered shaking the President's hand once when he was in primary school, as part of the National Primary School Milk Project promotion. There was an old photo of Kandle drinking from a small packet of milk while the President beamed at him. The image had been circulated nationwide, and even now people stopped Kandle on the street, mistaking him for the Blueband Boy, another kid who had been a perpetual favorite in 1980s TV ads.

When the noise died down, Guka turned to him.

"Ah, Mr. Karoki. Kandle Kabogo Karoki. After keeping us waiting you have finally allowed us the pleasure of your company. I am sure you know everybody here, apart from Mr. Malasi, from personnel." Guka stretched his arm toward the bald-headed man in the non-prescription spectacles. His back was highly arched, as usual, his eyes were those of an old tribal elder who brooked no nonsense from errant boys. Kandle suddenly remembered who the bald-headed man was. He was the recruiter who had endorsed him when he had first applied for his job.

Guka turned to the shop steward. "Mr. Kimani, this committee was convened to review Mr. Karoki's conduct, and to make a decision—sorry, a recommendation—to Head Office Personnel." He gave Kandle a long, meaningful look. "This is not a complex matter. Mr. Karoki decided he was no longer interested in working for Eagle, and stopped coming to work. Before me, I have his attendance record, which has of course deteriorated over the last two months. Prior to this, Mr. Karoki was an exemplary employee. We have tried, since this trend began, to find out what was wrong, but Mr. Karoki has not been forthcoming. What can anyone say? I am here to run this branch office, and eventually, as the Americans say, something has to give." He paused, cleared his throat, and looked out the window with self-importance. Then he turned back to Kandle.

"The British, whom I worked for when I joined the bank, would have said Queen and Country come first. Eagle next. At that time, when I joined, I was a messenger. The only African employee at Eagle. I worked for a branch manager named Mr. Purkiss, a former D.C. who made me proud and taught me the meaning of duty. I have been here for *forty* years. I turn *sixty* next year. It seems that young men no longer know what they are doing. When I was your age, Mr. Karoki, no one my age would have called me Mister. I was Malasi's age, *thirty-six*, before anyone gave me a chance to work in Foreign Exchange. I was already a man, a father of *three* children. Now look at you. You could have been in my seat, God forbid, at forty. It is a pity that I did not notice you before this, to straighten you out." He paused again. "But before we hear from you, let us hear from the branch accountant, Mr. Ocuotho."

By now everyone from the branch was trying to hide a smile. Mr. Malasi had a slight frown on his face.

"Thank you, Mr. Guka," Ocuotho said, clearing the chuckle from his throat. He spoke briskly.

"Mr. Karoki is a good worker, or was a good worker. But after he received his June salary, which was heavily supplemented by the furniture loan he took, he never came back. We received a letter from a Dr. Koinange, saying that Mr. Karoki needed a week off for stress-related reasons. After that week, he did not appear at work again. This is the first time I am seeing him."

Mr. Malasi shifted in his seat at the mention of Dr. Koinange. Kandle was looking at his boss, Kimani, who wore a grave expression. Feeling Kandle's eyes on him, he made the most imperceptible of winks.

"What was the exact date of this doctor's letter?" Guka asked. Everyone waited as Ocuotho referred to his diary.

"Friday, 24 June."

"Today is Thursday the 15th of August. So not counting his sick and annual leave, Mr. Karoki has been away for two weeks with no probable reason. And after eight weeks, he doesn't seem to have solved his problem." Mr. Malasi coughed, but Guka ignored him. The manager stretched and stroked his belly. "Let us hear from the shop steward, Mr. Kimani."

Kimani straightened up. "I have worked with Kandle for a year," he said, "and in all honesty have seen few hardworking boys of his age. A few weeks ago he failed to appear at work, as Mr. Ocuotho has mentioned. He called in later and said he wasn't feeling very well, and that something had happened to his mother. He said he would be sending a doctor's letter later in the day. I didn't think much of it. People fall sick. Kandle had never missed a day of work before that. I told him to get it to the accountant, give the department a copy, and keep one for himself. Then, of course, he went on leave. When he didn't come back as scheduled— I was to go on leave after him—I got worried and tried to get in touch. When we spoke, he told me his problems weren't done and that he claimed to have talked to Personnel. I told him to make sure that he kept copies of his letters."

Mr. Guka was getting agitated. It was obvious he was not aware of any contact with Personnel, with whom he'd already had problems. After he had accused the legendary Hendrix of insubordination, Personnel had decided otherwise and transferred the man to Merchant Services, which was a promotion. Hendrix was now Eagle's main broker. Guka had been branch manager for eight years; his old colleagues were now executive managers or had moved on to senior positions at other companies.

Guka loosened his tie. He remembered that he was due to retire at the end of the year. He wished he was on the golf course, or out on his tea farm, and reminded himself that he needed to talk to Kimani later, to find out whether there was any chance that the currency deals would start up again. It had been two months since he had received his customary twenty thousand shillings a week. He needed to complete the house he was building in Limuru. This was not going the way he had expected.

"I am not aware of any such documents or communication," Mr. Malasi offered. "But as you all know, we are a large department. It's certainly possible we overlooked something. I will check up on that."

Guka cleared his throat. "I think the facts are clear—"

Malasi interrupted him. "I think we should hear from Mr. Karoki before we decide what the facts are." Head Office Personnel had paid out millions of shillings to ex-employees for wrongful dismissal, and Malasi was starting to wish he had stayed away from this one and sent someone else. It was looking like one of those litigious affairs. For one, the boy seemed too calm, almost sleepy. And what was the large sheaf of documents he had in his lap? The reference to one of Nairobi's most prominent psychiatrists, Dr. Koinange, had introduced a whole new element. Dr. Koinange happened to be on Eagle Bank's board of directors. The belligerent hubris of one old manager would be, in the face of such odds, ridiculous to indulge. Even if they managed to dismiss the boy, Malasi decided he would pass on word that Mr. Guka should be quietly retired. As the oldest manager at Eagle, he was well past his sell-by date. Malasi decided he would recommend Ocuotho as a possible replacement.

Guka cleared his throat again. "Young Mr. Karoki, you have five minutes to explain your conduct." His easy confidence had become a tight and wiry anger. "Before you start, maybe we should address the small matter of the furniture loan you took out."

Kandle quietly removed the white envelope from his pocket and placed the shillings, together with the contents of the large brown envelope, on Mr. Guka's desk. Malasi reached for the documents and handed copies to everyone. Kandle spoke in a quiet voice.

"Over the last year, my mother has lost her mind. Being the first-born, with my father's constant absences, it has been up to me to look after her. My sister is in the U.S., and my brother lives in a bottle. Two months ago my mother left my father's house in Buruburu and moved to a nearby slum. At the same time, I started to get severe headaches. I could not eat or sleep, and even started hallucinating, as Dr. Koinange, our family doctor, explains in one of these letters. He has expressly told me that he would be in touch with the bank's personnel department. That is why I haven't been in touch. My doctor has." There were tears in Kandle's eyes.

Guka sat back in his seat and glared at the ceiling. He tucked his top lip into the bottom, re-enacting the thinking Kikuyu man's pose. The Kikuyu Lip Curl.

Malasi looked up from the documents. It was time to end this, he thought. "Yes, I can see that Personnel received letters from your doctor. I also see there are letters here sent to us from your lawyer. Why go to such lengths if you were truly sick?"

"I thought about resigning, because I did not see myself coming back to work unless my mother got better. But my lawyer advised that that wasn't necessary." One tear made it down his left cheek. Kandle wiped it away angrily.

"Do you still want to resign?" Malasi asked, somewhat hopefully.

"I'd like to know my options first."

"Well, it won't be necessary to bring in your lawyer. No. It won't be necessary. We will review your case and get back to you. In the meantime, get some rest. And you can keep the money, the loan, for now. You are still an employee of this bank." He turned to everybody. "Mr. Guka?"

The manager glared at Kandle with a small smile on his face. He remained quiet.

"Mr. Karoki, you are free to leave," Mr. Malasi said.

As they all trooped out, leaving Mr. Guka and Mr. Malasi in the office, Kandle realized that he had just completed one of the greatest performances of his young life. He hummed Bob Marley's "Crazy Baldhead" and saw himself back in Zanze till the early hours of the morning.

"Can I see you for a minute in my office?"

It was Ocuotho. Before Kandle followed him down the hall, he shook Kimani's and Koigi's hands and whispered, "I'll be at Zanze later." Then he walked after Ocuotho, into the glass-partitioned office right in the middle of the bank floor.

"Why didn't you tell me about your problems?" Ocuotho said when they were inside. "I thought we agreed you would come to me. I know people in Head Office. We could have come to an arrangement. You know Guka does not understand young people."

"Thank you, sir. But don't worry. It is taken care of."

"You now have some time. Think carefully about your life."

"That is exactly what I am doing, sir."

Ocuotho sighed, and looked at him. "I have a small matter. A personal matter. My daughter is sick and I was wondering whether you could lend me something small. Maybe ten thousand shillings?"

"No problem. The usual interest applies. And I need a blank check."

"Of course." Ocuotho wrote a check and handed it over.

Kandle reached into his back pocket and counted out twenty five-hundred-shilling notes from the furniture-loan money.

"Well, I suspect we won't be seeing you around here, one way or the other," Ocuotho said, with some meaning. "We'll miss…"

They both laughed from deep within their bellies, that laughter of Kenyan men that comes from a special knowledge. The laughter was a language in itself, used to climb from a national quiet desperation.

DUST AND MEMORY

by YVONNE ADHIAMBO OWUOR

ONE
RETURN TO WUOTH OGIK

DEATH SLOW-MARCHES at half past three. On the branch of a deformed Grevillea, a metallic-mauve bird tweets. Inside the morgue, the chill makes hands pale yellow, the same as Odidi's long, thick fingers. He's been nattily dressed up by his father and sister: olive khaki suit, black socks, and tan leather shoes, purchases from a half-closed, guarded, nearby mall. There are rumors of chaos out there. But in this other place, documents signed, all protocol observed, Moses Ebewesit Odidi Oganda is officially dead.

Outside, gray skies. Darting shadows, a pair of Bateleur eagles. Prophet birds, like Marabou storks. They know when a body is cooling. Savannah birds, circling a city tottering on the edge of a chasm. Below, four men advance in step toward a white hearse. Red, tattered ribbons flutter from the windows.

Arabel Ajany Oganda shivers. Breathing into her hand, she hunts and pecks at words. Emerges empty. Inside her body, she feels blistered and bruised in hidden places, eyes on her father's still-shiny, always black shoes, shoes that underline his out-of-placeness. Nyipir Oganda, tall and slender and dark and old-world dapper in his 1970s coat and 1950s brown-leather fedora, with manners to match. As with so many men of Kenya from his time, his mien is genteel colonial, almost Churchillian English, complete with board-stiff upper lip.

"Baba." An arrangement of letters. What she wants to say is, "Look! The birds." Anything *other than that* to talk about.

A beige wood coffin containing all that remains of his son possesses Nyipir's eyes and voice.

Oombe, oombe

Oombe, oombe

Nyathi maywak

Ondiek chame…

Baba's guttural breathing of a lullaby.

Ajany moves one foot toward the men. Stops. Head tilted, listening for directions in a now deformed world. *Baba*. Her mouth forms the word. No sound.

Nyipir, Ali Dida Hada, Dr. Mda, and a snaggle-toothed mortuary attendant lift Odidi's coffin up and slide it into the hearse. Harmony in step. Bruised faces belie their outward peace. There was a tussle inside the morgue, next to the silver autopsy bay, when Nyipir had said, "I'll take my son home now."

Dr. Mda had retorted, "A police case. The cadaver belongs to the state." The sympathetic but superior tenor of a creature with moral advantage. The tone led Nyipir to grab Dr. Mda's neck and squeeze as a python might.

Ali Dida Hada sauntered over, watched a bit. He said, "Me, I say there's no case."

Dr. Mda's eyes popped. He made bleating sounds. He choke-grumbled to Ali Dida Hada, "You brought me here."

"To show how this is *not* a police case."

Outnumbered and practical, Dr. Mda found a proper cause of death for Odidi Oganda. *Exsanguinations caused by pneumothorax and heart failure.* No ill will. Odidi was going home.

Distant sirens. Disorder approaches.

A thump in the hearse's boot. Ajany's body jerks. Odidi's coffin is pale behind the rear window.

The driver, Leonard, thin face bones casting defined shadows: Charon's acolyte. He has wrapped a white handkerchief around his coat's upper arm and assumed a funereal look. It suits his temperament. Earlier, he had brought Ajany and Nyipir in from the airport in a green saloon taxi. It is gone.

A searing ball works its way out of Ajany's throat, becomes a nose tickle, and scatters as tears. She scrubs her face dry with trembling hands.

Before-Now was a green car. That was five hours and forty-three minutes ago. *Before-Now* was rained-upon earth mingling with smoke and age and dust and sun and cows on a father's coat and her head tucked into its folds in welcome. It was the scent of coming home from Far Away.

Now is an icy season, thick with dread. It is a youthful quartet oozing a ragged, old-clothes smell. Their wet eyes a counterpoint to life-hardened faces. It is an unadorned, rough-edged, empty coffin on the ground nearby, next to a shaggy-haired woman in red. A wife? Mother? Sister? Grief-stripped, soul-bared, panel-beaten features. Under the weak sun, her look speaks of a hemorrhaging. Ajany Oganda averts her gaze.

There are no manuals showing safe maps through human messiness. A lethargic, white-striped lizard pauses for something between the tiny yellow flowers of a medicinal weed. Ajany sees how her blue-painted toes peep out of absurd, dark-blue Brazilian high heels, and for half a second she imagines how best to cut them off.

Where is Odidi?

Sorrow gallops in, seizes and inserts itself into her body from the left side. It hooks claws into her heart. Ajany rakes her right arm with broken-nail fingers, grunts at the naked, gauzy outline of cold shadows in an afternoon made of fear. A pungent clutch of ghosts shimmers, gripping unanswered questions like a threat. From inside comes the hollow sound of a baby crying, lamb-like. She doubles over.

A small explosion somewhere. It has begun. *I'm going to die*, Ajany thinks. In the sadness, the baby's cries stop.

Shuffling footsteps. No flowers. No cortège. A brother leaving a sour morgue where other corpses wait for their living to take them away. Orange daylight. A prepubescent girl with a tank top, belly ring, and red sneakers hurries off somewhere with her Nakumatt white plastic bags.

Ajany faces the Hurrying One. *Run! Run!* She thinks.

She cannot move.

Not without Odidi.

Nyipir says, "*Wadhi.*" Let's go.

Ajany and her father approach the hearse, slip in, and take their seats, a new, pulsating ghost between them. Like all the others, it is molded out of hard, deep, and buried silences.

* * *

Massive clouds rush in from the eastern coast. Ambushed by a warm wind in Nairobi, they scatter, a routed guerrilla force. At Wilson Airport, a *miraa*-carrying Cessna Caravan weaves its way out of the apron. The last small plane out of Nairobi without top-level permission for the next seven days.

Above the airport din, egrets circle and ibises cry *nganganganga*. A father, daughter, and son are going home.

Clouds like purple dots against a blue sky.

The dusk is Odidi's time.

An image. Ajany and Odidi sitting on a rock to spy the sun's decline. She leaning over Odidi's shoulder, pretending she could see the world as he did.

Onboard the Cessna, Ajany says, "Baba…"

Nyipir turns.

Twisted fingers rub wetness from his face. Even now, he rearranges new silences. She had once believed he was omnipotent, like God. He had, after all, summoned a black leopard to hunt down the inhabitants of night dreams who had tried to throttle her. And now… *Stop it!* A screamed-out thought.

She cannot give it sound.

Not without Odidi.

Beneath the plane, coffee and pineapple plantations. Greenhouses and flower farms. Ol Donyo Keri, a sentinel that looms like a revelation.

Ajany shivers.

Folds of Nyipir's skin gather on his forehead. The shape of a worry tree.

"Cold?" he says.

She shakes her head.

The light of the sky bounces on her thin face, all bones and angles. Nyipir notices bloodstains on Ajany's sleeves; the edges of her orange skirt are also soiled. Mud and blood. She is tinier than he remembers. His daughter has always been such a small, stuttering thing, all big hair and eyes. More shadow than person, her head tilted as if she was listening for answers to an old question. Nyipir frowns. The years have sloughed off her chubbiness, increased her wariness. *Ah! What remains for a man who cannot protect his children from the past?*

From the gloom of his soul, a hoarse voice. "Mama..." Nyipir says. "Er... she would've come to see you."

Ajany hears her father's lie. Draws it into the fog that is swirling inside. She sketches invisible circles on the window, glares at the mountain beyond it, waits for the saltiness and the ball in the back of her throat to ease.

"The mountain!" Nyipir shouts to the pilot. "We must see the mountain!"

The pilot glances back, frowns.

"My son... uh... he likes..." Nyipir's voice cracks. His face crumples. It is a strange thing. Seeking reassurance from the presence of a mountain.

The pilot scans the horizon and swings the plane right, to circumnavigate Mount Kenya. "Batian, Lenana, Macalder..." he intones. The late afternoon sun has colored the sparse snow crimson.

Ajany squashes her face against the windowpane. They turn northward. They are going home.

Half an hour later, flamingos-on-oyster-shell-colored water next to milk-blue Anam Ka'alakol. Lake Turkana.

"And there, Lake Logipi," says the pilot.

They know. This is their territory.

Teleki's volcano, a brown bowl, a labyrinth of landforms, the turns of which they know. They pass over Loiyangalani, toward Mt. Kulal. Shift northeast, toward Kalacha Goda. High places become low. They level over the salt flats fringing the Chalbi. Hurri Mountains in the dusk light and then, below, a wide unkempt stripe carved into the land.

Home.

Wuoth Ogik.

Home.

They were offspring of these northern drylands. Odidi and Ajany. Hemmed in by geography.

A river—the Ewaso Nyiro—four moody winds, the secret things of parents' fears, the throbbing shadow of histories, assorted transient souls, a massive canvas of vivid, rocky earth upon which anything could and did happen. Anam Ka'alakol, the lake that drank down three rivers—the Omo, the Turkwel, and the Kerio. The terrain of their lives dominated by the absence of any real elders with their names.

No one to tell them "how it *had* been" or "what it *had* meant." They had pieced together tales from stones, counted footsteps etched into rocks, peered into crevices to re-create myths of beginnings.

"The first Oganda was made of fire." Odidi once said.

Ajany believed him.

The plane sweeps past old lives.

A hollowed brown rock below, like that from which Ajany and Odidi would survey the rustling march of desert locusts. Dry, brown pastures where they'd herded cows and goats. She tastes again the creamy, hot milk of their animals, goats and cows and camels, gulped in mirth and mischief when the herdsmen were not looking. Running after homemade kites and not crying when one of Wuoth Ogik's visiting winds ripped them into shreds. Chewed-grass-slime-layered goat tongues on skin as she and Odidi fed them with salt stolen from the kitchen. Black pebbles falling into holes carved into the ground. *Ajua.* She was always losing to Odidi. He would gloat, of course, gloat until she cried. *Ajany yuak, yuak, yuak.*

Ajany scratches memory shapes on the Cessna's window, biting hard on her lips, needing to feel Odidi's presence. That's all.

The pilot swoops down.

Odi, we're home, Ajany mouths.

First landing aborted. They veer upward. Ajany scrunches her eyes shut, grits her teeth, and prays they will stay suspended in space and lost to time. Second descent. The plane evens out, crabs into a soft landing. Dust twirls on their tail.

Wuoth Ogik.

TWO

Pilot, Nyipir, and Ajany lift Odidi out of the plane. They walk in time to Nyipir's *March, march, march, left turn, march, march, halt*, zigzagging across rock and sand. The coffin edge digs into Ajany's right shoulder. *Halt!*

Beneath a stunted Acacia tree, they steady the coffin, then lower it to the ground. Dizzy, weak-kneed, hair matted, Ajany kneels, inert. "I'll…" she starts. Then she hunkers down next to the box, staring at the dust, at the progress of safari ants.

Nyipir looks down at his daughter, then trundles away to retrieve her travel bags. The pilot follows him, clasps and unclasps his hands, clears his throat, and says, "My condolences. My sincerest condolences."

Nyipir nods so he will not bawl. He nods as he hauls down orange and red luggage, clinging to it, nods at the pilot over and over again until the man boards the plane. Then he waits, a solitary form, watching the Cessna find its height. When he sees its lilt and waggle, he brings his hand up to his forehead in a salute.

Nearby, life churns. It is a violet-yellow evening that stinks of sadness. The electric sense of a threatening storm. Five kilometers away, a slow-moving dust-devil giant lops over the land. Ten minutes later the once green, now rusted family Land Rover, long in tooth and loud in rattle, bounds toward the waiting pair. Nyipir turns to face the car, not breathing. The Land Rover grunts to a stop and emits the smell of a burning clutch. The season of Life-After begins.

Nyipir drops Ajany's baggage.

Galgalu and Akai Lokorijem slide out of the car. Akai is magma, a moving rock become flame. Galgalu carries a lit kerosene lamp behind her. Nyipir moves toward his wife, ducks the ricochet of a conversation that began in August 1998, when a distant-living coward detonated a bomb in Nairobi.

Nyipir lowers his head. *How was he to know it was a forewarning?*

"My son!" Akai-ma wailed then, as a BBC news bulletin retold the story to arid land dwellers. "Where's my son?"

In response Nyipir embarked on a journey toward the city he hated. *The city of my dying.* He'd made it to the North Horr airstrip when he found Ali Dida Hada, who was also on his way to Nairobi, summoned by police headquarters to support efforts to handle the lunacy.

"As if we don't have enough fools of our own," he'd frowned. He did not comment on Nyipir's trembling, sweating body.

"He's my only son," explained Nyipir.

"I'll look."

"She would die…"

"I'll find him."

"Moses Odidi Ebewesit Oganda."

"I know him. Akai has told me."

A sort of admission of a situation that neither had dared to acknowledge before.

"I'll call you," said Ali Dida Hada.

They did not shake hands.

Nyipir headed off to Maralal to monitor the news. Eight days later, with a crackle of the radio set and a laugh in his voice, Ali Dida Hada told Nyipir that Odidi was safe, and was doing well in his work as an engineer in Nairobi.

Now dusk's shadows accompany Akai-ma as she approaches Nyipir. For a moment the massive sun of the evening, the dry grasslands, and the chirping of the crickets absorb him.

He returns to the horror of the story he must repeat. The roiling country, the murdered son. He eases away from the retching in his gullet.

There are patches on Akai-ma's scalp where she has torn out her hair. Scratches and tear marks on her face. Blood cakes her body in thin strips. One of Nyipir's AK-47s, the four-kilogram 1952 with a wooden buttstock and handguard, is strapped to her body, cradled in a green kanga with an aphorism written on it— *Haba na haba hujaza kibaba*. Little by little fills the pot.

The fire in Galgalu's kerosene lamp wavers. Ajany moves closer.

Nyipir might have blocked Akai's progress if it were not for some preternatural power she uses to push him aside. She reaches for the coffin, falling against it.

"Who?" Akai screams.

A wind hurls dust and pebbles around.

A single creamy butterfly.

Silence.

Nyipir enters the breach. "Our son. It is Odidi," he says, his head bowed.

"Yes, but who is it?" Akai insists.

"Odidi."

"Who?"

"Akai…" says Nyipir, sounding like small stones falling on a tin roof.

Akai whirls and takes off. Up and down a portion of the field, arms thrown up and down. Returns, clutches her waist, grabs Nyipir, eyes sly. "Where's my son?" Her tone is stern. She licks chapped lips.

"Mama," says Ajany from the side.

Akai waves a hand at the noise, strides backward, grabs at her head, hits her stomach. *"Where is my son Odidi?"*

Nyipir's head swings left, right, left, right. "I tried everything, I tried," he croaks, hands gesturing upward, open-palmed. "Akai…"

Akai scolds him. "Nyipir! I said *bring my son home*. Didn't I say that? Did you hear me?"

Nyipir's hands move upward again. His mouth opens and closes. Saliva clings to his jaw.

"Nyipir—*where is my child?*" Akai's eyes bulge.

"M-mama?" stutters Ajany.

"Ahhh! Nyipir!" Akai throws her hands up and turns again, facing the coffin. She points at it. Fingers waggle. She points again.

Galgalu moves closer, lantern aloft. Tears. He props the lantern against the tree.

Akai advances. "Show me."

"Mama?" Ajany tries again. Her mother glides past her.

Galgalu unscrews the large bolts and opens the coffin lid.

Akai-ma falls, arms stretched forward. Turns to face the sky, a choking wail in her throat. She crawls forward, leans over Odidi's body, reaches in, takes it by the shoulders, holding him to her breast, keening in small groans, lips on Odidi's forehead, and rocks her son, strokes his face, rocks her son and groans. *Odidi*, she croons. *Odidi, wake up.*

To name something is to bring it to life.

A roiling heat like heartburn with a rusty aftertaste is stuck in Ajany's throat. As if she has licked dead iron. *Cry*, Ajany tells herself. An ugly sense of jealousy, of wanting to be the dead one being held by her mother, being summoned to life by such sounds. Shame.

Akai-ma's moan.

Cry, Ajany tells herself.

Her brother limp in her mother's arms. *Live*, she commands Odidi. Her eyes are dry.

Akai-ma lowers Odidi, adjusts his shirt, moves his headrest, swabs invisible fragments from his face. She mops her face, rubs her eyes, and then she turns to Nyipir. Ajany feels the tangible spark that hurtles between them.

Nyipir shakes his head, palms out. "Akai." His voice is a plea. A gray shadow descends on his body and from his mouth, the whistling sound of deflation. His face is pinched, sunken and ancient.

Akai-ma stoops, scratches at the dust.

Nyipir lumbers toward her.

Akai screeches, lifts her hands. "No!" she says, low-voiced, firm. "No!"

Nyipir pauses.

Akai-ma spits indecipherable curses and prayers.

Sits on her heels.

The Not-knowingness takes a hold of Nyipir's body.

He droops.

Behind Ajany, Galgalu screws in the coffin lid. He places the lantern atop it. His arms go around the wood, his face against the surface. An embrace.

"Mama," creaks Ajany.

Akai-ma recognizes her at last. "You?" she says. She gets up.

The stone inside Ajany's stomach flutters.

"Arabel Ajany," Akai-ma says. "Arabel Ajany." Her voice fades and returns.

Ajany takes three steps toward her mother, a history of longing in the movement.

Akai's arms reach out.

Ajany moves close, inhales Akai-ma's rancid, sad warmth. Incense, hope, and softness.

She almost touches her.

Akai drops her arms, eyes dart left, up, and right. "Ajany," she says, "where is your brother?"

Ajany goes rigid.

Nyipir intervenes. "See, Akai, see, Ajany came home, too…"

Akai-ma sucks air. "Why?" The sound is childlike. "I want Odidi."

And me?

Ajany throws herself at her mother, grabbing onto her back. *And me.* The thought pushes at her mouth. She clings to Akai's neck. A tight hold, mucus mingling with saliva, choking her. Blood and acid taste from a palate cut.

Akai recoils, breaks away. Her eyes are thin slits, her nostrils flaring, and when Ajany looks again, her mother is a still, steady point with a finger on a trigger and a smile on her face. *Click-clack.* Rifle cocked. Clear gaze. Gun pointed to heart, a glint from the barrel like light on a pathologist's scalpel.

Certainty.

Akai will pull the trigger if Ajany moves again. Her daughter drops to the ground, flat. Her hand scrabbles at the earth. Mind roaming around the barrel of a gun, sensing its position with tenderness because a mother is on the other end. Hearing Nyipir's soft chant. *Akai, Akai, Akai, Akai.* Sensing the soft departing of day.

A shift of pressure, a rush of air. Running feet, a scream, the slam of doors. The car engine revs. Nyipir shouts—*Akaaai!*

Akai Lokorijem is leaving. Down a tunnel of memory.

Ajany scratches her arms, peeling the skin. Not feeling anything. She waits for her body to come back together, those parts she can no longer sense—hands, feet, face. She stares at the rusting car, lurching and stopping and starting and stalling. She tells herself that she too will leave. She too can go away.

And then she is in pursuit of the ramshackle green Land Rover.

Galgalu picks up speed behind her.

The car jolts ahead of them. Low-lying thorn bush scrapes Ajany's left foot. It stings. Galgalu overtakes her. Ajany grabs hold of his arm, tries to push him away. She bites into his wrist. Galgalu snarls and pulls her down. He wipes his face with the edge of his shawl. Ajany take his wrist, wipes off her saliva, and rubs at the teeth marks.

On the coffin, the lantern's flame dies.

Galgalu pats Ajany's back. *"Ch'uquliisa,"* he croons. *"Ch'uquliisa."* He grasps for clarity of heart. *"Ch'uquliisa,"* Galgalu says, deciphering Ajany's sobs. He knows the ways of her tears. After all, it was he who helped bring her into life. He received her first cry in the world. And her second outraged one.

Fida Galgalu is an intermediary between fate, truth, and desire, a cartographer of unutterable realms. He has lost faith in tangible things, certain only of a dialogue with landscapes. Now he scrutinizes the skies. The portents are cruel. A pale orange veil shrouds the heavens. He recites *"La illaha illa 'lla Hu. La illaha illa 'lla Hu."* And then Galgalu mutters to his dead father about what he sees painted upon the earth and in the lives of those whom he serves.

Isaack Galgalu, his father, had been an *ayyaantu*—an astrologer, in Hargagbo. After a gruesome drought he predicted would be the worst—it was—had passed, and a locust invasion he foretold would destroy all available pasture had done so, and the water wells yielded salt as he had said they would, rumors of sorcery and deliberate mischief began to rain upon the family. Wounded by the sacrilege, Isaack disintegrated into mad prophecy, railing in mud holes, shouting predictions that fewer and fewer people wanted to hear. He screamed maledictions. And then he predicted his death during the waning of a moon.

Galgalu tried to pray his father back into sanity over a week of confused winds, almost white skies, and orange dust casting a pall over everything. As they were now, the portents had been mean. He prayed while his mother, Umi, covered his father with herbs, smoke, and hope. Chants, silence, and darkness. Galgalu watched as life's signals sneaked out of his father one at a time, until one moonless night, in the light of a single wick, he heard his father cough and breathe out. The shadow of Isaack's potent essence got up from the body on the mat, brushed against Galgalu, and headed out without looking back.

"*Ch'uquliisa*," he sings now to Ajany. "*Ch'uquliisa*." His arms around her, rocking her. His mind elsewhere.

One wild afternoon, by decree of the elders, he was appointed scapegoat for all clan guilt. He had been bringing home a kid that had sprained its leg. Its mother bleated behind him while men surged around and the ritual curse was inflicted. The words wounded the inside of his soul. He tore at his heart to break the curse's hold. The scars are still curved lines across Fida Galgalu's chest.

The kid tumbled from his arms as Galgalu was kicked away, driven back with sticks, stones, dust, and dung. His goats cried in sympathy. Under the sensation of unwantedness, he sought wilderness cairns pointing to somewhere-anywhere by day. He chased after falling stars at night. He kept moving. A solitary bow-legged creature intending to walk itself to death.

Until the soft dusk of December 12, 1963, when Galgalu came to a stop in front of a coral-hued edifice. *Wuoth Ogik*. A brown-black-patched cattle dog that had a lot of hyena in it appeared and wagged its tail at him. Galgalu stroked its head. It licked his hand. He would learn that its name was Kulal, after the mountain.

By the time he saw the dark, tall, long-limbed spirit flowing toward him, its arms swinging in wide swoops, he welcomed dying. *Ekhaara*. It carried a headrest and club—things men carried—and a gourd of sour milk, herbs, and grasses. Its feet were dusty in *akala* tire sandals. It had hitched its sarong up on its thighs. Its eyes took in everything.

Akai Lokorijem bent over him.

The dog whined.

Galgalu quivered. A dead, restless, hungry ghost.

Akai stroked his head. "You're just a bone, boy!" she clucked. "What's your name?" She laughed. He wanted to laugh with her, but then he cried out because he saw that he would live.

"She'll return." Galgalu tells Ajany now. "Always, she comes home."

All through their childhood, Galgalu would scoop the soil where Ajany and Odidi's daylight shadows fell, and cast it into holes where the dusk shadows gathered, so that the departing sun would take with it with any chaos and evil that had entered their lives. Galgalu tried to collect enough of Akai-ma's shadow, too, to exorcise the ghosts that made her wander. Odidi and Ajany tried to help him. They failed. Akai would never stand still in one place for long enough.

Footsteps. Nyipir hobbles forward and joins them, peering at wheel marks. When the fear of death afflicts, people pull together. He has experienced it a thousand times. He glances at Ajany.

"Mama… she… uhm…" Nyipir's voice is hoarse. "She's happy you're here. Just…" He waves in the direction of the coffin.

Ajany nods.

Dalíesque darknesses drip giant aches into the hollow expanding inside her. "We forgot Odidi's flowers," she says.

Nyipir says, "Oh!"

And three people hear four winds creeping through the rattling doum palms. The winds cover the car's tracks, sprinkling dust over them. They race southward, to the part of the nation where unsettled ghosts have set the land afire and a gang of men are howling and dancing up and down a city street, dangling the head of a man they have just beheaded. The dead man's fingers, with their stained voter's mark, are scattered around his new blue bicycle.

IT IS ONLY THE BEST THAT COMES OUT

by ANNETTE LUTIVINI MAJANJA

PRECIOUS BLOOD RIRUTA SECONDARY SCHOOL
"FORWARD EVER, BACKWARD NEVER"

*T*HE CATHOLIC NUNS *of the order of Precious Blood Sisters established the Precious Blood Riruta Secondary School in 1964. The weekly student routine, which must be followed to the letter without deviation, is as shown:*

	MON.	TUES.	WED.	THURS.	FRI.	SAT.	SUN.
5:30 A.M.	WAKING UP						
6:45 A.M.	BREAKFAST						
7:45 A.M.	ASSEMBLY						
8:00 A.M.	FIRST LESSON					PREPS	MASS
8:40 A.M.	SECOND LESSON					PREPS	MASS
9:20 A.M.	THIRD LESSON					PREPS	MASS
10:20 A.M.	FOURTH LESSON					PREPS	MASS
11:00 A.M.	FIFTH LESSON					CATHOLIC HOUR	MASS
11:40 A.M.	SIXTH LESSON					CATHOLIC HOUR	MASS
1:30 P.M.	SEVENTH LESSON					FREE TIME	PREP/ FREE TIME
2:10 P.M.	EIGHTH LESSON					FREE TIME	PREP/ FREE TIME
2:50 P.M.	NINTH LESSON					FREE TIME	PREP/ FREE TIME
3:30 P.M.	TENTH LESSON					FREE TIME	PREP/ FREE TIME

	MON.	TUES.	WED.	THURS.	FRI.	SAT.	SUN.
4:10 P.M.– 5:00 P.M.	GAMES		CLUBS	GAMES	CLUBS	SINGING PRACTICE	
5:00 P.M.– 5:30 P.M.	EVENING DUTY						
5:30 P.M.– 6:00 P.M.	SUPPER						
6:45 P.M.– 9:00 P.M.	EVENING PREPS						
9:30 P.M.	LIGHTS OUT						

It is a serious offense to be found awake after lights out. Talking of any form is strictly forbidden, and all students must be totally silent.

There is a fifty-lesson week, and all other scheduled activities are of extreme importance. However, form fours are excluded from any activity after term one.

STUDENT ROUTINE

It is only acceptable to be loud when performing on stage with a proper rounded voice in choir, at the school assembly during an official school celebration, on the field when applauding teammates, and when Superman in *Lois & Clark*, Pharaoh in *The Ten Commandments*, or Hlestakov (in the video of the Saint Mary's production) in *The Government Inspector* appears on the television screen. At any of these times you can get away with screaming, clapping, whistling, and all other forms of acclamation.

On ordinary days, even when silence is not officially imposed, one must always wonder when the decibels will become unacceptable. Every shout, laugh, whisper, and exclamation has to go through an internal vetting process before its release. Almost always, there will be noisemakers undergoing silent punishment, or *groundation*. Students assigned this form of punishment are not allowed to speak or to be spoken to. *Groundation*, as we call it, means one must stand facing a blank wall or concrete support pillar for a set period of time. Sometimes entire classes are on silent punishment, thereby forcing their eerie stillness on the entirety of the space they occupy.

The weekday starts with a shrill bell at 5:30 a.m. To be caught awake and out of bed before that is inexcusable, unless it is for a trip to the toilet (*not* the shower). Once you get up, there is a mad rush for the bathrooms to finish all one's morning duties, and then to the classrooms to get some work done during the optional silent prep period before breakfast. During the tea-less 10:00 a.m. break, you must either be quiet or leave the classroom, because "they" will be trying to catch up on reading or homework. Outside you will be hard-pressed to find space to sit idly, because along the grass lawns, corridors, stone benches, and concrete slabs there will be students trying to read in the fresh air and natural light, or having study-related group discussions.

The lunch-hour routine will mirror break time, except that if you are fortunate enough to have tablemates who are not in a hurry to go and study, you may have a short conversation before being inundated by incomplete assignments, singing, or drama-practice sessions to be attended before afternoon classes start.

Back in class, you may find yourself daydreaming about the end of the day, when you might chat with the people you share evening duties with. If you are a hockey player or a choir member, or the people with whom you share duties are, then you will either be on your own covering up for them or attempting to finish a thirty-minute duty in five minutes so that you are not late for practice.

After the 5:30 p.m. supper, whatever you do, remember not to be too loud. There will be people saying the Rosary at the shrine outside your classroom, and Mass will be in progress at the nearby convent.

Night prep is particularly difficult: two and a half hours of rustling pages, muffled coughing, scribbling fountain pens, sighs, dragging footsteps, flushing toilets, doors creaking open and shutting firmly, glaring prefects, ticking clocks, and daring whispers until the bell rings.

When the bell rings, at 9:00 p.m., you must be careful not to make too much noise when walking to the assembly for night prayers and announcements, and to the hostel after that. Quiet talking is tolerable at the hostel, but only until 9:30 p.m.—compulsory lights-out. To protect you from the temptation of slamming your door, the hostel doors have padded pin-cushion-like gadgets we call door sausages attached at the point where the door latch meets the wall.

There are also prefects who lurk along the hostel corridors to catch students talking after lights out. My three roommates and I were always sleep-talkers, but there is nothing in the rules against that.

NUMBERS

I was laundry number 250. The laundry number was the first number assigned to me; it was in my letter of acceptance to the school. Your laundry number was the number with which you labeled your school uniform, your laundry bucket, and your box, packet, or tin of detergent. Some people even found it necessary to label their hangers, and anything else that was likely to end up on the clotheslines, or simply anything worth stealing; stationery, even. That made sense: with as many as 360 students, each with identical uniforms, one or two similar buckets each, and lots of identical initials, it was impossible to keep track of who owned what in the lost-property bin.

My bed number was 167. Like all my year mates, I received a rainbow-striped polyester bedcover, a mattress, and a plain white mattress-cover marked with that number. My roommates' beds were numbers 168, 169, and 170. I was assigned one metal hostel locker as well, also number 167. For four years in that school I slept on bed and mattress 167 but with sheet-and-blanket set 250. My second locker, kit locker 167, was located in what we referred to as the new wing, above the junior classes. This locker was to store whatever possessions could not fit inside my hostel locker or class desk. According to school rules, I could only access this locker between 5:30 a.m. and 6:45 a.m., unless special permission was granted.

My bed, 167, was located in Room 32, on the top floor of the hostel, which was known as Kenya House. Room 32 had red walls, a tiny framed picture of flowers, a sink, two double-decker beds, four neatly numbered lockers, and, in my first year, a twenty-five-watt bulb that made it feel like we were using candlelight. For cleaning, we had a dusting cloth and a floor rag, each embroidered *RM 32*.

My third locker, a wooden one, was located in the dining hall downstairs. The DH locker was where you stored your cutlery, crockery, and limited supply of foodstuffs. My DH locker was number 151. It contained the following implements: plate, side plate, cup, saucer, glass, stainless butter knife, and spoon, each inscribed with the number 151. In addition, and as required, it held two packets of Marie biscuits, five hundred grams red plum jam or honey, five hundred grams of Blue Band margarine, five hundred grams of powdered glucose, five hundred grams of tomato sauce (never ketchup), and some fruit. I also had a DH chair, marked 151. For all four years I used that same locker and chair. We sat in long rows based on houses, but every year your house moved to a different row of tables. You took your chair with you when you moved.

The Essence of a School #1
by Mr. Odida P.O.
Mathematics and Physics

School is the institution for educating children, granted that children spend the greatest part of their life in school. It is incumbent upon the school administration to ensure that they receive their training, control, and discipline in an atmosphere of extreme tranquility and inherent goodwill.

It is indeed perfidious to imagine that good character will be an indwelling commodity through peremptory and fallacious doctrines. Dogmatic presentation of rules has proved counter-effective as a means of inculcating elements of proper interpersonal relationships; as there is always a way in which they can be circumvented.

RED PLUM JAM, MARIE BISCUITS, AND TOMATO SAUCE

The school shopping list that comes along with the letter of acceptance specifies the items described above. No juice is allowed.

Even if the only jam you can carry is red plum jam, you still have a wide variety of red plum jams to choose from. There are the cheaper varieties, which are closer to liquid than the thick paste that the phrase "red plum jam" calls to mind. These have one advantage, and that is that a small amount can cover a wider section of a slice of bread. Thick and lumpy jam, though it often tastes better, requires a lot more of itself to cover the bread.

Whichever you choose, the jam will come in a tin can, a plastic jar, or a glass jar. A tin can is cheapest, most of the time, but it will end up with a layer of mold on it unless you are the kind of person who doesn't try to make your five hundred grams of jam last through the ten weeks before half term. You can buy the tin can and transfer the jam into a used jar, but be sure to do this in school, because the prefects will not believe that you haven't tried to smuggle in something if your jar does not have the manufacturer's seal on it and they have not seen it empty.

Just by the look of the plum jam, you can tell who is cheap, who is stingy, who is broke, who is practical, who is loaded, who is a wannabe, and who just doesn't care. If you opt to buy or keep your jam in a jar, it is important to remember that though the glass jar is nicer to look at and has a certain prestige, this will not matter if it accidentally falls out of your DH locker or slips out of your hands.

Marie biscuit packets are always green or red, though it seems there is a new variety of them available every time you go biscuit-shopping. Family biscuits taste the same and usually cost the same, but the school does not allow Family. A good packet has twenty-six biscuits inside; sometimes, if you are fortunate, there will be twenty-eight. Biscuit habits can vary widely: half a biscuit per meal, a biscuit a day, three biscuits at the end of supper, biscuits on weekends only, biscuits with jam, biscuits with Blue Band, biscuit sandwiches, biscuits dipped in tea. Anything to make them last longer, to make them tastier, to make them different.

Tomato sauce looks like ketchup, but disguises the taste of the food less well. You need more of it per plate of food. It is sold in plastic or glass bottles, and comes in various shades of reddish, from crimson to burgundy to chocolate. Sauce can be liquid or semi-solid, sweetened with too much artificial sugar or nothing to taste at all. School will teach you that tomato sauce is not just for chips and sausage. Tomato sauce is what soup was in your toddler years: it belongs in the *sukuma wiki*, in the beans, the boiled peas, the *ndengu*, the *githeri*, the pseudo *pilau*. It can even be licked fresh out of the bottle when nothing else is edible.

The rule about fruits is so reasonable that it seems like a trick. They forgot to say how much you can spend on your fruits, they forgot to say what fruits you can carry, and they forgot to say whether a tomato is a vegetable or a fruit. Your only limitation is the size of the DH locker, and even that can be worked around. Apples and oranges from South Africa are expensive but very practical, because their DNA has been enhanced to ensure that they will not rot after a month in your locker.

Even if you do not like glucose, you will meet many who are willing to buy it from you. It does not occupy much space in your DH locker, so I would buy my five hundred grams—there is only one brand—and sell it.

The Essence of a School #2
by Mr. Odida P.O.
Mathematics and Physics

Proper time management diminishes retrogressive eventualities such as unnecessary punishments, inadequate syllabus coverage, lateness for appointments, and panic. An institution worth its salt takes it as part of its responsibility to make its charges aware of their place, have a defined job description, and perform independently and perfectly without undue atten-tion and follow-up.

Everybody should realize that they have a great role to play, and should they not do it to the satisfaction of their immediate superiors, then they will definitely face the conse-quences. The trophies and awards on the school cabinets and shelves are but an embellishment of an ingrained tradition that perfection is the name of the game. Repeated rehearsals, con-sistent training programs, and a thorough revision process ensure that it is only the best that comes out.

PROHIBITION

The most convenient thing is to get your parents and doctor to write a letter to the school saying that you have anemia, stomach ulcers, or some other condition that requires an extra supply of Marie biscuits, UHT milk, and fruits. At the 10:00 a.m. tea-less break time, you will be able to eat in peace without wondering when you will get caught.

As it is, not all of us have parents or doctors willing to conspire with us for just a few extra packets of Marie and UHT milk. Innovation is the key to getting away with your contraband crisps, biscuits, chocolates, peanuts, chili sauce, and sweets.

Put your stash into a plastic bag, seal it to ensure that its contents are safe from the elements, then flatten it as much as possible and hang it on the clothesline under a wet sweater, a pair of sheets, or some other bulky washing. It will be safe for some time. With limited access to the laundry, collecting it may be more complicated; it may mean sneaking out of class at prep time, or rushing to the lines on the way to the hostel at night or in the early morning.

Another trick is to use your laundry bucket. Once your stockpile is watertight, put it in the bucket, soak your washing as usual, and pour in detergent for good measure. Park the bucket among others in the laundry. Watch out for the prying eyes—everybody knows this trick, and you will have nobody to blame if you lose your food.

Truly determined students arrive earlier than expected on opening days and at the end of the midterm break. It is not because they love being in school. Rumor has it that they bury junk food in the agriculture plots behind the hall. Such students can be seen constantly going to the plots to attend to the weeds and water their crops, as if theirs are the only areas that are weed-infested or have refused to respond to Mr. Wakesa's ammonium-sulphate and single-superphosphate fertilizers.

There are also two incinerators. The one that is used to burn paper and other trash is far out beyond the agriculture plots; with nothing around it, it is a place that draws too much suspicion. The other incinerator, close to the convent gate, is where all the sanitary buckets are emptied and their contents destroyed. Yes, if you have no fears, if smells do not bother you, then make use of the shelter the empty furnace provides. Along with the ash and emptied buckets, your food will be safe.

CONTRIBUTORS

JAMIE ALLEN has published fiction and nonfiction in outlets like the *Missouri Review*, *Salon*, *Slate*, *Paste*, and *New South*. His humor pieces appear occasionally on *McSweeney's Internet Tendency*.

STEVE DELAHOYDE is a writer and filmmaker in Chicago, where he plies his trades at the creative firm Coudal Partners by day and at lots of other places on nights, weekends, and holidays.

JAMES FLEMING is a college literature instructor and writer, and the author of the bi-weekly "Cosby Codex" for *McSweeney's Internet Tendency*. He lives in a fortified apartment somewhere in Central Florida.

JONATHAN FRANZEN is the author of four novels, most recently *Freedom*, and two works of nonfiction. He lives in New York City and Santa Cruz, California.

J. MALCOLM GARCIA's work has been anthologized in *The Best American Travel Writing* and *The Best American Nonrequired Reading*.

HALLIE HAGLUND is a writer for the *The Daily Show with Jon Stewart*, and a co-author of that show's *Earth (The Book)*. She can also be seen in various comedy clubs around New York City.

JOHN HYDUK has made his living on the paint line in a scaffolding factory, cutting patterns in a sweater mill, repairing railroad cars in a freight yard, and as a receiving clerk in a big-box store. Born and raised in Cleveland, Ohio, his writing has appeared in *Ohio* and *Cleveland* magazines. He currently resides in the city of his birth.

BILLY KAHORA is the managing editor of the Kenyan literary journal *Kwani?* and the author of *The True Story of David Munyakei*. His writing has appeared in *Granta*, *Kwani?*, and *Vanity Fair*.

ETGAR KERET's short story collections have been published in thirty-five countries, in thirty languages. In 2007, Keret and Shira Gefen won the Cannes Film Festival's Camera d'Or Award for their movie, *Jellyfish*, and the Best Director Award of the French Artists and Writers' Guild. In 2010, he received the St. Petersburg Public Library's Favorite Foreign writer Award and, in France, the decoration of Chevalier de l'Ordre des Arts et des Lettres.

EDAN LEPUCKI is the author of the novella *If You're Not Yet Like Me*. She lives in Los Angeles, where she was born and raised.

KEGURO MACHARIA is a poet and literary critic. A member of the Concerned Kenyan Writers collective and the Koroga collaborative, he blogs at *gukira.wordpress.com*. He teaches English and Comparative Literature at the University of Maryland, College Park.

ANNETTE LUTIVINI MAJANJA was born and raised in Nairobi. She left Precious Blood Riruta Secondary School in 1998, having completed her O-levels. That year, the class motto was Operation Stay in Position Again Jishinde Ushinde (conquer yourself to conquer). She has a B.A. in Language and Communication from the University of Nairobi.

JOE MENO is the author of five novels and two short story collections, including *The Great Perhaps*, *The Boy Detective Fails*, and *Hairstyles of the Damned*. A winner of the Nelson Algren Literary Award, a Pushcart Prize, and a finalist for the Story Prize, he is a professor in the Fiction Writing Department at Columbia College Chicago.

KEVIN MOFFETT's second story collection, *Further Interpretations of Real-Life Events*, is forthcoming from HarperCollins.

CHRISTOPHER MONKS is the author of the *The Ultimate Game Guide To Your Life* and the editor of *McSweeney's Internet Tendency*.

LARAINE NEWMAN is a founding member of the Groundlings Theatre Company and an original cast member of *Saturday Night Live*. Her film, television, animation, and writing credits can be found on her website, *larainenewman.com*.

BRENDAN EMMETT QUIGLEY is the sixth-most published crossword constructor for the *New York Times*. He lives in Cambridge, Massachusetts.

JOYCE CAROL OATES is the author, most recently, of the memoir *A Widow's Story*, and is a recipient of the National Book Award and the PEN/Malamud Award for Excellence in Short Fiction. She is on the faculty at Princeton University and has been a member, since 1978, of the American Academy of Arts and Letters.

RICHARD ONYANGO's work has been exhibited in Africa, Europe, Asia, and North America. He lives in Malindi, Kenya.

YVONNE ADHIAMBO OWUOR writes when she is not plotting with others to develop arts-friendly structures all across Africa. At present, she lives in Nairobi, Kenya.

JAMIE QUATRO's fiction, poetry, and essays have appeared or are forthcoming in the *Alaska Quarterly Review*, the *Antioch Review*, *Bomb*, *Blackbird*, the *Cincinnati Review*, the *Hopkins Review*, *Oxford American*, and elsewhere. She lives with her husband and children in Lookout Mountain, Georgia.

NELLY REIFLER is the author of *See Through*, a collection of stories. Her work has appeared in *Post Road*, *Jubilat*, *BOMB*, and *Nerve*, as well as in previous issues of *McSweeney's*. She teaches at Sarah Lawrence College, and codirects the Writers' Forum at the Pratt Institute in Brooklyn.

MIKE SACKS has written for the *Believer*, the *New Yorker*, *Esquire*, *Vanity Fair*, *Time*, *GQ*, *Salon*, *Vice*, *Mad*, and other publications.

TED TRAVELSTEAD is an actor and writer working at *Vanity Fair*. He is a co-author of the book *SEX: Our Bodies, Our Junk*, and has appeared in music videos for The Fiery Furnaces, Superchunk, and The National.

CHRISTOPHER TURNER is an editor at *Cabinet*. His book *Adventures in the Orgasmatron: How the Sexual Revolution Came to America* is forthcoming in June from Farrar, Straus and Giroux.

JESS WALTER is the author of five novels, most recently *The Financial Lives of the Poets*. Among his other books are *The Zero*, a finalist for the National Book Award, and *Citizen Vince*, a winner of the Edgar Allan Poe Award.

BINYAVANGA WAINAINA is the director of the Chinua Achebe Center for African Writers and Artists at Bard College. His memoir, *One Day I Will Write About this Place*, will be published by Graywolf in July.